CRAZY WOMAN

What is the reason for her lush imagination?

A young couple has everything that many others want. They are missing only one more thing for all their dreams to come true.

But life is not a peaceful sea for anyone, not even for them. At the same time, a tragedy strikes them - the spirits of the past and a forgotten sin - " Once sworn, sworn forever ... "

How much love is in the love stories really? Do we all measure it the same?

An unusual story of one unconditional love and complete acceptance of the person, although the madness remains unaccepted forever. Patience, secrets, protection and promises that are fulfilled at all costs. When beliefs are so conflicting, it may be best to never discuss them again. It is better just to love and be silent, until the lumps of black earth start speaking, shocking everyone around ...

PART ONE

1

The alarm on the digital clock on the bedside cabinet rang: Beep, beep, beep, beep, beeeeeep....
Before it could do that again, a man's hand reached out to it and pressed the button to stop it. Then the hand returned under the covers with a slight motion.

The man struggled to get himself in a sitting position. He put his hands next to his body and tried to open his eyes, at the same time turning his head to the right. His eyes were still burning and everything was blurry, but he managed to look at his wife's face on the pillow next to him.

Closing his eyes again, he threw his head back on the headboard of the bed. He thought that it was good that she didn't hear the alarm today too, and he managed to turn it off fast enough.

A lot has been bothering her lately. A lot of things made her angry. But his patience with her was not a test. He loved his wife anyway, and when she laughed and when she was angry. He even felt nice when she yelled at him for little things, like when his alarm in the morning threatened her ears. She liked to sleep longer. She wouldn't be in a good mood from early morning till the evening if her sleep was interrupted. And all that for him was only hope - maybe she was really pregnant this time. Pregnant women behave like this - they are constantly angry, overbearing, they don't know what they want, but they want it right away. He would endure all this without a problem, if only her pregnancy would bring them the sun in the house.

A smile covered his sleepy face again. Even the thought of having a child was the most beautiful thought he could start with. His closed eyes, his head leaned on the headboard, and the most beautiful thoughts were more than enough for the dream to take over him again. But he knew that, and that's why he was always getting up in a sitting position immediately after the alarm went on. Then the same thing always happened - as soon as he would fall asleep again, his head would lose its balance. At first moving gently, and then, as soon as it couldn't find a suitable support, would slip abruptly and it would wake his whole body.

This second part of waking up would be like a cold shower. After that, he no longer had the will to take a nap.

He would slowly get out of bed, put on his robe and slippers, and as he fastened his belt, he would quietly sneak to the other side of the bed and start looking at his wife.

She slept on her back this morning. Her black hair was scattered in contrast to the white pillow. The silhouette of her slender body was painted under the covers. One arm was over her stomach and the other one was above her head next to the pillow.

She was as sweet to him as a child with her long lashes, her beautiful hair over her small forehead, and she was breathing calmly on her long nose. Her cheeks and her bulging chin made her face long and her mouth was thin. If he was sure that he wouldn't wake her, he would kiss that mouth sweet and tender.

But he wasn't sure, so after admiring his wife enough, he headed for the bathroom. After the morning hygiene ritual, he went to the kitchen to have his tea and biscuits. There, he could be loud because the bedroom where his beloved Patricia slept, was on the other side of the house.

It was a large house built by Patricia's parents for their only child. They had a smaller house on the other side of Krapina, where they gave birth to and raised their daughter. After she got married, Patricia wanted to live with her husband in a house built for that purpose. She regularly visited her parents alone, but also with her husband. They also regularly visited his mother. She was living alone in a small house on the way out of town. She did this to maintain family contacts, but also for their irreplaceable

cooking.
Patricia didn't have time to cook. She had her dreams - to become an opera singer and she spent her time singing, enjoying other people's operas and studying in Zagreb, which took a little bit longer, but she still managed to graduate. Unfortunately, there has still been nothing serious on a professional plan. But she was only 25 years old, life was ahead of her. Her parents said that often and she blindly trusted them and therefore she always agreed with them.

Her husband was to her liking. She was happy with him. She loved him. That's why she wasn't overthinking when she fell in love with him. She was so brave and free that she proposed to him, and he started crying of happiness.

At first, it was hard for him to let his mother live alone, because it wasn't long after his father's death, but he got used to it over time. And her father was such a good diplomat that he explained to him clearly that the time had come when it was unacceptable to live under the same roof with your parents. After all, his mother is close to him and he can visit her every day. That is why they, and because they could afford it, built a house for Patricia where she would run her own household. They wanted to have a lot of grandchildren, so they built it a little bigger, just in case.

Unfortunately, after 3 years of marriage, there was still no sign of the grandchildren they eagerly awaited. For a long time they thought Patricia wanted to finish her studies first, but now they were a little worried about it. Because since they retired, it has become a bit monotonous and quiet in the house. And for some time now, Patricia's singing was not there either.

But Patricia wasn't obsessed with the thought of having a child. She never seriously thought about it, but it was true that she wanted to please her parents, as well as her beloved husband, who also kept saying that he wanted a child.

And the child will come. It should not be rushed. Life is so beautiful, Patritia thought.

She got up without knowing why and how, put on her slippers and looked for her husband in the house. She found him where she thought she would find him - in the kitchen. She came up behind him, leaned over his back, and crossed her arms over his chest.

A gentle smile spread across his face. He pressed his cheek to her warm face and said:

- Hey darling, what a pleasant surprise!

She kissed him on the cheek with a smile and sat across the table.

- Good morning, darling, - he said.

He looked at her with a smile on his face. He was so glad he could see her before he went to work. This didn't happen very often, and he was already used to leaving without saying goodbye because he wanted her to rest as much as possible. He didn't care that he didn't have tea with her, her peace and rest were more important to him. He was not one of those men who fought for his wife's attention, even if it didn't suit her.

Suddenly something dawned on him and he raised his eyebrows, so he hurried to ask:

- Patricia, is everything ok with you?

She looked at him gently, yawned, and said:

- Of course darling, don't worry! I just woke up and couldn't sleep anymore. So I got up to iron your shirt, but you're already ready - she pointed to the chair where his work shirt was.

- Yes, I ironed it last night before I joined you in bed!

- You could have told me!

- You know my mom taught me to be independent. But thank you anyway!

She looked at him with a gentle look. She loved him. She was glad to have him. It was true, he was very independent and he was not boring at all. Whenever she couldn' go to her moms and bring some lunch, he would silently make a sandwich, and of course he would make one for her. He never minded if she wanted to go out with her friends, if she went to see her parents alone.

He helped her with everything. He even packed her things when she had to go to Zagreb. A man that every woman would wish for. He was only two years older than her, but he really acted like an older brother.

He had her support for what he was doing. She even admired his patience with which he went to Trakoscan Castle every day, driving about 50 kilometers every day, standing there for hours between tourists and telling again and again and again the same story... ..

Yet another proof of how patient he is and how his monotonous work doesn't bother him.

Honestly, sometimes, not so often, something interesting happens at his job, as it happens when a person works with people. Most often with children whose insufficiently attentive parents leave them behind, and they like to touch the weapons there or throw themselves on the bed of a count and check his elasticity by jumping.

Her husband usually resolved such incidents peacefully. And he suppressed his anger. Then he would be more quiet at home than usual, and she would know that as a caretaker there, he would have to fight for order in the castle again.

These and similar situations made his work less monotonous, although he claimed that it was not monotonous. He loved what he was doing, he loved the castle, he loved the lake around it, the greenery around it, the blue sky above it.

He also loved to travel back and forth to work.

He also loved his mother.

He loved his wife.

He wanted to have a child with her.

Getting up from his chair, he looked at his watch, then hugged his wife again. She just looked at him gently. His light brown hair was almost covering his eyes. With a nod of his head, he tossed it aside and stared with his blue eyes into her green eyes. His white teeth came behind the smile as he said:

- I have to go! But you are always in my mind!

He kissed her softly, and she watched his beautiful male figure walk away, putting on his jacket and putting his shirt into his pants. He fastened his belt with his long fingers and as he was ready to go out, she yelled:

- Philip! Kiss me again!

He returned without hesitation and fulfilled her wish to her and his own satisfaction. Then he told her that he really had to go.

- Watch out for the resurrected countesses! - she was joking with him.

He heard her. He laughed and went outside.

It was the end of winter, so it was no longer very cold and his car started at first. He was looking at the road, but his wife's face was in front of his eyes. Her hair, her warm cheeks, soft mouth. And her last words. And that took her face away and he wandered off with his thoughts.

All he told Patricia about it was that one of the tourists, in a conversation with him, claimed strange things - in fact, crazy things! Patricia gave the story a name, but he never told her exactly who that person was...

"The Risen Countess" was the name his wife came up with for a slightly comical, a bit creepy, but certainly unforgettable story from his youth. After managing to find a job as a caretaker in the castle and doing it with pleasure, he met an eighteen-year-old girl in town with golden hair and brown eyes. It was hard for him to believe she was an adult, but it was true. Her face, white as a snowflake, was saying that she was only a girl.

She had an enchanting childish look, just like the girls on the New Year's cards. Especially when her soft long hair covered half her face and fought with one eye to reach his blue eyes. Her little mouth laughed like when you give a child candy, and she had these small dimples in her cheeks.

She was of average build, but she stood out above all the girls he had known until then. Only a year younger than him and not doing anything special, but after the first meeting she left a strong impression on him and he looked for her for days, until he saw her again and ran frantically towards her. Thank God she had not returned to America, from where she came to the country of her roots for a short visit.

She told him that her, now unfortunately deceased parents had left the country and took her to America as a small baby, leaving nothing behind. Before leaving, they sold their house and everything they couldn't take with them. They raised her in America, working very hard at the same time and creating their own little fortune. However, the hard work always stopped them from visiting Croatia. Fortunately, and she was very grateful to them for that, they all spoke Croatian to each other in their home until their deaths.

It was very important to them that she knew where she was from, who she was and that she held onto her origins.

They died one after another. First the mother, then the father only a year and a half later. As she was of legal age when she was left alone, she had no problems with the inheritance. But she still didn't want to study. She wanted to give herself time to ease the pain and then she would surely make history.

- I'm very sorry - Philip said quietly - their death is still fresh.

- Yes - she said - especially my fathers. After my mother died, he taught me that it was okay to cry and mourn. I had the freedom to do it whenever I wanted. He never condemned me, he would just hug me and most of the time, he cried with me. He was very sad too, so we gave each other time and understanding. I still wonder if his death was hastened by grief. But certainly, I was again at the beginning, crying and mourning all over again.

She wiped away the tears that ran down her cheeks and than she raised her head and said proudly:

- But he certainly had enough time to teach me how to deal with pain. It was his idea for me to come here, where they never did after they left, although they wanted to. He wanted me to grieve for him right here, because that would make the pain easier. They took me away when I was very young and I don't remember anything from our life together here.

Philip, out of compassion, but also out of the strange attraction he felt towards her, began to call this girl out more often. On the long walks together, he tried to start a cheerful topic, only to keep her grief away from her, at least while he was with her.

At his mother's suggestion, he invited her to their home several times. His parents did their best to make this poor child feel like she has a family again. Until late at night, she told them about life in America, about her parents' successes, but also about the love they felt for each other. Philip's mother absorbed stories of the distant land, but the highlight was when this young girl named Elena said that they, as a married couple, remembered her of her parents.

They loved her. And that's why they were very happy when Philip admitted that Elena was his girlfriend.

- I've never believed anyway that a boy and a girl, two young people, can be and remain friends, -his father was joking with him.

- I believe they can,-Mom said, -but I'm glad you didn't,- and she Mom.

Her only fear was that this little girl would return to America with or without Philip, but she admitted that to him only after their story was over.

But before it ended, this love story was the main episode in his life. With Elena, he felt like in a fairy tale. Until the fairy tale got really tangled up and destroyed everything.

He wanted to spend as much time with her as possible, so he always stayed and slept with her in her rented apartment. He hated the mornings that separated him from her, until he got a really good idea - he started taking her to work with him.

He will never forget her first day in the castle. As she looked at the castle, she was speechless.

She stayed home the next day because she had a headache. The headache lasted for a couple of days, and when it was gone, her desire to visit Trakoscan Castle returned.

The next day in the castle she was silent again. This time she asked to separate from Philip and do a little independent research. He didn't mind, but when they returned home, she wanted to go straight to bed. She didn't get up until the next day. Philip wanted to make a joke and he asked her:

- Don't tell me you saw a ghost!

She turned to him with a sudden movement, her face was all of a sudden covered with sweat and all of her hair was clung to her face. He realized it was a bad joke, but he couldn't take it back. Then she asked him to spend the night with his parents because she wanted to be alone.

He didn't even offer to take her to work with him again the next day because, although he couldn't explain it to himself, the castle seemed to be having a bad effect on her. It was exhausting her in a strange way. But when he returned from work straight to her apartment, because he could not wait to hug her, she got angry with him.

He redeemed himself with the warm hugs and the silence

she needed, as well as the promise that she could come with him whenever she wanted.

And she wanted to go to the castle all the time. Almost every day. As much as he was glad to know that he was somewhere in the castle near him, he was sad that the castle had become more important to her than him. She kept moving around and sneaking around the rooms. It used to take him a while to find her after work and beg her to go home.

She has changed. They were still very much in love with each other, but her smiles faded slowly, and the long conversations between them became irrevocably shortened as she wanted to spend more time just thinking and dealing with herself.

For three months he struggled to regain their relationship as once was. He knew and he could feel that she loved him, but she wasn't the same anymore and that hurt. And she knew that too. And since he was the only family she had in this world, she decided to tell him the truth. She was sure he would understand, he became a part of her, she thought to herself. She knew it was time to save him from this pain, reveal everything to him and begin to enjoy his support.

After spending half of the day telling him how much she loved him and that she didn't want to hide anything from him, as well as that she would do anything for him, and she knew that he would do the same for her, she finally told him what she carried within herself, and after these 3 months, she was more than sure that this was her truth:

- My love, I know that this will shock you, but I would never have told you such nonsense if I wasn't convinced completely that it is the truth. I am still out of myself, but I know that it is one hundred percent true. Philip...I am one of the Count Drashkovich family.

Philip, after holding her in his arms for a minute in silence, encouraged her that she didn't even have to hide such a thing from him. If she doesn't mind a noble heiress being in a relationship with an ordinary mortal, even less. She shouldn't be scared at all.

- Philip, dear...Please don't leave me...
- No, love, I didn't even think of it!
- But you misunderstood me. I'm not a heiress. I...I lived

there...in the castle. I know it sounds crazy, I'm sorry, but I remembered everything!

- Elena - he took her face in his hands - no one has lived there for centuries. It is not possible that you were born there. 18 years ago and many years before that, the castle was just a museum, a cultural heritage!

She looked at him sadly. But she was still hoping that he will embrace her as she was and she tried again:

- Yes, darling, I lived there many centuries ago!

He waited for days for her to tell him that she was just joking. He had hoped in vain for days. At first he would tell her to wake up, cold, but with love, because she must have had bad dreams.

But as the time went by, her story became more and more embarrassing. When she went to the castle with him, she took him around and made up situations that happened to her there. She was telling him about her life there, her love stories, the child she easily gave birth to, how she died young. She tried to persuade him in every way possible, and the more she tried, the more her story repulsed him.

As time was passing by, the real Elena never came back to him. Unfortunately for him. And unfortunately for her, she never managed to convince him of her story. That story, day by day, made them strangers.

Then she disappeared. She only left a short message - I'm going back to America.

He never saw her again.

He never even got over her.

Patricia didn't know that the "crazy" tourist was in a relationship with her sweetheart. The truth was that, although Philip loved her too, it was not the same way he loved Elena. His wife was the person who made him believe in love again, but he never called her "my love". That title, as long as he shall live, belonged to Elena. But he could not do things differently. If it was Elena's dream, he couldn't ruin it for her. But he couldn't dream with her either. He could never believe in this madness. Never!

When he lost her, it was as if his heart had been torn from his chest. But he couldn't accept her madness. He tried everything.

He promised her that no one would ever know, that it would be their secret, but that it would be best for her to see a psychiatrist.

Of course, she didn't think such a thing was necessary. She didn't get what she needed. Philip didn't believe her even though she was telling him and showing him things about the castle that no one knew. He believed that that was only her imagination and her digging around the rooms in the castle. She had the opportunity to discover the undiscovered parts of the castle, but that she lived another life there centuries ago....He will not believe in that nonsense in a hundred years.

It was hard for him to watch the woman he loved losing touch with reality. There were times when he thought it was all because of her grief over her lost parents. Later, whatever the reason for her madness was, brought him to exhaustion. If only she had accepted his proposal and talked to a psychiatrist. But a problem whose existence is not acknowledged cannot be solved.

He did not reveal the reasons to his parents. He just told them that she had left and that he did not know if she would ever return.

Patricia brought them hope again, but being brutally honest, they never accepted her like Elena. Maybe they will succeed, if God gives them grandchildren.

This is what everyone expects and hopes for.

And their hopes came true only a week later. The doctor congratulated them. She was pregnant.

2

Eight months after the wonderful news, almost everything was ready to welcome the baby. The room was freshly painted, new curtains were installed, new furniture was bought, a beautiful wooden bed, a cradle, a changing table and covered in white to match all the other furniture in the room, Particia's favorite armchair, because she claimed it would be the most comfortable for her to breastfeed.

The plush teddy bears had already been lined up, they were also white or light beige, rattles, pacifiers, bottles and blankets, everything was there. White was for joy, happiness and anticipation, and at the same time calming. Grandparents were just thinking about their grandson.

- I would like to buy so many more things, but I really need to know if it's gonna be a girl or a boy, because I want to use a little more color than white only - Patricia's mother was impatient.

Secretly, all of them had decided what they wanted to be,

except the father. For Patricia it was certainly a beautiful time and she enjoyed her pregnancy without worrying too much if she is gonna have a girl or a boy, but deep inside she wanted to be a girl. Raised as an only child and later truly loved as a woman, she always got the attention of the people around her. And yet, she didn't expect this much attention. Everyone was running around her like crazy, and of course she liked it.

Philip repeated several times and asked Patricia for her opinion on this, but still, mostly on her own initiative, the days off and his vacation, he decided to take when the baby would come. Then his wife will need him much more, even though there are older members of their family to help.

He paid maximum attention to her every move, to every bite she took in her mouth, and strictly adhered to the doctor's recommendations, although there weren't too many of them, because it was, after all, a normal pregnancy.

However, every morning when he locked the door of their house behind him and left his wife to sleep inside, he felt guilty for leaving her. His thoughts were with her at home, he skipped parts as he shared the history of the Thracians with the tourists. He thought that he shouldn't be in the castle now and that he wanted to be next to Patricia, to laugh together with her when the baby moved. But on the other hand, he wanted to keep his job. And although he didn't want to be in the castle right now, he loved his job. And in the end, it never occurred to him to live at the expense of Patricia's parents.

Those were the days when he drove faster, even though he didn't like to. Before leaving, he would stay home as long as he could listening to Patricia's steady breathing in front of the bedroom door. He wanted so badly to kiss her on the forehead, her arms and her belly! When he would come from work, he wanted to be at home as soon as possible and after he was convinced that she was well and happy, he would do all the things he wanted to do in the morning and much more.

Then he would take her for a walk. They walked as long as she could, and he would ask every now and then how she felt and if she wanted to stop and rest. When they returned home, he would tidy up, cook for the next day, spread the laundry, give her fruit, make her fresh squeeze lemonade and oranges, and set pillows under her back.

Patricia was aware of his kindness, but she was also aware that she was carrying their child, so she was not embarrassed. She was bored while he was gone because a lot had changed, she didn't live like she used to, and her friends didn't come to see her every day. She missed him and was happy when he would come home. She enjoyed the weekends when he was at home and after he had done everything around the house, he would sit down, take her hand, bring it to his mouth and hold it for so long, sometimes until he had to get up and do something for her.

When they would go to bed, he would touch her face, her hair and her belly for a long time. He praised and exalted her for the life she carried to make her proud to be a mother, although she was a little frightened by the question of how her singing efforts would progress afterwards, with the baby. However, to her it was more important everything to be OK with the birth and the baby. For everything else she would think afterwards. Her family will come up with something clever anyways.

She would lie down for a long time in the morning after waking up, and every day she would find breakfast in the kitchen, which Philip had already prepared for her before he left for work. Her dear Philip! She is so happy to have him!

That morning she wanted for him to be there to share with him that something was not quite right, but she would have to wait for him to return. By the time he returns, things may be different.

Because he has just arrived at the castle. Groups of tourists were just starting. He has been especially kind to them recently, because he couldn't stop thinking that soon he will be holding his and Patricia's child in his arms. He was smiling more than usual, and it was difficult to attract his attention in any way.

And today, everyone in the castle, except him, turned to the red shoes worn by one of the tourists.

Those leather shoes had a strange red color. Nothing was strange about the red, but the shade of the color was a little bit different, not like the other red shoes. These looked a little bit sophisticated, what a woman's eye would usually notice. And their cut, that bizarre style, no one could explain, and everyone who met this young lady today at the castle stared in amazement.

- Mom, where did this lady get these shoes - a girl's voice rang out - I want you to buy me the same ones, please, mom!

And these goth shoes have been walking around the castle for the longest time today. Philip caught them with the corner of his eye, but they didn't reach his brain because the only thing he cared about was that this last female figure got out, so he could go to his wife.

In the meantime, Patricia's mother came to see her and she wanted to share with her that she had not felt the baby inside her all morning. But just as she was preparing to say it while her mother was making her tea, the baby moved and signaled to the young mother that she hadn't realized that someone had slept inside her longer today. At that moment Patricia forgot about that.

On the last day of that week, Philip couldn't wait to go home. But one of the visitors today persistently delayed leaving the castle. After a short conversation with himself in which he reiterates to himself that the woman doesn't really have intention to go home soon, he decided to remain kind while he approached her from behind in the room where she stood under the hanging pictures on the wall... She did not show with a single movement of her body that she was not a statue, but he knew, so he said loud enough:

- Dear Madam, I am very sorry to tell you that today's time for visiting the castle has expired. I will be glad if you enjoyed it and I hope you will visit us again!

For more than a minute, the figure of the woman remained like a statue and heard nothing. Philip stared at her, trying to think of his next move. Maybe a woman doesn't hear well, he thought. In that case, the worst thing would be for him to appear behind her back and scare her. To make sure, he tries again:

- Ma'am?

This time, with a barely perceptible twitch, the female statue became alive again. She sighed softly, not turning her head, nodded a few times, and then walked really slow toward the exit. If she meant to annoy him with her slow gait, she failed. He is more patient than any woman in the world can comprehend, but this time he has a pregnant woman at home and he can't wait to see her.

This made him look at this woman again, and then his gaze fell on her shoes. It was as if he had already seen them. No, no, Patricia doesn't have these kinds of shoes. Nor would she ever put those on.

He didn't even care if he'd seen them before, after the feet in them finally began to walk a little bit faster and rushed out of the castle.

That evening Patricia wanted him near her more than usual. This is not usually the case, but motherhood changes her as well. Now that these days of her pregnancy had come, it was time to talk about names. Since childbirth is so close, it is time to decide the name of the child. They should talk about both, boys and girls names, because although they have heard about it, but not only in their vicinity, but in the whole country, as well as in their republic, there are no new devices that can determine the sex of the child before birth.

Like all other decisions, especially since she was pregnant, Philip leaves it to Patricia. So she almost chose the names for each gender of the child alone. She told him that she had thought many times while spending her days alone and that she finally knew what names she wanted.

And he? He would never contradict her, except in extremely unacceptable situations, this time when he heard the name she wanted for a girl and shook him to the heel, but also to his heart.

- But darling, he protested in the most gentle way possible, Elydia, it's kind of unnatural to me. I mean, I've never heard ...

- That's why - Patricia interrupted him - I want our child to have a unique name.

- You know I always support you, but why not just Lydia?

- Because I don't like it. It's simple and too common!

Philip's palms were sweating. He didn't want that name. As much as he wanted to please his wife, but this time he didn't agree with her. That same name she chose herself could hurt her if she knew his story with Elena.... Okay, she'll never know, but he didn't like that name. For years he has been struggling to forget the past and fortunately he is doing well and now his beloved wife, to her detriment, wants to take a step back by forcing him to say half of Elena's name while saying their child's name!

- Patricia, please, it's weird! I would not want anyone to make fun of our child one day for the name we gave her!

- Make fun of her? The only thing that could happen is that people start giving this name to their children, because the name is beautiful and no one has remembered it yet, but us!

- Darling, everything is fine, but just Lidija is....

- I don't want just Lydia! I don't want it! That's not it then! And just so you know, this is not ok, you supposedly leave the choice to me, and then you argue with me!

She straightened in her chair, put her hand on her back, and supported her head by turning it side and casting a disappointed look at the floor.

- No, Patricia, I didn't mean that!

Philip knelt beside her and tried to find her gaze. She refused to look him in the eyes.

- Honey, please, I don't mean anything bad! Here, I'll let it be your way, but I don't really agree with that!

She turned her head abruptly and swung her black hair.

- You don't agree? But I want this name! I chose it!

And his mild nature emerges on the surface. So many times he has given in and suffered damage compared to many other people, so many times to his wife, so how could he protest now when his child is growing in her stomach. But it's hard for him. It is unacceptable to him! He doesn't want that name! No way! But he also doesn't want his wife to get upset, especially not in this state. Not now. That's enough for today. He will drop the ball. He will surrender. If God allows, he will try to reason with her in the coming days, when she is not upset like now. And he sincerely hopes that her parents will not accept that name either.

In the worst case, he can only hope that the child is a boy. That's it! If the child is not a girl this will be over! But we have to wait until then. Not long, but still! Will that waiting time be enough for him to accept the name? Because to hope that Patricia will change her mind is madness. No! He will not accept it. He will not agree with that name, he will call his daughter by the wrong name many times, and he would not like that to happen.

Or, worse, in his memories he will call the girl he loved

more than himself, after his daughter. Not at all! He must not connect them! They have nothing to do with each other! They are both the most beloved beings in his life, but they have nothing to do with each other!

For the first time, to his great surprise, Philip thought to himself: God, please let it be a boy!

-Patricia... Darling, everything is fine - he whispers, running his fingers through her hair - If that's what you want, ok! Just don't get upset!

She calmly rested her head on his chest.

When did she not win? When didn't she get it her way? This man is to be loved!

3

As he walked toward the castle, Philip enjoyed the song of the birds rejoicing in spring. The greenery enchanted his gaze. He allowed his lungs to maximize the breathing in the fresh spring air full of the scent of fresh grass and spring flowers. He missed coming earlier and walking around the lake, but he didn't want to do that until Patricia gave birth, and certainly after that either. All that was left of those walks was this admiration as he was walking to his workplace.

The lake calmly embraced the hill on which the castle stood. Chirping birds flew over it.

Walking along the path, Philip saw a female figure standing on the pathway, at the very edge of the lake, staring at him. She wore a long dark brown robe, with the hood pulled over her head. Her head was completely covered and she was facing the lake. Her arms were crossed over her chest. The only thing peeking out from under her robe were her slender legs. The white skin shone in the gentle spring sun.

Like it or not, her covered head got Philip's attention, but it didn't hold it for long. His mind was preoccupied with getting the castle gates open in time.

But just as he walked down the path just behind her, his head turned in the direction of the woman. He noticed a familiar detail on her. Her shoes on her little feet looked as if he had already seen them. Without slowing down, he tried to remember — yes, it is the silent lady who had already visited the castle.

And that was all that he thought about her. He was back on his way. Suddenly, it seemed that she turned to him, ready to ask him something. He decided to answer her as briefly as possible, so he started walking backwards towards her.

But as soon as he looked at the woman, he was relieved. She didn't turn to him at all. Still calm, with her head slightly bowed, she was still just standing there, looking at the lake.

He paid no more attention to her, until, after a few hours, he saw her little feet walking through the castle again.

There are some people that are never fed up with the castle. He is also one of them, but fortunately he works there. It happened all the time that he saw some people coming there more than once. Some returned again and again each year. He was glad to recognize them, as they were to see him again. Some of them he wouldn't recognize, and then they'd tell him how they were there last year with a baby in a stroller. That's why it's harder to recognize them now, because it's not a baby anymore, it's this little girl who walks around curiously.

His child would soon be walking around, he thought, and it was warming his heart. Those tender thoughts led him to the wall, and he began to look at the lake through the crown. That majestic gaze drowned in his majestic thoughts. Although there were still visitors to the castle here and there, his thoughts left the place and he went into their house for a moment to spend some time with Patricia.

- How did the lake come to be here? - he heard a familiar voice.

He quickly managed to get his spirit back into his body, at the same time thinking about how he could hear Patricia's voice, just because he thought of her.

- This... - all confused, moving quickly at the same time thinking what to answer, he started to look around to see where the voice was coming from.

Only a meter and a half from him, with a hood on his head, stood the now well-known female figure. She wasn't looking at him, she was looking through the crown at the bottom of the hill, and her hood was completely covering her face, even her nose wasn't sticking out.

Philip wiped his sweaty palms on his jacket, making sure she didn't see him, squeezed the shirt sleeves between his palms and fingers, and began to say the things he had engraved in his head:

- The abandoned castle from 1850-1860, was restored by Marshal Juraj Drashkovich, turning it into a residential castle. The renovation was in the spirit of romanticism, carried out in the neo-Gothic style, with the simultaneous restoration of the entire environment, so on that occasion a forest park with rare trees was arranged, an artificial lake was created - he emphasized his last words and then continued — and some garden facilities. The elements of the restored castle are highlighted - the entrance tower with a drawbridge, the knight's hall with complete knight's armor from the 16th century and the flags of Drashkovich from the 18th century. Collection of weapons with heavy beards, rifles and pistols on the wheel, and Turkish weapons.

She didn't move. He did his job, though he was aware that she had asked about the lake. He therefore added:

- That with the lake was a very good idea. The castle is beautiful, but with the lake it is even more beautiful. It is about one and a half kilometers long, and its depth is up to a maximum of 2 and a half meters. In summer, the water warms up to 22 degrees. It is also a pond, but aesthetics is a much more important part. It is a decorative element common in romantic park architecture. There are hiking trails everywhere, and sport fishermen always enjoy it, in addition to walkers.

She sighed. At least she reacted to something. He thought that by telling her that he had seen her enjoying herself near the lake this morning, he would have provoked her to look at him. But he didn't really need her look, so he gave up and remained

Crazy Woman

silent and waited for her to go away.

Apparently, her eyes widened and she had no intention of leaving, so he relented.

- Now excuse me - he said, only not to leave without saying goodbye.

The older couple was the next to seek and receive his attention. After them, the working hours for that day were over. He couldn't wait to see Patricia. He rushed down the path, with his thoughts already in his house, when someone called him by name:

- Philip!

He turned around. There was no one. Before he could turn to the left and to the right, the voice said:

- I'm here!

The woman in the robe descended from the back path. In his head, he was already working on a defense strategy. That fact they met by chance and talked officially several times, as well as the fact that she tried to find out his name does not give her any right to keep him after the working hours. No matter what her plan is and what her questions are, he will apologize for being in a hurry and really had to go home, and has a long way to drive and kindly he will try to get away from her.

- Greetings, ma'am, - he waved his hand, and without slowing down, he continued. She understood. She waved at him as well, as she stood like buried on the path. She watched him go, then lowered her hood and continued walking through the woods.

Philip rushed home. After he parked the car in front of the house, he didn't even have time to lock it. He decides to do it later and hurries to the entrance. He pulled his key out of his pants, unlocked the door with quick movements, and shouted:

- Honey, I'm home!

He throws his jacket on the cupboard by the entrance and runs across the ground floor. Patricia was not there.

He didn't want to yell too much because she might have fallen asleep, so he headed for the upstairs bedroom. He opened the door as hard as he could, but when his gaze managed to cover the empty bed, he burst inside. He even searched the terrace, but found no sign that his wife had been there today.

Then a slight smile appeared on his face. He knew where she was.

He strode to the door of the baby's room. He knocks and calls softly:

- Honey, are you there?

Patricia didn't answer, so he pushed the doorknob lightly, sure she was asleep in her chair there. Before he could open the door and go inside, he heard the phone ring. Although they made sure that the place where the phone was is far enough from the door of this room so it would not wake the baby in the future, he hurried because he did not want the phone to wake Patricia or make her hurry to answer if she is somewhere else in the house.

- Thank God you're home — he heard his mother's anxious voice. - Honey, come and get me right away, I'm ready. Patricia's parents took her to Varazdin. She complained that she couldn't feel the baby and they didn't want to leave it just like that. They called to inform me that she wouldn't be back soon and that we should go there as soon as you're home from work. Patricia wants you there. Come, baby, hurry! I'll wait for you in front of the house!

Good thing he didn't lock the car. He grabbed his jacket from where he had thrown it and ran out.

About 5 o'clock the next morning, he returned his mother to the place where he had taken her. She took him in her arms, as dirty, sweaty, and almost sick as he was and held him for so long, until she begged him to spend the night there. She wouldn't have peace if she left him alone in the state he was at the moment.

Philip was also happy to nap a little with his head in his mother's lap. But the pain didn't let him sleep for long. It woke him and slapped him mercilessly. His tears came down his cheeks like when he was a child and he cried in this same lap. And his mother cried with him, stroking his hair with her fingers.

He wanted to pull that hair out. He wanted to bite out his own flesh with his teeth. He wanted to feel physical pain that would silence this other, emotional pain for the lost child for a moment.

His daughter Elidija was born dead yesterday before he arrived at the Varazdin Hospital. He took the news with a grieving groan and all of a sudden all the doctors ran to him. After they managed to calm him down with pills they put in his mouth, they sent him to see Patricia.

All he could do was sit next to her and hold her hand. All she could do was stare blankly at the wall in front of her, with no desire to say or do anything.

The forensic medicine doctor, Mr. Sinchic, a short and polite man, accompanied them for a while, explaining that nothing could've been done. His kind voice spoke with measured words. There was an experience in him, but also an innate kindness to share bad news with understanding for the pain of the listeners. His round face had a line on the forehead that showed that certainly was not easy for him to tell the hard truth. His palms were clenched and that only showed that words were barely coming out of his mouth, but he had to tell them anyway.

The baby was already dead when they arrived at the hospital. He examined her and confirmed what the gynecologist had said before provoking the birth.

Patricia saw the child. Who knows if that was a smart move, but at least she'll be at peace and never wonder if it really was true.

Two days later, Patricia could go home, along with the document: "Female child, in the thirty-fifth pregnancy week, born dead on May 14, 1984..."

Everything was gone. They were alone again. Again, they belonged only to each other, although in these moments they did not care to whom they belonged.

Philip blamed himself. Himself only. If only he hadn't been so persistent against the name Patricia chose. If only he hadn't felt the fear and disgust wanting to have a boy. How much better it would be for him to be able to hug a little girl with an ugly name now than for their child to die! He couldn't control his pain. He had never before believed that man's thoughts had power over his life, but this convinced him by breaking him. Will he ever be able to forgive himself!

He hid from Patricia because he feared she could read everything from his eyes. What would he tell her then? How would he defend himself, redeem himself, compensate her?

How? She worked so hard and was obedient to everything that the doctor said, and no matter how hard it was for her, she did her best to bring the child according to the rules and healthy into this world. She left everything, her music and her singing and her company, going out, going to Zagreb, everything! And in the end, she didn't even bring him alive into this world! How much must she be hurting by what happened to them, and he can't save her from her pain! He can't take it away from her, he can't reduce it in any way! There is no way he can help himself or his beloved wife.

He felt helpless as never before. He took days off from work to be with her, and they ended up avoiding each other inside the house. The laughter between them was gone. They did not meet inside the house for hours, and when one came to the bed next to the other in the evening, the one who went first pretended to be asleep.

They would share a few words only when their parents visited and brought them something to eat. They did not stay long when they visited them, because everyone was speechless, and you can not be silent with everyone.

A glimmer of hope came when Philip noticed that Patricia was showing interest in her mother's menu. Most of the food was still thrown away, but at least she tried to eat a little. Then Philip offered to set the table for her, make her fresh lemonade, and sit silently beside her, barely touching his plate.

As hard as it was for her, Patricia noticed his attention and was grateful to him, and one afternoon she even got up, approached him and hugged him tenderly. She held his head to her chest as he used all the strength left in him not to cry and upset her. And he knew that tears would come down like rain if he hugged her too. That's why he did not. All he did was squeeze her wrists with his palms.

When he came to the bedroom, he allowed himself to approach her from behind for the first time and hug her, burying his face in her hair. With a sigh, she let him know that she was still awake. It was the first time they had fallen asleep hugging after losing the child.

Her father suggested a psychiatrist from Zagreb with

whom he would personally arrange meetings to help them return to normal again. They refused unanimously, determined to try to help themselves first. But as the days were passing they knew less and less the answer to the question how would they do that.

Working, her dad suggested. Philip should go back to work and Patricia should go back to Zagreb and to her friends and coworkers.

He was right. Only a preoccupation with other things can take their minds away from their sad reality.

After the first day, he came home really tired. She was waiting for him at the table and over dinner told him that she was going to Zagreb for 2 days the next day. She hopes that the company of her friends will make her feel better.

He was pleased with her decision. She made a smart choice.

She got up in the morning before him. They didn't talk much as he drove her to the bus station. They hugged each other when the bus came, and as he traveled to work he was aware that this hug was not like before. He had to admit that he hugged his beloved wife as if he was afraid he would insult her if he squeezed her a little harder. Or did he still think she was still in pain, the consequences? But taking everything into consideration, he was aware that he had not given himself to her as before. He blamed himself for that and promised himself that he would make it up to her when she comes back.

The spring was coming, and he was home alone, so he allowed himself his long desired walk around Lake Trakoscan. The pain was still there, but it was easier to be in this place. It was much easier to think that he and his wife were, not because everyone said so, but they are still young. As much as they were trying to understand why this happened to them, they were only opening more of their wounds. It is good to give yourself time, but it is wise for them to return to a life that may heal their wounds and take them further. They will have a child. And now no one will care at all for the gender or the name! This pain will never go away! But there is still hope that it will at least diminish. And then hopefully they will live a normal life.

He took off his shoes, layed on the grass and stared at the sky for a long time. The blue color was bringing hope, but he tried to chase it away. It was too soon to be hopeful. Way too soon!

So he got up and sat down on the grass. He wrapped his arms around his knees and closed his eyes in front of the greenery that was reflected in the lake like a mirror. He breathed evenly, deeply and calmly.

It was getting dark over the castle and the lake when he heard:

- Philip, you're back!

Apart from his name, he wasn't sure he heard the rest of the sentence exactly. But sure that the voice was addressing him, he abruptly opened his eyes and turned in the direction from which the voice was coming.

He wasn't sure how he felt when he saw the woman he had met several times. The woman in a dark brown robe and whimsical shoes stood no more than three feet behind him.

He wasn't really sure if he was glad or if he felt it was better that she didn't find him there. That it's okay for someone else to be there, or that he should talk to her and he wasn't in a mood for a small talk. He just stayed there as if he hadn't even seen her. He kept gazing into the lake, not bothered at all that he was extremely rude. Until he saw her shoes in the grass right next to him The scent of the grass and the wildflowers suddenly mingled with the scent of the velvet of her cloak.

Philip would be embarrassed if she came so close to him. He felt worse as she bent down and sat down in the grass beside him. But she was determined.

- I hope you're okay, she said.

He didn't want anyone to question him, no one! He didn't want to talk about his pain, not yet. Especially not with total strangers.

He tried to compose himself, but he was aware that he had to speak to this woman, whatever her intentions were, in order not to leave a false impression. He is not a weirdo who does not talk, nor is he someone who avoids the human race. He is a normal human being who lives and works among others, and it is time to start behaving that way. He will grieve in his house, between its four walls.

However, he did not dare to lie, so he just said:

- Thank you for asking.

He had never before allowed himself not to answer such a question, especially to a woman. But he has never been in the situation he is in now and he sincerely hopes that he will never lose a child again.

- You haven't been here for days - she didn't give up.

Why does he need to be informed about something he already knows?

- We also have a life besides our job, he said.

Before he could say anything, she said:

- I missed you....

He turned abruptly to her. Not because of what she said. He was not yet aware of it. Her voice! Her voice sounded so familiar that it seemed to lift him half a meter above the grass on which he sat. He stared at her hood and for the first time he wanted to see her face. To see that he had not been deceived and that this woman is a complete stranger.

She seemed to want to get him to do that. She let her wide velvet sleeves fall to her elbows, revealing her white arms, raising them toward her hood. Even he could see them trembling as they removed the velvet from her hair, which was another continuation of covering her face. Her long hair, only an inch above the grass on which she sat, was shining like gold and covering her side.

He tilted his head toward the lake in an attempt to get a better look at her face, but that didn't happen until she made an effort to help him and turned slowly but firmly toward him.

It would be good for him to have someone to put those pink pills in his mouth again. In that mouth that remained wide open as his eyes, and his forehead wrinkled, sweating and making his light brown hair wet. He dropped on his knees to the grass, turned to the woman, supporting his body with his hands, as he spread his palms over the wildflowers, in an amazement saying almost without a voice:

- Elena ......

She covered her face with her palms and her hair was falling over them. She shook her head from one side to the other as she begged him:

- Please forgive me, Philip!

Philip was turning around as he was asking for help. Seeing that he would not find help around there and that he was alone with this woman there, he jumped to his feet and began to walk nervously in a circle. He raised his hands above his head, trying to protect her from thinking, but the longest train in this world at the highest speed and with the loudest noise just passed through his head, bringing back in its carriages all the memories, all the pain and suffering associated with this thing standing in front of him.

He felt like the blood was running out in his face and he was struggling for air, so without thinking, letting his body do whatever it wanted just to help itself, he knelt again and his body just fell to the ground.

- I'm sorry - he hears the familiar voice again- I had to let you know I was back!

Those words changed everything inside him. Now all his blood came to his head, his hands went down next to his body, squeezing his palms, and his lungs began to inhale and exhale quickly. Through his teeth, he strained his first words, knowing consciously who he was talking to:

- You couldn't? Really nice of you to remember that you should call people! It's nice that you've finally decided to let people know that you are coming. Just tell me one thing, one damn important thing - have you finally learned that you have to let people know when you're leaving too? Or you still leave behind yellow papers that can be torn, set on fire, destroyed, but it can't do you no harm? Have you learned not to run away without explanation? You know what? I don't believe you have!

With her head bowed, she was silent. She didn't answer a single question, which made him even angrier, made him raise his voice:

- Have you ever wondered how the ruins under which you leave the living souls when you leave suffocate them? With how many wounds and bruises does a man get out from under them, if he ever manages to get out, with parts of him remaining there, rotting forever? Have you?

She pulled the hood over her head again, covered her face, and tried to push back the unruly strands of hair with her fingers.

She crouched under the covers like the greatest sinner at the time of the trial and began to tremble, but she did not have the courage to speak until he grabbed her by the shoulders, shook her, and yelled at her and his cry flew across the lake. :

- Have you?

- I have, she barely whispered.

He held her without a grip for a moment, then pushed her back slightly.

- You're lying, he growled at her.

She could take everything he said, but she could never bear for him to call her a liar. Him thinking that was a liar was exactly why she left him leaving her heart here. She never found peace, she was haunted day and night by this castle, this story, this man. She was bleeding more than he was, but he didn't know that. He kept leaving his life and everyone accepted him. He could fight back and get back on his feet. He was able to continue to live after her. She never moved on. Somehow she managed to get her degree in history, but there was no place for her under the sun. She had no choice but to come to the only place where she felt alive. She knew she wouldn't live long, even if she survived here for a while.

Her only wish was to return to this place where she belonged and to see Philip for the last time, but even more than that she wanted him to believe her. That everything she told him was the truth. And now, after 7 years of living in a vacuum, after she managed to return to her castle and find the only man who had touched her in this second life, he told her that she was lying.

Repentance tore her soul. Why, why did she not keep silent, realized her intentions and secretly watched him? Why did she allow her feelings for him to win and take her into his mercy? Did she really expect to find the same man or, worse, a man who would trust her this time?She just wanted to jump in the lake! But she didn't want to die like a coward! She didn't die like that last time! She will continue to love, she will give birth to a child out of love, and then she will leave this world and she sincerely hoped, this time will be the last time. And how did she know? It's crazy to ask.

- You're lying, she heard again, much quieter, but much

closer to her ear.

She closed her eyes. She just wanted to disappear. Instead of the joy she expected, she got pain. Strong as fire. It burned all over her body. It was as if she could hear her skin and flesh burning. When the pain reached her bones, that was the end of her endurance. She jumped to her feet, let the tears come down her face, and as the cloak fluttered behind her along with her long hair, she ran along the wooden path. The further she was from Philip, the more strength she had to run. She hoped she had already run out of his sight, and then she heard him yelling:

- Elenaaaaaaaaa!

She jumped from the path to the grass in panic. Struggling to stay on her feet, she was running through the trees without turning. The fire that was eating her inside gave her the strength to overcome the slippery terrain with her shoes and escape further into the woods.

She felt the cloak was slowing her. She stopped and took it off with sudden movements. Throwing it to the ground, she staggered and slipped in the grass. With her whole being, she instinctively tried to hold on to something, and then the tree caught her.

With quick and short inhales and exhales she was trying to come to her senses when she saw Philip sliding closer to her, struggling to keep her cloak in his left hand.

- Go away! - she yelled at him.

Even if he wanted to, physics wouldn't let him. He slid to the same tree that held her and clung to it.

- I'm sorry!- he said.
- Go away! - she yelled again.

Philip let go of the tree, raising both hands in the air. Then, with a slight motion, he spread her cloak and covered her body.

Although she liked that he cared, the fear and all the other emotions were still there. She only managed to lower her voice when she addresses him again:

- Don't touch me!

He had no intention of touching her. He had no intention other than to save her life, when he suddenly felt that he was the one who put her in danger in the first place. True, he was really shocked, but it was not okay to scare her and make her get hurt in the woods. He was sad. Really sad. Him making Elena get hurt because of him? Elena, whom he once loved so much and never really stopped loving her? And now when God sent her back to him, even if this was only a dream, he would make her hurt herself!? Any other person could do it, but not him. Realizing his enormous mistake, he started begging her quietly:

- Elena, all I want is to help! Please give me your hand!

She would rather roll straight into the lake than give him her hand! Her look made that clear to him.

He was afraid to leave, but he was also afraid to be there because of how angry he made her. He never believed before that the line between love and hate was so thin. But he had a lot of problems in his life and a lot of shocks, so he had to make an effort to make things right.

- Elena - he tried again - I'm sorry! If it's easier for you to understand, just put yourself in my shoes. After all that happened, you just appeared out of nowhere! I, myself, am surprised that my wound has opened again and started bleeding with your appearance, but try to understand me. I'm not me these days, Elena! You are not the only thing that drained the blood from my body to the last drop. I lost a child just a few days ago. I've been out of my mind ever since, so I accepted your presence in a wrong way. Please forgive me!

Her already wet eyes lit up again. It was as if an invisible hand had carried away her anger and replaced it with pain. He had a child? He loved again after her?

Her body clones. As much as she tried to gather her thoughts and remind herself that when she secretly left him, she was aware of the risk, yet this was the strongest slap across her heart. But losing the child he had after daring to love again saddened her. She did not think about his pain or the pain of the woman who should feel only pain in her life because she dared to take her place. All she could think about was the lost life, no matter whose child it was.

- You lost a child? - she whispered.

He nodded.

She still didn't reach for his hand. Picking up her cloak,

she managed to stand up and mechanically clean her dress of the grass and the wildflowers on it, and she stood up in front of him, very close to his face.

- How? - she whispered and he could feel her breath.
- My daughter was born dead in the eighth month of the pregnancy!

Her greatest fear came true to him. She remembered very well how children were constantly dying and how panicked she was when she had her child.

But nowadays, everything is different. Child mortality is much lower, but it has not yet been eradicated, unfortunately. And his child died, among others. How much does it hurt? She absorbed him with her eyes as if she believed she could see his pain. There was no change in him. The pain is not visible. Usually. But it can be bigger than anything visible.

- Maybe someone thinks it hurts less when a child dies before you get used to it alive, and probably that is true, but a death of a child is a death of your child!

A tear came down his cheek. Then another one from the other eye. Then another one and another one and he bent down to the tree, putting his hand on it, and rested his head on hers. This is not Patricia. He has to hide his pain from Patricia not to make her sad and not to look weak in her eyes. This is Elena. As much as she had changed in all these years since he had not seen her, he could not have imagined that she wouldn't be the woman in front of whom he could not weep from the depths of his soul. For her all human beings were equal in pain and she never divided them into male and female.

He shivered leaning against the tree as he felt her palm on his back. The miraculous warmth spread through him and he shivered even more, but at the same time his tears calmed down. He still felt neither shame nor discomfort. When he turned to her, he felt only deep gratitude for her understanding. He wanted to say it, but when he turned to her, her embrace paralyzed him.

He felt her face on his chest. Under his chin he could feel the familiar smell of her hair. He put his cheek into her hair and dared to give her a hug back.

Her tiny figure in his hands after so long.... And it was as if he had held her like this for the last time yesterday. How many times had he wished she had hugged him like this before she left. Or that she came back like this. Everything, just not that he will be hugging him out of pity for the lost child.

- I'm sorry, - she said, pulling herself out of his arms.

And then she slipped and fell. Letting go of his emotions for a moment, he grabbed her arm and, holding on to the tree with his other hand, managed to lift her up. She bent over her cloak with her free hand, then obediently followed him. Darkness had already covered the woods when, watching her every step, he managed to get her back on the wooden path.

- Don't you dare to go there again, ok? - he looked her straight in the eyes.

- Ok - she replied, still standing with her hand in his.

She looked him straight in the eyes and admitted to herself that those were still the most beautiful eyes she knew. Their blue color absorbed her and she sank into them like in a deep abyss. That abyss, however, had a bottom, and she fell hard when she remembered that these eyes, while she was gone, looked at another woman and he went after her. She gently pulled out her hand and released it from his grip.

- Sorry to keep you! Probably you want to go home, - she said, trying to hide her pain.

- I'm not in a hurry this time!

She felt happy. Although he will later go where he belongs. But if that means that she will be able to enjoy his company a little bit more, it is enough for her to be happy. A happiness that screams because it is not permanent, because it is transparent and fake to its core. But it is still happiness!

Neither of them knew how many times they were walking in circles around the lake while talking about the past seven years. She got a degree in history, she even found a nice job in America. But Trakoschan kept calling her irreconcilably. And even knowing that she might be returning to her death, she could not resist.

There was a hint of disappointment while he was listening to her talking about her beliefs again. Nothing has changed. And he sincerely hoped it was, for her own good. Why torture yourself with impossible stories and crazy believes? Why not help yourself by accepting reality as it is?

And later that night, their conversation began to be accompanied by laughter. The holes in her cheeks still had a strange power to warm his soul. Even now that he is so wounded by the death of his child. Even after the shock of seeing Elena again. The same Elena. Nothing has changed, except that he no longer calls her his! Elena, with whom he doesn't have to pay attention to what and how he talks. Elena, who absorbs his every word, never forgets what he was talking about, how he felt. Elena who is the only one, irreplaceable. At the same time, Elena who killed part of him.

When it was getting really late, more for her than for himself, he asked her:

- Where do you live? Shall I give you a ride?
- I'm closer than you think, don't worry! You just get home safe!

He did come safe, but more confused than ever. If only he would fall asleep instead of the bears that are waking up now. No, no! Maybe after that dream, the pain for the lost child would decrease, but he would certainly sleep through the time of Elena's stay in this country. He doesn't want to sleep. He wants to fight. Combine these two things, combine them and survive. Both!

If he manages to stay on his feet, he will know that a new life is waiting for him.

4

Patricia didn't return after those two days as they agreed before. She enjoyed herself in Zagreb and Philip was glad for that. So he visited her on the weekends and brought her the belongings she needed.

Her face was glowing again and that made him happy. He had already been informed of postpartum depression, and to be honest, he seemed to be noticing the signs when she was at home. But here it looked like his wife was going to make it.

After they lost their child she has never spoken so much to him. She was telling him waving her arms about the meeting with her former college professor and how impressed he was with the great development of her mezzo-soprano. The professor encouraged her to keep working on her voice, because she can really make it.

Her friends Magda and Jasmina, sisters, did their best to help Patricia move on. Their parents were constantly out of the country for work, so they accommodated her during her stay in Zagreb and offered her the opportunity to invite her husband.

Philip thanked them for their generosity, but he had just returned to work and it would be some time before he could have his days off again. However, he spent the weekend at their house and was delighted with their hospitality.

He was glad to be with Patricia somewhere else and not in their house where everything reminds her of her pregnancy, and oh my God, there is still the baby room that no one dares enter. He took his wife for a walk in Zagreb and enjoyed her company, although he felt even more tense when he spoke as he hugged her from behind, dipping his face into her black hair.

What was he afraid of? That she might recognize in his words that he had met someone after seven years? That is impossible. That maybe he could call her by someone else's name? That is more than impossible. Then why does he think that Patricia will see in his eyes what he doesn't want to tell her? And it would be much easier if he just told her. That's for sure. But even more than that, he is sure that it is not a story for now, no matter how much he simplifies it. His goal is to help his beloved wife get through the pain she has experienced, and it seems to him that she has found the right path. Her friends accepted her and worked hard for her, the professor praises and motivates her, and him, her husband, who cares most about her well-being, to pull her back, it really wouldn't be right.

Or is he finding excuses only? Maybe he's just afraid of her reaction. After all, he never told her the whole truth about Elena because he knew he would not be the same anymore in her eyes. Patricia would surely make fun of Elena's personality, and he wouldn't be happy about that. Then, what would he say when she would ask him why he waited for such a woman to leave him and why he hadn't left her long before? As if he never wondered! But how could he explain to anyone what he could not even admit to his mother, that although he had seen the severe disorder in Elena, she was and remained the most gentle being he had ever met, and she drew him to her with some kind of magic. How can he explain to anyone that he never intended to leave her? It is true, he wanted to help her, he wanted more than anything to get her out of her fantasies. But he never wanted to leave her. If you ask him, even if she never got rid of her fantasies, he would have stayed with her. How to explain that to the people? To himself?

How could he stop that pain because she left without a word? Did she come back to play by the old rules? This time it would be much more acceptable to him, but if he wants to be honest with himself, from that day forward he can't stop thinking about her.

With his head bowed, he approached the visitors, looking for her shoes. He stood by the window looking out at the lake, looking for any sign that he was still there. But it wasn't until couple of days later that he heard behind him:

- Philip...
- You are here! - he said before turning and seeing her.

She stood with her hands down next to her body, her face a little frightened.

He approached her in two huge steps to make sure it was really her and then asked without delay:

- Is everything all right?

She remained silent and motionless in front of him and he could not help himself. He held out both hands to her, his palms clenching her upper arms gently, looking straight into her brown eyes, he asked the question again:

- Elena, are you okay?

She shook away the strain from her face and said:

- Yes, I'm sorry!

She pulled herself out of his arms, turning her back on him briefly, then turned back to him with a slight smile on her face. Then he bowed his head and pressed his fingers to his temples.

At first he was happy to see her again. He suddenly resented himself for thinking that she had run away again without saying goodbye. He recalled the last time how she reacted when he attacked her for being a heartless liar and now he was ashamed of himself. He looked at her in her dress without the robe and tried to make sure there were no bruises or scratches on her hands. But she was covering her face, and suddenly revealing it, she said:

- Sorry - and put her hands next to her body again.

He came closer and grabbed her hands, pulling her behind him. He took her to a small hallway where people rarely came across because there was nothing important to see.

- Why do I have to forgive you? - he asked.

She pulled her hand out of his and tried to cover her laughing mouth.

- I thought….You looked like you couldn't wait to see me again, - she said directly.

When she pierced him with her brown eyes, she convinced him that it was not Patricia standing there in front of him, so he discarded the restraint and allowed himself to talk to Elena:

- Yes! I wanted to see how you were after that night! Do you have bruises, scratches, any physical consequences?

- Very kind of you! Forgive me for not being able to return the favor, I do not show the place where I was hurt to a married man, even if you have seen it so many times!

At first he felt the urge to see it, to react, to help if it was serious. Then her gaze calmed him and showed him that there was no need to worry, it was nothing terrible. And in the end, the laughter she held back showed him that he had fallen for her provocative joke and that she was not hurt at all, at least not in the place where he imagined it. When she realized he got her joke, she started to laugh and the echo in the hallway was mixing with his.

- You naughty girl, he pushed her against the wall, stabbing her gently with his index finger all over her body, making sure the touches were far enough away from her private parts.

She was laughing frantically and, raising her tone of laughter, let him know that she would invite all visitors here if she did not stop. Her message was clear to him, he still knew this woman well enough to understand her even when she wasn't speaking. So he stopped and put his index finger on her nose, whispering close to her ear:

- Shhhhh ……

And when it seemed that she had calmed down for a moment and was about to walk away, she began to laugh again. Surprised, Philip squeezed her body with his, and covered her mouth and nose with his fist.

- Shhhhh… - he whispered in her ear.

As she calmed down, he loosened his grip, but he didn't move. His hand was still over her mouth and he could feel her warm breath. The smell of her skin set his brain on fire. As if that scent had never disappeared, as if it had always been there. As if it hadn't been seven years since he had last smelled it. He stood motionless as if time had stopped and as if he had forgotten where he was. Before his eyes, he saw Elena completely naked in his arms. He liked it. Until Elena, dressed in her brown dress, pushed him away hard and since he didn't expect this rejection, he staggered down the narrow stairs.

- Philip! - she grabbed his jacket as fast as a lioness.

She stared into his eyes with a frightened look to make sure she had really saved him from falling. Surprised by her reaction, she felt remorse. Let her push him away, for she could no longer bear his body over hers without kissing him, but that did not entitle her to throw him up the stone steps and break him. She breathed a sigh of relief and dropped his clothes from her grip.

He looked at Elena questioningly, who had never pushed him away like this before.

- I'm sorry, - he said, - I overreacted!

- Me too - she whispered. - But don't come so close to me again, please!

Of course. He knows he can't. He knows he doesn't belong there. He knows he's overreacting. That he took for granted something he shouldn't. This is Elena. That's right. But the years have passed and they did what no one else could have done - they separated them. Where did he get the courage to come so close to the woman that left him and after which he allowed himself to fall in love again and get married. And is it okay to get so close to another woman while his wife is still crying over her lost child and he is the one to comfort her, to be by her side? Shame on me, he told himself.

- I'm sorry, Elena! Forgive me. I was just glad to see you again!

She looked at him curiously.

- Are you serious? - she asked, looking at him with her brown eyes.

- Of course!

The man she knew like she knew her own heart stood in

front of her, showing her that he is not ashamed of his change? The one who told her he would stay with her even though everyone declared her crazy, but yet he married someone else only a few years after she tried to help herself and him and was back on her feet in America! Well, she knows how wrong she was, but cursed once, you are cursed forever! She came back, deeply remorseful, and what did she find? And he still allows himself to be happy to see her!

Who else can look forward to two women at the same time?

She turned and ran up the steps. He couldn't control himself and run after her, but her determination gave her the strength to disappear like dust before his eyes. As he turned in the middle of a not-so-small room in the castle, looking for her, an older lady approached him and addressed him in a kind voice:

- I would like to see the kitchen, please!

Damn kitchen!

- Come with me, he said calmly, - it's located away from the apartment building!

After introducing the lady to the kitchen, he tried to concentrate on the story:

- Since the Middle Ages, when food was prepared on an open fire, until recent times when masonry stoves are used, they are located in the middle of the room, so they can be accessed from all sides and easier to prepare daily meals for the family, but also feasts for many guests. There are numerous records of the hospitality of Zagorje nobles, which was widely known. Some dishes were prepared for days, and they were eaten for days. The menu included meat, fish, vegetables, fruits, and in the hands of imaginative chefs, the dishes were decorated to please both the palace and the eyes of discerning guests. For this purpose, in addition to utensils, they needed various tools that you can see here.

The lady obviously enjoyed looking around the kitchen and soaking up what she saw and heard. With a sigh, she informed Philip:

- I like to cook!

- I don't doubt it, he said politely.

After getting rid of the older lady, he wandered around the castle hoping to find Elena. She did not show up until closing. Before heading home, he sat for a while in the grass by the lake. This time, he didn't just enjoy the peace and the view. He waited with his whole being for her to appear. And why? He wish he knew!

But at least he knew something. He knew it was wrong to show her affection when he told her the truth that he had a wife at home. True, she is still in Zagreb, but she chose her. His intention, together with his wife, is to get over, as much as they can, the death of their child and to continue living as before. Elena 's absence in his life opened the door to that life, and if she intended to return to close that door, she was mistaken! He and Patricia will have a child, this time it will live! They will raise that child and maybe more children, raise them together, educate them. He determined his path, as he thought was best, after he had managed to put his broken pieces together and start living again. His life is not a bus station and Elena or anyone else can't just go in and out whenever they want. She hurt him once, she doesn't deserve a second chance.

And again… Ever since he made sure she was really back and hadn't seen her ghost, he thinks less of his lost little girl. His thoughts are occupied with her appearance or her non-appearance, and he has begun to eat more. He feels the urge to clean the house again before Patricia returns. And hug her tight when he sees her. To share with her their new will to live even after the tragedy that happened to them. They can do it, together. And where is Elena in all this? Where is she? Nowhere, she only made him love his wife more. He should thank her.

He imagined the bare shoulder of his wife while looking at her as she slept beside him in their bed. Then she becomes aware of his presence, slowly waking up and turning to him, extending her hand and pulling him close to her. And he leans over to kiss her warm cheek, he just has to get her hair off her face first. He puts her hair behind her ear with a light motion and kisses Elena in her closed eyes, and she smiles because she likes it.

Suddenly he jumps to his feet and taps his feet on the grass like a little angry child! He doesn't need this! This confusion in his mind! He has to react as soon as possible, even if he has to visit the psychiatrist Patricia's dad was talking about. But only after he confesses his sins to his mother. Mom! That will be nice. How many times he has forgotten to call her, to ask how she was in her loneliness. But she is the first one he thinks of when something goes wrong, like now when he thinks his head is messed up. And mom is not getting mad. Mom opened the door wide and stretched out her arms. He hugged her warmly and, as if she had been waiting for her whole life, absorbed his words. All of them.

- Mom, I need you tonight, he thought, running toward his car.

From the whole story he had set up in his head to be at least painful for his mother, sure that she would die first than betray him, he only said:

- Elena is back!

Mom smiled silently and made him dinner, joining him at the table. Her soul was full when she could eat with her child, and even more so that he wanted to share with her the things she knew he would not share with anyone else. She waited over the food for him to continue talking, but then she realized that she had to encourage him:

- Did you see her? - she asked him.

He nodded silently.

She waiting and when he didn't say nothing, she asked another question:

- How sure are you that you really saw her?

Philip wiped his mouth, drank some water, and before taking another bite, he said:

- We talked, Mom!

She nodded that she understood.

Elena was back! And if only her child could talk a little more about how he feels now that he's sure he saw her. The mother struggled whether to ask or to be silent, to wait when he was ready. He may need time, but if he ever decides to talk, it will be to his mother. His dad's advice is gone. His wise mouth is silent forever. And their child still needs support of all kinds. And he will need it for a long time. Now left alone, she will have to do this by herself.

- Patricia will be back soon, he interrupted her thoughts.
- Nice. How is she doing there? Do you think it was useful for her?
- I believe so. She connected with a former professor, noticed her progress, and persuaded her to use her voice more. He introduced her to his pianist and I see that she enjoys it. I'm glad. Her friends are just as wonderful and I see them working hard around her. I'm starting to miss her a little, but it's more important for me that she feels better!
- You have me!

He got up from his chair and knelt beside his mother, hugging her.

- And you know you can tell me everything - she added.

He strengthened his grip as much as he appreciated her support.

- Thank you, Mom!
- At any time, honey!

When he leaned back in front of the TV after dinner, she asked him to sleep there. He accepted with a smile. She kept an eye on him and for as long as she knew him, she noticed that he was distracted.

- Is something bothering you? she asked softly.
- Mom, he said softly, - I need time.
- Of course!

The moment he fell asleep in his old bed, his Patricia was still singing. The young pianist followed her, while the professor absorbed every note, sincerely admiring this connection. He expressed his admiration for them when they were finally done for the day.

Of course he wasn't a stranger and he knew well what had happened to Patricia lately. Wanting to motivate her a little more, he allowed himself, in the presence of a pianist, to tell her about his friend who had lost his 26 - year - old son. Let her be grateful that she lost her child now, although everyone understands that it is not easy either. The young pianist, Michel, himself well acquainted with the story of this young man, nodded his head all the time. After supporting the professor, as he was in

the foreground, Michelle drove Patricia to her friend's house. He stopped the car in front of the entrance, turned to Patricia, and as he kissed her hand, he said sympathetically:
  - I'm sorry this happened to you!

5

A Baroque concert was held in the ceremonial hall of the Drashkovich family. A lot of people took their places and enjoyed the beautiful performance. Philip's duty today was a little higher than usual because attendance on that day was different. People crowded in front of the portraits of the Drashkovich family and the creaking of the old wooden floor could be heard everywhere.

Filip enjoyed this day because the time was passing quickly, and Patricia was coming back from Zagreb tomorrow. He was kind to everyone and only here and there, and especially if he saw a child, did it occur to him that the pain for his daughter was still present. Fortunately, although there were many people in the castle, there were few children today. At the very end of the concert, before people began to leave the castle, he saw the well-known strange shoes.

He knew everything he had to know. But something like a magnet made him follow her around the room and watch out for her not to see him. Letting go of all the other visitors and not caring about his obligations, powerless to fight against his desire, he walked behind her like magic. Why is he doing this to himself and to her? In an instant he stood as buried. Isn't he mature enough to see the consequences of the things he does? A lot of people and situations can get involved in our lives, but we need to know our way and we must stay away from what would excite our journey.

He turned abruptly and stepped back. He wanted to make sure he did it because he decided to, not because he lost her. But he knew he wasn't right.

In the same way he fought against the thought of the child's death, he fought against the thoughts that reminded him of Elena too. Ready to return to "his" life, he greeted Patricia the next day, happy that she was back home.

He has already managed to clean the house. He did not cook because today they were going to eat with her parents. He was glad that her parents saw that she had recovered a lot after her stay in Zagreb. What he didn't like was that they paid too much attention to her wanting to go back to singing. He assured himself that he was not jealous and that he certainly wanted to support his wife, but against his will he noticed that her mother and father absorbed the news about the professor and pianist with such attention that he had not noticed for a long time concerning their marriage and plans for the future.

He tried to reason and not think like a small child, telling himself that he is in fact acting immaturely. True, the recent events broke him, but it would be more than wrong to expect her parents to understand him the way his mother understands him. In the end, they are her parents. It is not their fault, they have never been a working class people like his parents and it is understandable that they would be more interested in the health and work of the old university professor than the construction worker who built them both houses. This cannot and will never be justified, but people should be allowed to be what they are and not sulk at each other's differences. His parents always told him that, but he seems to have fallen into another puberty, in some late years when he needs to understand the world around him and that that world understands him.

The desire to be close to his wife made him gently pull himself up and hug her from behind. He noticed that she was still awake by the way she was breathing. He stroked her hair gently. He missed her. Patricia shuddered and he asked quietly:
- Honey, is everything okay?
Not turning, she replied with a lazy voice:
- Honey, I'm just trying to fall asleep!
He wanted to be at her service of course. He covered her shoulders with the light blanket and let his wife fall asleep alone.

In the morning she waited for him with a smile. Thank God, life goes on! But sometimes not as we plan. With that same smile, she asked him to understand that she would have to spend more time in Zagreb in the future. She didn't want to force him to move there because she knows he doesn't like living in a big city, but she begged him to be patient with her.

Of course he will be patient. Who wouldn't be for the woman he loved? Who wouldn't push her towards making her dreams come true? But he will miss her. Very much. Fortunately, he has his mother here, his wife's parents, as well as his job. And she will come often, of course. She didn't say exactly when she was going and when she would come back, and he didn't want to bother her. As long as she is happy. And he is hers! Only hers!

Soon the two of them are going on a vacation by the sea. Everything between them will be as before. But there are still three weeks until then. Him being in the castle, sitting by the lake and expecting Elena to show up at any moment, while he prays that she doesn't.

But she was nowhere to be seen. And as usual he did not know if he was happy or sad about it. But he was very angry when one day he approached his car and found a piece of paper under the wiper. The familiar handwriting. Fear shook his whole body. He turned pale before he could read because he knew it wasn't good. Why did he believe she had changed? How could he be so naive? She is leaving again! In the same way, the same damn paper! For God's sake, how should he read it? Isn't it better just to throw it away?

He crumpled it between his fingers. He clenched his fist. He wanted to throw it away and step on it with anger. He was sweating on his forehead and under his nose. When will he find the courage to end it with Elena once and for all and take her out from his heart? Yes, he needed the help of the damn piece of paper, and he managed to open it with trembling fingers. His teeth were ready to chew it and his mouth wanted to spit it out with all the pain Elena had inflicted again, but he begs for himself and her, one last time.

He read the short text quickly and was left petrified.

- I am watching you every day, my love!

No one in his twenty-seven years had ever been able to change his mood so quickly. No one ever managed to make him sit behind the wheel and start crying instead of leaving. No one made him look at the castle, the forest, the lake, the road, the city and not see the brown eyes. Nobody. Nor will he allow anyone.

That is why he is leaving for Zagreb right now!

He hoped for a warm embrace, he hoped to find a cure in Zagreb. That his wife's warm arms would embrace him and bring him back to life. And that's all he wants. His life back.

When she saw him at her door, Magda was surprised.

- Philip! We didn't expect you! Patricia is still with the professor, you know?

In just a few minutes, Philip was with the professor too. More precisely, in front of his house. It was wrong to ring and disturb them, so he stayed in his car waiting for Patricia, until dawn if it's necessary, he thought.

The piece of paper, which he did not want to throw away, but to hide among the documents in the car that Patricia never touches, kept him awake and fought fatigue instead. She knew what she was doing. No one knows him better than her. She knew those few words would make his whole body, soul, and past years tremble before his eyes. She knows everything, that little witch! She came to destroy him, and unfortunately for him, she has the strongest weapon with her. If only his child had been born alive. That little bundle of joy he would be given to take home from the hospital would have been so powerful that even the memory of Elena would have faded. Or is he just lying to himself and nothing can fade away the memory he has of Elena...

They must go on that holiday by the sea! With his wife and

as soon as possible!

His wife! His dear wife just came down the steps that connected the professor's house and the road to the sidewalk. The young gentleman offered her his hand so that she could go down the stairs safely in her high heels. Philip would be glad that Patricia was well accepted and treated in Zagreb. Full of anticipation, he got out of the car and, ironing his shirt with his hand, said in a polite voice:

- Patricia!

She raised her head and looked at him in surprise. Her hand was still in the young man's hand, so when she saw her husband, she gently pulled it out and showed her friend in the direction of Philip, losing her breath trying to explain:

- It seems that my husband came to visit me!

She felt uneasy in her movements, but she brought her friend to her husband.

- Philip, this is Michelle! Michelle, this is my husband, Philip! He surprised me!

Michelle leaned over to Philip, and after a few seconds, rising up, greeted him politely:

- Nice to meet you. I follow your wife on the piano and I can tell you that you should be proud. Her voice is beautiful and if she works on it, one day you will have a very famous person as your wife!

Philip received his words, looking into his wife's eyes, as he kissed her hand tenderly. At this moment, he was not really interested in whether and how much Patricia would be famous one day. The only thing that mattered to him was to stay in the same relationship with her as before and get a child that will live.

- Nice to meet you too, Michelle - that was all he said.

Patricia thanked Michelle for the offered ride, but she will definitely go back with her husband. Michelle greeted him politely, and Philip held the door open as Patricia got into their car.

- You surprised me, she said
- I hope you liked it!
- Well, yes, and on what do I owe this pleasure?
- I missed you!

The car started, and after thinking for a moment, she said:
- I missed you too.

That softened him and he reached out with his hand to hold hers, but she pulled back.

- You're driving - she told him sternly.

This time she was right. But he could not explain her rejections even on their vacation at sea. He was consoling himself that he was only imagining that, that he was acting like a child, expecting more attention. He blamed himself for resenting her for not trying to comfort him because of the situation that loomed over him, but she didn't even know what was happening to him. So he tried to compose himself, get himself out of his head, and dedicate himself to pleasing her, to make her feel satisfied. He succeeded, he succeeded very well, but the trace of the new Patricia was on her face, in her speech, her posture.

He forced himself to understand. For eight months she was carrying a heart under her heart and hoped for the best. She has never said and probably she would never say if she feels guilty about their child's death. It is not difficult to imagine. So he was aware that she needed more time and freedom to get back where she was before, at the very beginning. And she will. She is a strong woman. And he will be her support. He has already seen the results. They returned to Krapina after the holiday, and two days later she didn't even mention Zagreb. He liked that, except that he felt bad spending so much time at work, and she felt sorry for herself at home. He was happy to hear that she had spent the day with her parents or her aunt. He was willing to do absolutely anything for her. Except for one thing - he couldn't stop waiting for Elena to come, now knowing that she was watching him and he just wanted for her golden hair to shine from around the corner.

And it happened! Finally, one hot day, he saw her hair in the library. He felt even better when he realized he was standing just a few feet behind her well-known figure. She was wearing a simple dress, her hair was down and her head bowed. She was standing close to the books, holding one in her hands. He didn't know how to react. What would be the smartest thing to do? He wanted to greet her, to run to her! But he also wanted to stay there behind her and watch her this time. His doubt was interrupted by her voice:

- You're back!

He became paralised. His palms were sweating. And as he always did, he tried to wipe them off his jacket so that they would be dry in case he had to shake somebody's hand, and now it would be her hand.

- Did you see me in the glass? He asked quietly when he saw his reflection in the glass in front of her.

- Since I don't have eyes on my neck, she said. - Vacation again? I hope it was peaceful this time.

- Your message was the last thing I read before I left, I must admit. I respect your desire for books, but, unfortunately, I must warn you, as well as all other visitors, that you are not allowed to touch the books from this library.

She turned to him with a serious expression on her face.

- Is that so? - she asked and then added- Well, just so you know, I touched them while you were gone. I read it and returned it nicely, don't worry!

- You took books outside the castle?

- The books are back in place now -s he reassured him - It will be the same with this one too, don't worry! I found something mine again, so I'll borrow it!

He gave up. Although he was breaking the rules, he could not treat her like all the other visitors, and he knew her, he knew she would keep her promise.

- I will take that as if you had found a book that you would like to read, and not that it used to be yours and belonged to your collection!

- You can take it as you wish, - she put the book on her chest, hugged it and raised her head. Then she stared at him suspiciously, then took a few steps and came closer to him - What happened to you?

He did not allow himself to be confused.

- I got a little sunburned, he said.

She laughed sweetly. She tilted her head to one side and held out her hand to him. Touching his cheek with her fingers, she said with a smile:

- I always liked you and your love for the sea, the sun, the waves. I hope you enjoyed.... my love - she whispered these last words.

With a sudden movement, he squeezed her hand so hard that she knelt down due to the pain in her wrist and dropped the book on the floor. She tries to catch it, but halfway to the floor she realizes that he's holding her tight enough and not letting her get down, at least not alone. He knelt together with her, keeping his gaze fixed on her eyes, which, as she picked up the book, were trying to find out if everything was fine with her.

- You're going to destroy my book, what are you doing? - she yelled at him.

- What are you doing? - he yelled even louder.

- I'm trying to save the book because if I destroy it because of you, I'll have to take full responsibility! But you are not letting me go, you squeeze my caring hand without mercy! Where did all your tenderness disappear?

Realizing that he was really hurting her and that he was acting like a bully, he immediately let go of her wrist.

- Thank you! - she said calmly.

With both hands, he pushed his hair back, showing his face completely. He said calmly but very seriously:

- Elena, I have always supported my love for the castle. I'm glad you were able to come back and enjoy it again. But don't you think you're here a little too often?

- No, I don't! It's the only place in the world where I feel like I am home, even though you never believed me!

- I won't now either!

- I am not asking you anymore! I got used to it! I accepted that!

He felt the same grip around his heart. The same sadness as when this woman was his favorite being and when he tried his best to help her, to save her from those ridiculous stories. He felt as sorry for her as he had then. He absorbed her eyes as he screamed inside asking Heaven to help him so he could help her. He knew that it should not concern him anymore, that she was neither that young now nor his, and that she herself should try to understand, but it was obvious that she wouldn't.

- I would really like to help you - he told her honestly.
- No, you don't! If you wanted to, you would try to trust me at least a little bit. And then you would dig and search with me, and since there was so much evidence, you would've been convinced!
- Elena, this is crazy!
- I'm sorry these things happen to me too, but they happen no matter how much you ignore them! And no matter how crazy I look!
- You're not crazy - he couldn't bear hearing that word, even from her, - you just don't want to think any other way!
- I thought differently until the death of my parents put me back on track. Until you helped me and showed me who I was.
- It's my fault now! It's as if I haven't cursed myself a million times for ever bringing you here!
- Did I say it's your fault? On the contrary! And I am deeply grateful to you!

She rested her palms on his shoulders, clutching the book under her elbow.

She drew her tiny body close to his, then raised herself on her toes as much as she could and pressed her mouth against his cheek. She stayed like that for a moment, or two, or three.

He felt her breath on his face. He could smell her hair. He felt all that can be felt - life and fear, death and joy, madness in the body of the angel who clung to him. With his soul, and as loud as he could hear with his ears, he could hear being put back together again. Like the wind took the pieces like the pages from this book and put them back together. He felt healthy, and he hasn't been feeling like that in years. That he was light like the wind. That he was floating even though she was holding him with her hands. That he moves in such a way that he can no longer control his body, and surrenders. He surrendered. And then he saw that the breeze carried his arm around her waist. It fitted perfectly. He pulled Elena to his chest, and with his warm mouth found hers.

The breeze disappeared when she pushed him away, pulled herself out of his arms, and ran out of the library. His voice caught up with her on the stairs and she felt that it grabbed both of her legs like a hand when he yelled:

- Stop!
She managed to overcome the paralysis of her body and, running faster than ever, got lost in the castle.

6

While Patricia was in Zagreb, Philip used the time to maximum, fighting to expose Elena and her latest games. His mother realized that he had not even spent a few nights in Krapina. She prayed that he was wrong thinking that he knows who she really is.

She was wrong. Not quite, but in a way. Most of the time he just watched Elena. In all possible ways. He even allowed himself to hide in the castle furniture, only to win the game of cat and mouse. Whenever she would see him, she did not avoid him. Sometimes she would just sit with him by the lake for a long time. Sometimes they talked more, sometimes less. However, they both didn't mention his outburst since that day. She, out of respect for his new life, and he, of fear that he might repeat the same thing again. When greeting each other, they were very careful and stood at a sufficient distance from each other.

They both feared that the physical distance was the only distance between them.

She always insisted on walking him to his car. And the more she insisted, it became clearer that something bad was behind it. And he wanted more and more to find out what she was planning to do. This made him lie for the first time in his life. He would greet her and leave, and then he would secretly come back. If this is a game, they were both curious who would play it longer.

After several sleepless nights and days, tired and barely able to stand on his feet due to insomnia, it seemed that he was on a good trail. He went down the stairs to the lowest level of the castle, where he managed, after a supernatural effort to follow Elena, to see her crawling behind one closet. His once dearest person in the world was lying and although he was shocked, he admitted to himself the truth that Elena lived in the castle longer than he had imagined. Retreating behind the closet, she would stay until everyone leaves, and then continue her stay in the castle in silence and solitude.

After making sure that there were no living souls around, Filip peeked curiously behind the closet. In order to see how Elena was doing this, he carefully pulled all the weight toward himself, very carefully. At the same time, he felt sorry for Elena because she had to do that every night, and he knew it wasn't easy for her.

Philip pushed his slender body between the old wood and the wall, which was half-covered with wood paneling, and stayed that way for a moment. Easy to do, he thought, especially since this is a poorly occupied room. The only thing is that you have to stay with your head turned to the same side as when you entered. Because if you want to turn your head the other way, you have to push the closet forward a little bit more. And then his position would become suspicious.

After he found her secret hiding place, he turned to the second part of his mission - to find out why Elena stays here at night and what she does? Where she goes when she doesn't stay there after the castle closes. He found himself thinking a lot more about this than about what his wife is doing and how she is in Zagreb. She is, thank God, a normal woman, and she has been out of their home way too long not bothering him in the investigation and his excessive desire to find out what this less normal woman is doing here and what her intention is.

That summer evening he spent alone by the lake. This time the golden-haired fairy didn't come and didn't honor him with her smile. He got up and walked to his car in the dark. And then he left. But not too far. Only to the place where he used to hide the car when he wanted to trick her into leaving. If she watched him, she would be sure now that he left, that he is on his way home. He parked the car and opened the trunk. He took out the bag he had been driving around since yesterday and said to himself:

- Ok my dear, let's play, let's see who will last longer!

In less than an hour, Philip returned like a hunched old man, walking slowly in his old shoes. He wrapped himself in an old jute cloak and hung an artificial beard under his torn hat to cover his face. He managed to cover his blue eyes and nose as much as possible with glasses and supported his body on a wooden stick.

After walking the paths around the lake hoping that she is not there because he might scare her with his appearance, he exclaimed contentedly because he knew where to find her, if not tonight, then one of these nights. He climbs the hill and pulls out the keys of the iron entrance grate and then the wooden door of the castle. He unlocked the door silently, and even he didn't hear the key moving in the lock. Cautiously, after quietly detaining himself, he locked the heavy wooden door behind him. His plan was not to frighten her, but only to show her that he had discovered her secret, after revealing it to the end. So he left his props next to the door, returning to his real appearance again. Then he lit a candle, shoved it into the candlestick, and began to walk through the castle, yelling not too loud with every step:

- Elena, it's me, Philip, I don't want to scare you, just come out please, I know you're here! Elena, I won't do anything to you, I promise, it will remain our secret, you know I would never betray you or hurt you. Elena?

Walking on his toes on the red carpet, he managed to reach the library, and after listening carefully to hear turning off the pages of the book, he peeked inside. But there was nobody in there. If he could at least find her there reading, it would be easier for him. But it is not like that. Discomfort overwhelmed him. He raised his voice.

- Elena, please come out, I won't do anything to you, I promise!

But she was nowhere to be found. In his head, he was sure she heard him and was afraid of him. So he yelled and begged more and more to persuade her to come out. But she didn't. This made him angry, and he quickened his pace toward the closet behind which he believed he would find her. Coming, as he thought, near her, he lowered his voice and said:

- Elena, please stop! You can play with everyone, but please don't play with me, I'm your friend! I know where you are, I know everything, if I wanted to, I would have told everyone, but I don't want to do that! I just want to tell you that I know everything! I can't be against you, Elena! I just want to help you!

He approached the closet step by step, almost certain that she was trembling behind him. Starting from the side, Philip saw that the space between the closet and the wooden wall was so narrow that even Elena couldn't fit in. Hoping that she somehow managed to squeeze in and keep her breath there, he pulled the closet toward him with one hand and held out the candle with the other, sure that he would see her frightened face in the light. Unfortunately and in his disbelief, Elena was not there.

Disappointed to the point of pain, Philip began to breathe angrily. After clenching his teeth and eyes, he yelled abruptly:

- Elenaaaaaa!

His voice echoed through the castle, but no one answered him. The only one who reacted to his torment was the flame of the candle he was holding. It struggled with the air to stay alive. He instantly regretted yelling near the candle because it would leave him without light. He grabbed his pocket in panic and calmed down when he felt a match under his fingers. He played it smart tonight because it seems to him that the flames are really in danger. Although he no longer intended to yell, especially not near the flame, the flame did not subside. It staggered battling, but lost the battle. Philip remained in the dark, and the strong smell of an extinguished candle reached his nose.

He pulled the match from his pocket and again gave life to the candle in his palm. To his surprise, although he was quite calm, it seemed that the flame was in danger again. Philip stiffened his hand a little frightened and stared at the candle. What could threaten the flame in here, something behind the closet or something right next to the wall? His face was flooded with suspicion, but he was determined to fight tonight and wouldn't let himself get tired that easy. He brought the candle close to the wall to protect it from the suspicious draft and turned its flame toward the wooden rectangular panels nailed on the wall.

With light movements, Philip very patiently began to bring the candles up and down, and then to the left and to the right. The more he walked, the more unusual it was. With all his senses turned up on high, Philip clenched his fingers and knocked on the wood. The sound he heard confused him even more. It sounded as if there was no wall, but a cavity. If the search for Elena had not taken him to this position and to this part of the castle, he would not have known that their bases were separated from the wall. Leaving aside for a moment the reason why he was there, he wanted to see how great the damage was and his fingers began to squeeze the wood. Then he noticed that the wood would separate from the wall, and in an instant he was ready to accept the whole two-sided cladding with one hand when it fell out.

- The consequence of her being here, - he thought as he pulled the board toward him. He managed to separate it only at one end, while the other remained attached to the wall. Philip gently pulls, but it lets him know that it can't go in that direction. He then pushed it, and this time it was more successful. He patiently waited for the other panels to come off, and then in shock, his hand shook, the candle fell down and rolled away, leaving him in total darkness.

With trembling hands, he lit another match, and while the dim light lasted, he was shocked by the sight in front of him. There was an opening in the wall, and right next to it, stairs leading to the bottom. With the second match, he decided to be brave and stepped on the first step, then went down on the second, then on the third one. Only a couple of more steps separated him from his candle, and he jumped over them with trembling legs, grabbed the candle and managed to light it again. The draft was fighting with the flames and he was trying to protect the candle with his palm as he descended an abyss he never suspected was in the castle, behind this old wooden closet.

In the narrow hallway where the stairs descended in a semicircle, he saw old lamps that had not been lit for centuries. He struggled with his thoughts, convincing himself that this was not a dream, and that it was most likely a corridor leading somewhere and that someone probably knows more about this. And it probably leads to a dungeon or, God forbid, an old grave. Or maybe it just leads to the kitchen. There must be an explanation, there must be an end.

And it had an end. He came in front of a semicircular wooden door. The wooden planks on the door were connected by long - wrought iron. He would rather give up and go back, leaving the research for another day and more reasonable time. But then he remembered who he was looking for and his hands became sweaty when he thought that Elena knew about this hallway and even worse, that she used it. And if she wasn't afraid, why would he be and leave without seeing what was in there.

Then he squeezed the cold metal handle gently. With a short creak, the door opened and a slightly larger and more spacious space appeared in front of him. That space was dark, Philip admitted to himself that there was little and no air inside. But to be honest, if this was underground, then it is a normal thing. He starts walking slowly through the stone-paneled room, and to his surprise, the first thing that he saw was a closet. A wooden closet, apparently much older than the one upstairs in the castle. And of course, this one here smelled of wood and moisture. Across the closet there was a table and one chair, of a material very similar to the closet. Trying to compare them, he looked at the closet again and saw that one door was half open. Suddenly his jaw dropped! Hanging on the opened door, Philip saw the well-known cloak.

Not only did she know about this place, but she was using it. He could see now how those seven years separated them. She was really no longer the woman whose every step he knew, as she knew his. He really didn't know what she was thinking, what she was up to, just as she didn't know about him. Now, here, in this mysterious place, on this night when he looks for her, he feels that he cannot bear it. His Elena, the girl that once was his other half, had moved so far away from him and became a total stranger to him. They were strangers and when he got married, but at least he knew then that she was far away and would never return. That she was gone forever. Now, after she came back into his life and was often so close to him, the knowledge that she had become more distant from him than many other people hurt him in some strange way. He felt defeated, trampled and endlessly abandoned.

He lowered the candlestick on the table beside him, pulled out the chair, and lowered his tired body into it. Resting his elbows on his knees, he rested his palms on his forehead, that felt wearily down. He always avoided thinking about her and how close she was to him. He didn't want to admit to himself how much he liked her and how much he missed her since she was gone. Determined to bury the past, he was always trying to chase her away from his thoughts every time she came on his mind. He assured himself that she was not worth mentioning. But now, everything he tried to push in, was coming out. He started crying and his tears were falling on the stone floor. He cried like a child, and that's how he felt. He wanted to be hugged, warmed, comforted. Alone in this underworld, he gave in to his pain and the pain broke him. In this empty underworld he allowed himself to be who he is. And he cried until he felt that what was pressing his chest came out of his body through his tears.

After that, his vision adjusted even better to the light of the candle, and he managed to see the space that separated that room from another one. Seeing that his candle was about to give up, he decided to hurry and see what's behind it. And then he would have to go upstairs to get a new candle. He approached the wall and looked in the other part of the room. There was another closet, smaller than the first one, but with both doors closed. There was a bed in front of him, and in it, under a rough blanket, he could see the silhouette of a clinched body. With her legs folded in her arms, she even pushed her face into the blanket. The only thing left outside the blanket was her golden hair.

Without thinking, Philip whispered in a low voice:
- Love!

At the sound of his voice she started crying out loud. In panic, he ran to the bed and leaned over her. He reached for her shoulders with his free hand, wanting to make sure that his touch would calm her and awaken confidence in her. Still not moving, she asked:

- Go away, please!

He put the candle down on the cupboard next to her where he saw the book she had taken from the library that day and sat on the edge of the bed next to her.

- Elena,- he said, believe me, I won't do anything you don't want me to do!

- Then leave, I don't want you to be here!

- I don't want you to be here either, but here you are! I thought you were staying in a hotel, that you are leaving and coming from some distant place, maybe that you have bought a house somewhere, but that you will be stuck in this dampness without fresh air, I wouldn't have thought that in a madness! How did you get here?

She starting crying even louder and yelled at him:

- I will not allow you to insult me, my life or anything that is mine! I didn't get anywhere! I just know this castle much better than you know it, and I've lived in it for centuries before you got your job here! This is not my workplace, this was my house before my relatives rebuilt it and buried its parts and spilled that lake around! But that's none of your business!

Aware of how much he hurt her, without intention, he hugged her with both hands and pressed her head on his shoulder, stroking her hair.

- I'm sorry, I didn't mean it that way- he whispered - I'm just worried about you and your health!

- You should not worry about me, she said a little calmly, but there was even more sadness in her voice.

- You're wrong....my love....

She wanted to push him away. She wanted to throw him on the stone floor, then stand up above him, tell him to leave and never come there again... To watch him go, to throw everything she could at him, but not to hurt him, just to scare him and make him quicken his pace. She wanted to see him raise his arms and wrap them around his head to protect himself from her anger. She wanted to make him feel miserable.

But of all she wanted, she made only what she didn't want

- she sank into his arms and rested her head on his chest.

He held her like that for a moment, and when her crying stopped completely, he laid her down and covered her in bed. She already felt sad because of him leaving, and then she came to life when he lay down next to her. He reached under her, and placed her head on his shoulder, resting his chin on her head. As the smell of her hair intoxicated him, he decided to be brutally honest:

- I'm not planning to tell anyone nor to do anything that will harm you. I'm not your enemy. It's true, your behavior leaves me in awe, but as much as I want to be reasonable, I can't. I just want to protect you!

- And what will happen on the day when you come to your senses?

Philip squeezed her harder, then said:

- I don't think I will! Everything stands still in front of the memory of us!

They were both silent, lying totally still, and then he broke the silence:

- Elena, why did you destroy us?

Without any expression on her face, without wanting to cry again, she said coldly:

- I wanted you to be ok. After finding out the truth about myself and you not being able to accept it, I wanted to let you live a "normal" life!

How can he tell her that he does not accept such a truth even today?

- Don't you think that you mix your love for history in some way with the reality, love?

If he hadn't said that last word, she would have pushed him hard on the stone floor. Thus, she remained motionless in his arms and said coldly:

- No! I know I'm not mixing anything!

Seeking an even better position for her head, she turned her face a little more toward his neck. His sensitive skin was warmed by her breath. He put his fingers into her hair, drawing her shoulders even closer. The candle on the cupboard next to them was dim, and he didn't care. Tonight he would feel better not to get out of this hole than to get out of it. In fact, he would put up with everything except to leave this place. He hugged Elena as if he was begging her not to tell him to leave. She could do anything, but not that, and not now, when she felt his pulse near her temple. Closing her eyes, she tried to remember if the scent of his skin reminded her of her love from seven years ago, or had taken her incredibly far, centuries before.

Anyway, she inhaled his scent long and deep, then exhaled quickly and enjoyed inhaling again. If there was one thing she wanted at this point, it was for him not to let her out of his embrace, even if he never believed in her story.

Many times she tried to understand him, to put herself in his place and imagine how she would react if someone told her such a crazy truth. Ah, he calls it the truth because she believes it is, and what would she call it if she didn't? You can't, you just can't know how you would react if you were on the other, the opposite side. What we have not experienced, we can only imagine and assume, but we cannot "know."

One thing fascinated her the whole time. Sometimes it even made her angry, sometimes she was ok with it. Philip insulted her to the core, and she forgave him everything! She wanted to think that it wasn't true, but it was! It was rather strange to her and she tried to explain to herself how she could, and the only answer was love. Leaving him that way was not enough of a punishment for him. She wanted her departure to hurt him at least as much as he hurt her, and yet, when she thought she had succeeded, she felt sorry for him. But the desire to see him again when she returned to Trakostan never left her alone. Seeing him is one thing. Talking to him is another. But to lie next to him like this and even allow him to hold her in his arms, while he has a ring on his hand that confirms that he belongs to another woman... And worse of all, she enjoyed all of that.

Oh yes, he deserves such punishment that she should jump up and tear him to pieces with her teeth. " Sworn once, sworn forever" was the only thing she knew about promises from both her lives. And he trampled on his own and escaped by marrying another woman. And then he lied to her too. While she is waiting for him at home, he hugs his first wife, to whom he was swearing... Shame on him! He is disgusting! But she loves him. Is it true that love never dies and that it only falls asleep sometimes when we force it to do so?

The one who could once easily recognize her thoughts was so close that she seemed to be able to hear them. Or is she hearing his thoughts? Or do they both hear someone they can't see? Or all these questions should be set aside, come even closer together and in the dark, find his lips with hers.

All the bells of this world rang in the quiet underworld as two people on an old wooden bed joined together as if they wanted to make up for those seven years of separation.

7

When he opened one eye the next morning after rubbing it with his fingers, he could see a little better where he had fallen last night. The dim light illuminated just a little bit the underground room that Elena used for her crazy things. With a little trouble, Philip managed to open the other eye and looked with both of them around the room. A little bit of daylight was spilled over the modest furniture in that corner of the room, and he still couldn't understand where it was coming from. Not far from the closet near the bed, there was something like an old dressing table and a chair next to it. He saw his clothes on that chair, aligned and arranged. His dear Elena, meticulous and caring as always, made sure that he still looked clean and tidy by picking up his scattered clothes from the floor. Always one step ahead of him, she knew that he should still show up for work today, and at the same time, he should look decent and clean.

Elena!

The last thing he remembered when he last saw her flashed through his head like lightning. He closed his eyes again. He asked remorse to visit him briefly, but the only guest in his heart was pleasure. The smell of her skin reached his nose, and a smile of victory came across his face because he woke up in her bed.

The moment he felt her sitting to the other side of the bed, he removed his smile from his face. He looked through his half-open eyes, but he didn't see her, so he thought that she was sitting behind him. He remained calm and motionless, just like her, until she said:

- I made you a chamomile tea, after cooling it down a bit, I added honey and lemon. If you are still on the same doses, you will enjoy your tea. I sliced your favorite fruit along the way, look! I don't want you to go up hungry!

With a gentle smile that came up on the memory of old Elena, he turned his head towards her, saying:

- How did you know I was awake?
- I know you! I know how you breathe when you sleep and when you don't! I know that as soon as you rub your eyes, you can keep them closed for a half day more, but you can't fall asleep anymore. I have to admit, I was surprised that you still wake up at the same time, but this time it's good for me because I managed to prepare this for you before you woke up. Now, as you go up the stairs, all I have to do is to look at you and enjoy myself, after watching you sleep.
- You didn't sleep?
- Sleeping would be only a waste of time. I have nothing to do here but read and sleep, so I'll do it while you're gone. I am enjoying your presence. And I missed your head on the pillow next to me so bad anyway. And one more thing, no one can guarantee that I will see it again on the same pillow - she bit her lower lip, handing him the bronze bowl - today's vitamins, love! Don't let your tea get cold!

Rising in a semi-sitting position and adjusting the pillow under his head, he took the bowl from her hands and set it down on the cupboard. Then he turned to her and, with both hands outstretched, brought her upper body close to his chest.

- I don't feel hungry today!

At least not that kind of hungry, he thought.

- I also have toast. Milk, cheese... Do you want cereal?

Her humanity warmed his heart. He squeezed her harder, kissed her forehead, and repeated:

- I'm not hungry!

She remained still for a moment, then she squeezed his hand. Rising to be able to look him in the eyes, she suddenly changed the subject:

- I'm sorry I wasn't careful enough and you found my secret corner. For everything else that has happened since you entered here, I don't feel any remorse and I don't care. But if it's easier for you, feel free to put all the blame on me. After you've lifted me to heaven, I don't care if anyone curses me for that. I'm afraid I won't hear the curses, I've stayed there, under the sky, I'm too high. I just wanted you to know that.

- Good, he said, - I know now!

Pushing her head back, she stared straight into his eyes. She stayed like that for a while before, without taking her eyes off him, said:

- I'm glad you're happy too!

He laughed out loud.

- Is it that obvious? -he asked.

- If someone doesn't know you like I do, then they can not tell. But I can see a little bit further than the others!

- What else do you see?

- That, even though you are trying to fight it, you are wondering what time it is. Relax, I would have woken you up on time! And the light comes through the corridor that leads to the surface. It ends with a grilles and not even a squirrel can get through it. The only thing that can get here and peek is the air. The fresh air that you thought was gone last night. The Drashkovich family was smarter than you imagined. And please don't get angry, but you will never know the old parts of the castle better than I do!

His wide-open eyes remained on her face even after she fell silent, and then Philip burst out laughing.

- You still read me like an open book!

She laughed with him as loud as she could after seeing that time can not prevent to remain as one with the one you once were, even though an ocean separates you from him. Then she jumped up, crossed one leg over him, and sat in his lap. She raised his hands in the air above the bed and hold them there with one hand, while with the other, she brought a piece of apple to his mouth.

- You'll have to go upstairs soon,- she told him, - but you are not going hungry!

- Then feed me,-he said, moving his mouth aside.

She followed his movements, carrying the scent of apples under his nose, until he began to laugh again.

- You didn't understand me - he told her.

He freed himself from her grip and lowered his hands. With one hand he took her by the wrist, brought the apple over the bowl, and, shaking her hand, ordered her:

- Let it go!

Before the apple joined the rest of the fruit, he began to gnaw at her mouth and cheeks gently.

Half an hour later, getting dressed, thanking her for taking care of his clothes, he drank the tea even though it was cold, and ate a few pieces of apple and banana. As he was in a rush, she stood close to him, wrapped in a blanket and fixing his shirt and strands of his hair with her hand. She held his jacket with one hand, helping him to put it on easily, and he deliberately took off the sheet she was squeezing around her with the other hand.

- Oops, sorry - he apologized smiling

- Shame on you,- she said, glancing sternly at him and shoving the rest of the fruit into his mouth as punishment.

He wanted to kiss her before leaving, but she had already wrapped herself in the sheet and went in front of him. He followed her up the stairs after they passed the wooden door, and when they reached the end, she moved aside, holding the candle in her hand, letting him approach her, and then she wrapped her arm around him and put all her weight around his neck.

- If you never visit me again, I'm gonna ask you for two things,- she said, looking him in the eyes pleadingly, -do your best not to betray me. And... .. Never forget that you brought me back to life tonight.

The long embrace wasted their time. He didn't say anything to her, but after he got out of the closet and pushed it into place, finding himself back in his reality, he became aware that Elena, this night, brought him back to life too.

He worked that day, breathing with full lungs. He had an even greater reason for this when she found him in the castle again, bringing him a sandwich with prosciutto and cheese. Although her gestures were the gestures of Elena that he once knew, he did not take them for granted. Thanking her, he hugged her tenderly and kissed her cautiously.

- Did you sleep a little? - he asked her.

- I did my best. But the memory of you and your scent kept waking me up!

- Oh, I'm sorry,- he apologized with a smile. -But I think you really need a break. Rest a little and after work I will go to Krapina anyway, so don't wait for me by the lake!

A poisonous arrow pierced her, but she was too happy to fall down on her knees. She stood right in front of him and greeted him with the words:

- Alright!

She will do her best not to think of him after he leaves today. His suggestion is very clever. It would be best if she slept through the moments when he would be with his wife in an attempt to apologize and come up with the most convincing excuse about where he spent the night. With bitterness in her throat, she imagined him lying: "The castle was threatened by fire, thieves broke in, a bear drowned in the lake… .."

She waved her hand in an attempt to dispel her thoughts. She consciously accepted him back, even though she knew he could no longer be hers alone. That this night might be the only night he visited her. That same night could be the reason his wife would ask him to quit his job. And she will be left alone with her past again. She will embrace only her past. Because the past is her only friend. The truth is, she can't have him. But she is happy to have tasted, smelled and loved him again. That she didn't turn him down because she couldn't.

He did not leave her in the castle. He carried her with him in his head when he decided to greet his mother. He was afraid he was thinking so much of her that his mother would see her in his eyes. He was lucky because his mother was not alone. After looking for him several times at his home, his friend and godfather Goran decided to look for him at his mother's house. Philip's mother had already informed him that Patricia was in Zagreb and staying there to sing, and that her son was a little lonely and working.

The godfather, full of compassion, tried to come up with something fun for them to do together. He suggested matches, concerts, exhibitions, just to take his friend out of town and enjoy forgetting the reality a little bit. Goran didn't have a fun period in his life either after he was threatened with losing his job.

Philip was watched with much different interest by his mother than the previous days, but she did not want to sabotage him. She even tried to save him by saying:

- But if he's tired, leave it for another day!

She couldn't get him out and after Goran gave him time to take a shower and change, they were on their way to the "party".

- Don't tell me that one beer is enough for you again - Goran provoked him.

- No! This time will probably be too much- he frowned.

With a smile, Goran grabbed his arm and pulled him into his arms, punching him in the back.

- Don't think, old man, I don't know how you feel - he said. - But I'm glad you're trying, both of you. Especially Patricia. Let's be honest, everything around us says that it is much harder for women in these situations than for men. I'm so glad you're supporting her on her way to fighting the pain, but do you really think being separated so often is the best option? If I were you, I would let everything aside and go with her to Zagreb.

- With her friends? No way!

- Rent an apartment for you, man!

Philip scratched his hair.

- It's not that simple, man. She is not earning anything at the moment, and if I quit my job too...

- You'll find another job there. This is Zagreb, man. I think Patricia is right! If I lose my job, I will move to Zagreb. Let's be honest, the possibilities are much greater there!

- Not for everyone. I don't like big cities, and I'm more than happy with my job. And with other things. I also love being close to my mom. I have no desire to move.

- Well, you know what is best for you - Goran gave up over the loud music.

He had never seen Philip so sensitive before and with no topics for a conversation. The truth is, he had never lost a child before. That's why Goran did his best to keep him until the morning hours and watch over him.

- It will be better-were the words he greeted Philip when he left him in front of his mother's house.

Like when they were young, his mum turned on the light as soon as she heard the auto pilling up the driveway. Only when she knew her son was safe in bed , she closed her eyes peacefully and fell asleep. She greeted him with a delicious breakfast in the morning, and when he told her he had to go, she calmly accepted.

It was Sunday, so she thought she was probably going to visit Patricia. She didn't want to question him for things he wouldn't tell her himself. Sometimes she wondered if she was right, but it was easier for her than when she knew he was talking to her about things against his will. She watched him lovingly as he got into his car, after wishing him a pleasant Sunday. And when the mother wishes something, she does it with all her heart. So for her children, very often, it comes true.

Zagreb never crossed his mind. After yelling Elena's name in the castle and hearing no answer, he decides to disappear behind the closet and look for her there. Convinced that he would find her, he ran up the stairs, but was left without a smile. She wasn't there.

He sat down on her bed. Staring at the ceiling, he started thinking. He is now embroiled in her craziness. And not just that. He gave in to love that never died and fell into her arms again. He felt he loved her as if he had never stopped. But, my God, he has a wife!He is married and they recently lost a child! What is he doing to himself and to them, to both of them? Wasn't there enough pain for all of them already? Who needs salt on a wound when everyone has suffered enough?

Drops of sweat appeared on his face. Why did he do that? He first trampled on the promise he had made to Elena, and after he had risen from the ashes, he wanted to be sure that he would make sure that his love for her paralyzed him. He meet Patricia and thought he was really in love with his wife. Okay, there wasn't a day that she didn't remind him with her character and demeanor that she wasn't and would never be like Elena, but she loved him the way she knew him. He was sure that she gave him everything she could, even though it was not like what Elena could give him.

For years he fought and managed to fight against the fact that a man meets his true love only once in his life. And now Elena came back and rocked everything. Before she came, he was sure he had succeeded. The first day she showed up she brought an earthquake in his heart and in his head. After a night spent with her, she put the complete story with Patricia into question. Where does she get all that power from? But no one has so much power to cover up the truth - he is a happily married man and what he allowed himself to do is wrong, so wrong. And yet, how would he resist? What if Elena has a magnet in her blood that he couldn't fight against the first time, and he can't now either? Although he knows that she has lost her mind a little, she enchants him with her madness even when she is not talking about it.

He broke his marriage vow by falling under the influence of a mentally ill woman. That might justify her, but not him! He was supposed to stay cool-headed after she returned. He should have avoided her, ignored her! He should have told his wife, his mother, everyone who could protect him. He should have protected himself! But he didn't! He did none of that! He only surrendered and, like intoxicated with her wine, he looked for her until he found her. And then he went even further. And even worse, he enjoyed it! And he doesn't regret it! And while he thinks about it, all he wants is to do it again. For himself, for his heart, but also for her. To see the flame in her eyes again, to see her lips trembling as he touches her, to see desire in every cell of her body, and finally, to see despair in her whole being when the end is near. To see that she would continue to live, just because she hoped it would happen again.

- Love? - he heard her voice full of joy as she ran down the stairs.

Elena flew to him as if carried by a storm! She tossed the bamboo basket she had under her arm on the floor, and while her hair remained in the air above her, she jumped into his lap. She wrapped her legs around his body and forced him to hold her in his arms. At the same moment, she began to cry, and while he wondered what could have happened to her, the tears that came down her face, made his face wet too.

- Thank you, thank you, thank you for coming back! - she exclaimed with tears.

When he realized she was crying because he was there, his body weakened. He could no longer hold her in his arms, so he surrendered and lay back on the bed with her. So much happiness over his presence, it can only be his Elena.

- How did you know I was here? - she asked as she sobbed in his arms.

- You didn't put the closet back in place. I wanted to make myself think that you betrayed me the first day and that you certainly didn't come in the middle of the week when you can't get out of your house so easily, but I knew, I knew that, although you didn't support me in the most important way, you wouldn't have destroyed me. You wouldn't hand me over to the police, the psychiatry, the insane asylum. No, because deep down you either trust me or you love me so much that you can't do that to me.

- I love you, Elena! I've always loved you. I was just deluding myself that I am living after you. I was not! I was only surviving until you came back to me and I have no intention of losing you again! Just please cooperate this time...

- I'm not going to a psychiatrist! - she yelled at him.

He just squeezed her harder.

- Did I say that? - he asked.

She paused for a moment. She gave herself time to calm herself and said more calmly:

- Sorry love!

He stroked her hair gently, signaling that he was not angry with her.

- Just cooperate this time! Please, please - he continued - Don't leave this time!

She hugged him closer, raised her head and stared into his blue eyes.

- I promise - she said - I won't leave this time. At least not voluntarily!

8

Patricia got off the bus and looked in all directions. The sky waited wearily for people to hide where they could, so it could drop the heavy rain in the air. The wind was already blowing and threw her black hair over her face. She tried to control it with her hands, but it was more important for her to get rid of her bag, which the conductor had relentlessly pushed in front of her. She didn't want to drag it around, until the same conductor, in an attempt to control the situation, yelled:

- Please , those who no longer need to stay close to the bus,move forward! Let those who need to deal with their belongings and bags approach!

Trying to tame her furious hair with one hand, she dragged her bag with the other. Until now, she didn't know how heavy her bag was. Magda accompanied her to the station in Zagreb, and Michelle, who drove them, was also in charge of her belongings. He was so kind that he went all the way to her room and took what she had for the trip. He put it in the trunk, and then dragged them to the area where her bus was about to arrive. Even when the bus appeared and the conductor lifted the door from the passenger compartment, he placed her bag in the corner. Then he motioned for her to remember where he had put it. Now, in Krapina, struggling for the first time with the weight of her bag, she wondered what she packed in it.

She dragged it a little farther, then gave up. She set it aside, stood beside it, then looked nervously at her watch.

- Where is he?- she wondered, considering him very irresponsible when he could leave her alone in this weather.

She felt a drop of rain on her hand and it made her even angrier. She grabbed her bag again and tried to drag it indoors or at least under the canopy. Her handbag slid off her shoulder and fell in front of her feet, opened and her make-up rolled away in the wind. On the verge of tears, she started running, picking up and stuffing her things back in her purse, and, nervously, she threw it over her head. Then she returned fighting with her heavy bag. Her hair sabotaged her and made her even more nervous, closing her view and getting even into her mouth. It seemed that smoke was coming out of her ears in agony.

And then, someone finally took pity on her. A man's hand, gently pushing hers and struggling to better grasp the bag in her hand, lifted the bag with a brief explanation:

- Let me!

The man carried the bag under the canopy in the direction of which Patricia had already dragged it, and she, breathing in relief, followed him with small steps.

- Where do you want it? - the man asked over his broad shoulders.

Patricia quickly answered:

- Here, just so the rain doesn't make me wet until they come for me!

- Do you need a ride? - the stranger asked.

Before she could answer him, she heard a familiar voice:

- There's no need, thank you for your help! I'm picking her up!

The stranger bowed to her and Philip and stepped forward, fighting the wind.

- Where have you been? - Patricia yelled angry at Philip instead of greeting him.
- I'm late!
- I see that! I almost got wet like a wet cat, the wind pulled my hair and threw dust in my face, I dragged this horror behind me, and the bus arrived in time. But, no one was waiting for me!
- Sorry, I miscalculated!

She looked at him from head to toe with a brief glance, then continued her attack.

- Oh, did you? It's good that you realized at least that you didn't have time to go home and change, because as I can see, you're still in your work clothes. Then strangers would have taken care of me and driven me home. I wish I had spoken with my dad. But no, I called you only to be late on this awful day!

He stood in front of her and turned to her and without lowering the bag to the ground, his eyes flashed:

- OK, Patricia, you're alive and well! I am late once in my life, so I beg you not to act like I do it all the time and like I did God knows what crime!

Whether this calmed her down or made her even angrier, she decided to find out after they sat down in their car.

When they were finally close to the car, Philip hurried to unlock it, and while she expected him to put her safely in the car first, Patricia experienced another disappointment when he went to pick up the bag first in the trunk. Offended, she opened the door to the passenger seat herself and threw herself inside to get away from the wind as soon as possible. After a few seconds, Philip sat down next to her and, breathing rapidly, he said:

- Here we are, everything is fine!

She snorted angrily, and snapped at him.

- Can you please tell me something really dignified in self-defense? Why are you late even though you see it's raining and why are you still in your work clothes at ten in the evening?

Giving no sign that her sternness was disturbing him, he said calmly:

- Welcome to Krapina. And welcome to a reality that is not always as we imagine. We don't know when the rain and the wind will start, we don't know what awaits us next and we don't know when we will have to stay at work longer!

- Why? - she asked coldly.

- Because we are not perfect humans. It is not possible for us to know everything, although we are learning all our lives!

She rolled her eyes, and without any pity, asked:

- Why did you stay at work late?

The effort he had to make to keep the same voice and the same facial expression, did not betray him.

- Something had to be done in the castle!

He was ready for a rain of questions. It was not that he was afraid of them or at least tried not to think of the fear that would provoke him. He just wanted her to ask them quickly and not follow his confused answers. But that she didn't care about him and what he had to do because she was angry enough, she showed by asking one question:

- Why didn't you tell them you had to go?

"Because I was the only one to whom I had to repeat several times that I had to go. But I couldn't. I couldn't leave her, I just couldn't turn around and leave, even if I knew I had to go. "

- Some things can't be delayed!

She became silent. What a pleasant surprise! He convinced himself again, that there was something good in every evil. If he had arrived on time and was there when the bus arrived, she would have gotten off the bus straight into his arms. How? How would he pretend that it wouldn't be uncomfortable? She was angry that he was late, but it was the first time he didn't care too much about her anger. As far as he is concerned, this time it is in his favor. If only she would keep quiet, at least until tomorrow. And tomorrow he would start a conversation she wouldn't like. Neither would he, but he has to do it. As his thoughts drifted away, his hands on the steering wheel sweated. And like black birds in the gloomy night, her voice scattered him:

- Here, it started raining!. And I would have still been at the bus station!

- But you arc not!

- I would have gotten wet, and maybe gotten sick!

- But you didn't!

A cold answer, instead of begging for forgiveness? Oh, he

will remember this for a really long time!

By the time they got home, she didn't say another word. He dropped her heavy bag in the hallway. As she walked in front of him, he only allowed himself to ask her if she was hungry. With angry movements of her head, she replied that she was not. She ran upstairs straight to the bathroom. After removing the dirt from herself, she turned on the shower, letting the water run at its highest, staying under the stream of warm water that massaged her and made her feel comfortable.

After drying her hair, she felt calm. It only takes a few minutes in your own home, to feel that you were never gone. However, although she is glad to be there, she does not plan to stay long. She looked at herself in the large mirror where she used to look at her big belly. She did not like that deformation, but she was glad that life was growing inside. Now it is just a lost dream, a burning memory.

Fortunately, not all dreams were lost. She managed to go back among the normal people by singing and realized that it was, now, her even greater passion. And yes, no matter how Philip accepts it, she doesn't want a child now. She can't be a good mom now. Now all she wants is to sing.

She abruptly opened the bedroom door, ready to ask him if it seemed to her or if the bathroom window was closing a little harder. She quickly stopped the question in her throat when she saw that he had already turned off the table lamp on his side and, apparently, was already asleep. She doesn't like the way he's become. He used to celebrate her return, and now he allows himself to stay late at work, even though he knows she is coming home today,the work that is taking away all his strength.

A little angry, she sat on her half of the bed, still smearing the cream on her hands. Then she pulled back the blanket, threw herself under it, but she had no intention of turning off the light yet. She took the magazine from her night stand and flipped through it, when a suspicious odor reached her nose. At first she didn't pay much attention to it and continued going through the magazine, but the smell reached her nose again. She brought her fresh cream-smeared hands to her nose. The first thing she suspected was that her cream had gone bad after so long. But her hands smelled nice of musk. She got up from the bed, grabbed her slippers, and brought them to her nose. It was not them either. She went around the bed and smelled Philip's slippers. She didn't recognize the smell that bothered her there either. Before returning under the cover, she thought it had to be him. She leaned over his head and abruptly turned her head to the side.

- Oh my God - she whispered.

She angrily pushed the whole blanket close to Philip and took a new one for herself. Either something is wrong with this house, their washing machine is not working properly, or Philip hasn't changed the bedding in a long time. She will find out in the morning.

Still sleepy, Philip looked at her in the morning surprised. First, because she usually slept longer than him, and second because of that question.

- As far as I know, everything is ok with the washing machine - he said.

Patricia was already going through her magazines on the kitchen table and drinking her morning coffee. With her knees up to her chin, she couldn't wait to ask him.

- Does it mean that you haven't changed the sheets on our bed for a long time? The smell was not pleasant at all last night.

- I'm sorry, I was so tired and fell asleep, so I didn't notice anything. I slept in my mother's house a few nights, that's why- he defended himself scratching his head.

- I could have done it last night, but you fell asleep while I was taking a shower. I am just unpleasantly surprised by both situations, but that's no reason for you not to kiss me good morning!

Ah, yes! He knew very well that he had not kissed her once since he picked her up at the bus station, but she had helped him with that a little bit. Now called out, he bent down and kissed her lightly and briefly on the temple, and rushed to get his cup of coffee ready. She barely restrained herself from throwing her magazine at him and asked him if he would kiss that way the woman you had not seen for three weeks. Still, she manages to control herself and she puts her nose back between the pages of her magazine. Maybe he hadn't brushed his teeth yet, and if that is the case than he made a good decision to kiss me like that, Patricia thought to herself

He was quite silent as she later babbled about the dresses she wanted to order and which, if all went according to plan, she would need in the future. He was just not waking up today, good thing it was Sunday. He looked at her as if he was looking through her, barely remembering what she was telling him. And he was lazy. He didn't prepare breakfast for both of them as usual. He said that he was not hungry, but he did not offer to make breakfast for her either, and in some way she was a guest in their house.

After breakfast, for which she could barely gather groceries in the half-empty refrigerator, he showed her that he does care about her being there. He was alone and eating most of the time at his mother's house, she could tell that by the situation in the house. Suddenly he brought in a glimmer of hope that he was still willing to please her, when he said:

- I'm taking you out for dinner tonight. I would like to talk to you about something important.

Her stomach turned. She put her hand over her mouth and soothed the sudden change in her body. She knew, she just knew it wouldn't be long before he would start to oppress her about another child. She has known him and since they were together, the only thing that mattered to him was having a child with her. Fortunately or luckily, she has already arranged tonight's dinner with her parents. Of course she will take her husband too, but of course he can't talk about having another child there, in front of her parents. And of course she would insist that they stay as long as possible, so when they come home, they will go straight to bed sleeping.

She was also aware that she had to survive until then, so after she told him about her dinner plans, she said briskly:

- But first of all, let's go together and change the complete bedding, check the condition of our flowers, and then go shopping because I see that your refrigerator is almost empty. It would be nice to greet your mom along the way. Now eat something and then come and get me.

She flew away from the kitchen on her toes. He looked at her briefly and he was thinking, then shook his head and thought to himself, - "When we get home tonight then."

He let her guide him through the day as she wanted, because he knew she would need strength for what she is about to hear tonight. She was kind and smiled at him all the time, she was even defending him when her parents and his mother declared him as a little bit absent.

- He worked a little harder this week. I immediately realized that he was a little exhausted - she came to his help.

Of course, as she had planned, she prolonged the dinner with her family as long as possible, kindly asking him to understand that she had missed them a lot. He said there was no problem and that if she wanted to, he could even leave and come back for her. She liked that idea, but her mother got involved:

- I don't think that's a good idea! We are glad to see her, but you are still her priority and we do not want to steal your time!

"For God's sake, Mom," Patricia thought to herself.

By the time they drove back home, she was already yawning. She was pleased with how the pretending turned into a real need to yawn. He let her take a shower first, and while she waited for him to finish his sleep preparations, she acted a little, but she was really feeling tired. She remained calm in bed as he approached, sat down, and turned to face her.

- Are you sleeping? - he asked her quietly.

- No, darling, but I think I'll fall asleep very soon, I'm so tired - she said.

She felt that he remained sitting on the bed for another moment. But then she realized that he was already under the covers in a semi-sitting position. Even though her back was turned to him, she knew that he had his hands across his stomach and that he was thinking in silence. He can think all he wants, but not about a child and never try to talk to her about it. Not now when she is doing so well in Zagreb and when she sees a new chapter in her life. Not now that everyone there understands how talented she is and when everyone is, somehow, on the same length as her. Unfortunately, she could never expect anything from Philip on this topic. He is a good man, but he does not understand opera.

She felt him reach out, turn off his desk lamp, and lay down on his pillow. He laid with his back turned to her. Then he changed position. When he brought his body closer to hers, she expected that he would say something to her. But she was wrong. After lying in that position for a long time, he turned on his back again and probably put his hands on his chest again. She could bet he was looking at the ceiling. Something might have bothered him. Maybe he wanted to tell her, but was afraid he would wake her.

She decides to help him. Turning slightly toward him, she brought her warm body closer to his. She put her arm over his chest and made sure she was right about the position of his hands. She pushed her fingers between his. He didn't even move, and if he hadn't coughed softly, she would have suspected he was already asleep. After that cough, she was even more encouraged and raised her head on his shoulder. She kissed him lightly on the cheek and then bit his ear with her teeth,not gently.

He squeezed her fingers between his, and the grip only came loose when she let go of his ear. Patricia pulled out her hand and hugged him. Grasping his opposite shoulder, she tried to pull him and let him know that she wanted to turn him towards her. He didn't even move.

Then she lifted her body on her elbow and swung one leg over him. She started kissing his cheek searching for his mouth.

He suddenly jumped, pushed her leg away from him, pulled his head back, and began to block her shoulders with his hands, so that she would not come towards him again. It seemed to her that he had done this very rudely, but at least his voice remained soft when he said:

- You said you were tired, Patricia! I am too! Let's go to sleep!

A little offended, she tried to fix the matter in a kind way:

- But dear, you are leaving for work tomorrow morning, and I am going back to Zagreb!

- It's not a tragedy! You will come again! And I hope that it will be a little longer then, because we need time for some things!

- We can use this little time - she didn't want to give up easily.

- We're tired! For everything we need to do with each other, we are very tired now. Just go back to sleep, Patricia!

It was the first time she felt that he brought her to tears. But she didn't cry. She just made herself remember how angry she is, she'll need to remember that and not forget.

She carved it into her heart before she fell asleep.

In the morning she was happy that her dad was driving her to the bus station, because Philip had to go to work. Before she got into her dad's car, Philip hugged her and kissed her on the cheek, like he was hugging his mother. "He's angry," Patricia concluded. But she can't afford to ruin her dreams just because he needs to hold on to her skirt every day. If he can't do it alone without her, he can pack and go to Zagreb with her. It's on him.

She waved a smile at him, telling him not to give up. She knew he wouldn't understand her, but she would be happy to explain it to him one day.

He locked the house and jumped into his car. He hurried towards Trakoscan because he wanted to be there before his working hours started. He didn't have to move the closet, Elena was waiting for him and as soon as he entered the castle, she threw herself around his neck.

- You're back! You came back to me! - she muttered as she kissed him.

Good thing he didn't tell her what he intended, because it would be really hard to explain now Patricia outsmarted him and he didn't have time to tell her. And if looks a little deeper into his heart, he might find another reason - it's not easy to sit down and tell Patricia what is happening. How he feels around her and how he feels when he hugs Elena and all this sudden change in his feelings affects her as well. But one day, and one day very soon, he will have to tell the truth. The worst thing he could do is to be silent and tell no one. Out of self-respect, out of respect towards Elena and Patricia too, he has to tell her.

He grabbed Elena's thin figure and lifted her into the air. He turned her around, gently lowered her down, and kissing her lips, fighting for air, he said:

- I've been coming back to you my whole life! And I will be always coming back! I can't leave you even then when I think I have already left you!

9

Philip's mother wore her dark gray formal dress. Although it was made of satin, the dress was very decent in cut and length. Along its edges and the sleeves satin ribbons were sawn. Also it had lace around the neck. She sat down on the dress table in her bedroom in front of the round mirror and took out her modest make-up collection. Her son's wedding was the last time she put on make-up and today she had a reason for that again. She was hoping that the makeup would last long enough until they entered the Cultural Center in Zagreb. She put a pearl necklace around her neck and looked sadly at the clock on the wall. And then she heard Philip's car park in front of her house. A sigh of relief came out from her chest.

She waited for him at the entrance and in a voice that sounded a little worried she said:

- You didn't leave work on time again!

Closing the door behind him as he bent down to kiss his mother, he said briefly:

- I had to do something!

- Ok, honey, but you know we need to arrive there on time, and I don't like when you have to drive in a hurry!

- Mom, please don't panic, we have plenty of time!

His mom leaned aside and let him walk in front of her, pointing to the bathroom.

- Will you take a shower first or will you eat first? - she asked him.

- I'm not hungry, Mom. If my clothes are ready, I'll take a quick shower and we can go!

- But how come you're not hungry, honey? We have a long way to drive and probably we will not be able to leave right after the concert - she said worriedly.

- Mom, I ate! I'm not a child - he assured her before closing the bathroom door behind him.

Shortly afterwards, after asking her if she had anything to put in the car and after telling him that she had already packed everything in the trunk, they were on their way to Zagreb.

- I made a sandwich for you and I put it in the back seat, just in case - she told him.

With a smile on his face, Philip reached out his hand and gently pulled his mother's head toward him, kissing her on the forehead.

- Did I ever tell you that you're a very good mom? - he asked her.

She laughed contentedly but modestly before answering:

- I was hoping that was the case. I've been trying my whole life, I've been working on it, I know I don't always succeed, but my attempts are with the best of intentions. Like any other mom, I always thought I was doing the best I could.

He held the steering wheel with one hand and squeezed her hand with the other. She knew that that means he agreed with her, and therefore with the fact that she was not always successful. She had blamed herself for some time and tried to find a reason for his distrust, but she knew she had been hiding something from her for some time. Whenever she thought about it, tears filled her eyes and she thought for a long time how to change that. If she had promised him that she would never betray him, he already knew. If she said that no matter what happened to her, she had no other child and her love would not change anything, and she had shown that many times in her life. But obviously this time she was doing something wrong because he would not open up to her and she was willing to do anything to make things right.

Noticing that she had been looking at him for a long time as he drove, Philip could no longer remain serious and, laughing out loud, said to his mother:

- Mom, I think you have looked at me long enough!
- No,no! You are so beautiful and handsome that looking at you is never enough. It is not easy to look away from a masterpiece.

Her words warmed his heart. Only two women have really known him and looked at him in that way - his mother and Elena. Both from different reasons, but he knew they were both doing it sincerely and from the heart.

He had at least one of them with him tonight. And he was glad for that. It's not that he spends a lot of time with his mother, although Patricia is more in Zagreb than at home and he feels a little guilty about it, but he can't go against him and his love for Elena, that flared up in him so much and he thought that this time it was even bigger than when he had Elena for the first time. This time he was even more resilient to her crazy stories from the past, but it still seemed to him that he felt a crumb of pleasure as he watched her express her senseless beliefs with enjoyment. This time he showed to himself what it means to truly love someone and accept him as he is.

He was glad that this time he wasn't doing it from fear that not believing her might separate them again. That she will leave again. He was not afraid. He managed to find a way how they can function - he will not pressure her to go to a psychiatrist, because if he loves Elena, he will love her even if she is mentally disturbed. In return, she does her best, in a way that his mother has always done, to please him and, if necessary, to sacrifice herself for him. He doesn't force her to think differently, so she spares him from her stories and tries to talk with him only about things they experienced when they were together. And that was enough for peace in the house.

They found their peace. At first she was ready to get sick while leaving Trakoscan. After successfully establishing the mutual trust that had been lost after the first separation, he kept her informed of his every move, and she calmed down. Even without him telling her, she realized that whenever he returned to the castle, he wanted her more and more. And then he would share everything with her - that Patricia was building her career, and that he was glad she is not home that often.

Elena knew that Patricia had a concert tonight and that it was normal for Philip to attend. Totally convinced that the only thing he would enjoy was his mother's company and the music and singing, she let him go with her blessing. Sometimes people need so little to have confidence and feel peace in their heart - just to know that they have become one with another person, and even when one goes to the other side of the world, they will come back for their other half because they don't won't find it anywhere else.

- Her mom and dad went early today - his mom told him.
- I know! I't ok!
- If you could have taken a day off, we could have been there earlier too. Maybe Patricia would have felt better if you had lunch with her before the concert tonight. She would have been more relaxed.
- I don't think it necessary, mom! After all, we're coming to the concert. She is so confident in her voice, in her education, in the professor and the pianist she works with, that I clearly doubt she lacks self-confidence!

After a moment of silence, she said:
- I am glad for her, but all this is separating both of you!.

He fell silent. How can his mother interpret his silence now - and he doesn't enjoy it, but he doesn't want to stand in her way, and if he talks, even with his mother, his wound would open up again, or... it doesn't bother him that much, because he doesn't notice her absence that much. And in order to provoke him to say something more, she did not let him drive in silence:
- I can only imagine how she felt after what happened to both of you. I'm not saying, darling, that it was easy for you! But the mother carries the child under her heart and feels it moving all the time, - she said.
- Mom, I understand! Neither I nor she ever condemned me! It happened, we have no answer why! To be honest, I was

wondering if there might be any connection between what happened to us and the death of her twin sister who died at childbirth, but I never, ever allowed myself to to think in front of her on the subject, let alone talk about it! If I ever mention it in front of her, it will be to tell her that, even if it can be proven to us, I don't blame her! I know and I witnessed how hard she worked and was following all the rules. I know she is devastated and it is best to let time heal that pain in all of us.

She squeezed his hand in support. If the mother could, she would surely take all her child's pain, all the suffering, all the misfortune. And if she could, she would put all the beauty of her life in her child's life. Unfortunately, life does not work that way.

- You're still young,- she whispered.

He nodded in agreement. It's true, they are young, but now is not the time or place to say a word to his mother about the fact that he is pretty sure that he does not want a child with Patricia. He just couldn't say that to her now. He kept quite so far, so he will continue to do so. However, he was aware that one day he would have to admit everything to his mother. And then it will be harder and harder to start from the beginning of the story, mostly because the beginning is very simple. He would simply say, "You know, Mom, I once mentioned to you that Elena is back." That would be enough for an introduction, but what will he say next? How will he explain what happened next and why he allowed it? He doesn't have to explain to himself, all he has to say is that he listened to his heart and decided on what would make him live happily. But how can he explain that to someone who can't peek into his heart and figure out everything that is there, and he can't explain it in words, even if it was his mother?

It will not be easy, but if it is really impossible, he will simply give up. It is enough for him that he managed to understand himself, to find himself. He knows that the people will not justify him, but it is up to him to be honest and do his duty. The rest it's not on him.

- Mom, the most important thing now is to get to the concert in time - he said to close the topic.

The hall in the Cultural Center in Zagreb was almost full when they arrived. Strangers huddled in it, and he walked between them again, feeling grateful to his mother. As they struggled to find two empty seats, he thanked her:

- Thank you, Mom! It would have never occurred to me to buy her flowers!

- That's what the mothers are for - his mother winked at him, - don't worry, you will give it to her after she sings tonight.

He stood in front of his mother.

- Why me? - he asked, confused.

- Because, my dear, with you being here, it would be a shame for me to give her the flowers!

- But you remembered and you bought them!

- Just because I was pretty sure your pretty head wouldn't think of that tonight. But I bought them for you to give them to her!

He didn't plan that. He couldn't even imagine that. Ok, he came, out of respect for his wife, but to go out there with the flowers and kiss her in front of everyone... no,no, no mom... He didn't have the desire to do that for a while. The only woman he could kiss lately, to be honest, was....

- Philip!!! -Patricia's mom waved her hand from the front row.

When they saw her, she motioned for them to come closer and pointed to the two empty seats she had kept for them. She was smiling and seemed very happy in the chair next to her husband and turning impatiently in all directions, every now and then exclaiming:

- It's full! Everything is full! The hall is full!

- All right, darling, it's okay,- her proud husband said.

Of course, they came much earlier today. Her mom had to check Patricia's dress, make-up and haircut for tonight. She had to make sure that Patricia would not talk too much, that she would eat and drink only water, but not too cold. She even made her lie down and rest after lunch. Of course, she knew that Patricia couldn't sleep, but she insisted on seeing her in bed with her eyes closed, freeing her mind.

And this evening here, just minutes before the concert, this woman seems as if she would jump out of her skin. At first she panicked and fluttered her silk hand fan nervously and her husband warned her several times to stop. She would stop when people finally started to show up, but since there were no people coming in yet, she thought she would faint and the only thing that could save her was that hand fan. And then little by little she calmed down, got serious, and lost control of herself the moment people started coming in as if they had agreed that everyone would show up at the same time, so she started jumping and looking around with her eyes wide open, happy as never before.

Her husband seemed much calmer. He was not indifferent either, various emotions were mixed in him, but he was much more skilled in calming and silencing them. Like a true gentleman, he was sprawled in his chair in the front row, lightly touching his chin here and there, which his wife interpreted as pleasure. Of course he was both pleased and proud of his only child. He would have been happier only if his second daughter, a twin, had survived childbirth and now the sisters were performing together, but life has decided so, and they have been getting used to it for 25 years. Most of the time, they succeeded, but in situations like this, the thought and grief of a lost child came uninvited in their heads and hearts. What was worse, they have now lost a grandchild too.

However, they had to concentrate on this beautiful moment now and give their sweetheart maximum support, as they did so far.

After greeting them, their daughter's husband and mother-in-law took their reserved seats. Patricia's mother wanted Philip's mother next to her, and then she squeezed her hand with a wide smile, because it was only in her eyes that she saw the glow that mothers have in moments like this. The male part of the family was restrained.

- How was your trip? - Patricia's father asked.
- It was okay, thank you and thank God we arrived on time - said Philip's mom.
- Now our nightingale will come on the stage - Patricia's mother still shook her friend's hand. Philip was looking forward to the beginning of the concert like everyone else. But at the same time he was not feeling the same emotion like the others. He sincerely hoped it wasn't that obvious. His mother put the flowers she had for Patricia in her lap, while an even bigger bouquet was

in the chair next to Patricia's father. Patricia's mother kindly asked and then she put their flowers next to the other ones.

- You don't have to hold it all the time, she explained, - and if someone needs this chair too, we'll be happy to remove them.

She winked and leaned back in her chair contentedly.

There was a commotion in the hall. People took their places and talked loud with each other because it was so loud that no one would hear anyone if they spoke normally. Acquaintances greeted each other, strangers got to know each other, bowing kindly to each other. A black piano glowed on the low podium, and a microphone attached to it on a stand waited for Patricia's voice to spread to every corner of this great room. Around the piano and the microphone, there were artificial flowers on the floor.

The more people leaned inside, the more Philip felt alone. Alone with his mother. But his mother was just not enough. Not until she finds out what's bothering him.

The lights in the back of the hall dimmed, and the lights above the podium intensified. The talkative people raised their heads to watch the changes, and then, realizing that the beginning of the concert was near, they silenced themselves and turned their chairs up front.

Moments later, two young artists appeared in front of the audience. Michelle, in an elegant black suit and white shirt, with a bow tie around his neck, freshly shaved, and his shiny hair combed back. He held Patricia's with one hand. He walked in front of her, giving short glances full of thanks to the audience, but most of the time keeping his eyes on Patricia. He led her to the microphone, bowed in front of her, and sat down behind the piano.

Patricia was glowing. She wore a long silver dress with a wide skirt emphasizing her waist, and a wide collar that fell down revealing her cleavage. Around her neck, the singer wore a silver necklace full of small shiny stones. Her shoulders were not covered, but her hands were with silver-black velvet gloves up to her elbows. Her black hair was combed back almost in the same way as Michel's hair, except that hers fell almost to the end of her back. Although wide at the bottom, the dress still had an opening and her black velvet shoes with silver flowers were showing.

Philip noticed that she had put on make-up in a completely different way tonight. She loved make-up, but it seemed to him that she had exaggerated a little this time. But that didn't mean she didn't look pretty. He was honest, she was glowing in some special way. And she looked very, very happy, and her eyes shone like diamonds when she saw her loved ones in the front row. She bowed in front of the audience, and after complete silence took over the hall, the piano started. After a few moments, her mezzo-soprano voice took over the space.

Her dad had experience in controlling, or rather, hiding his emotions. He sat cross-legged, arms crossed over his knees. With his head bowed to one side, he looked at his daughter with slightly closed eyes. His gaze was serious, but the ends of his mouth betrayed him that what he heard was very, very nice and that he was very proud.

Besides him, his wife could not control herself. She stiffened her body because it seemed to her that if she allowed herself a slight movement, everyone in the concert hall would do it, and that would confuse her daughter. She also had her head to one side, but she pressed her legs to the floor because she was sitting on the edge of a chair, so she kept her weight on her feet. She kept her hand under her chin, squeezed to the point that her circulation was almost cut off and her palms looked pale. The singer's mother's eyes somehow managed to hold back her tears, not to upset her daughter.

The mother-in-law also absorbed every note and smiled gently, looking her daughter-in-law straight in the eyes.

The husband was the only one looking at the floor. He listened very carefully with his ears, his body calm, his hands folded over the arm of the chair, but his gaze flickered away from his wife's face. He was glad for Patricia. Her preparations and absence from their home were good for him too, so he was pleased that she had achieved such great results. In a way, though, he felt like a traitor. Like a hypocrite. Like the biggest coward who came only to avoid the countless questions and the answers he feared.

While he honestly enjoyed the tunes his wife performed, he was aware of his acting. He had the courage to follow his heart and turn his own life upside down, but also the lives of the people around him, but he still did not have the courage to inform all participants in a dignified manner. Patricia's grief for her lost child, her preparations to make her dream come true, the sensitivity to their parents because of their age, all of that he took as an excuse and he always hesitated to say that he had already gone where his heart had taken him. It was all kind and human, but it seemed to him more and more that it was just an excuse and it was just keeping him in a state of hypocrisy longer and longer.

His mother looked for his hand. When he looked into her eyes, she smiled at him and without a voice, only with the movements of her mouth she said to him:

- Wonderful!

He just smiled, and he knew that the woman who knew him too well would realize that he had done it because he had to, because it was expected of him.

Patricia's voice became stronger and stronger. Her confidence increased when she survived the start of the concert and remembered her professor's advice, so she took her eyes away from the audience and, looking at one point under the ceiling, imagined that she was singing only for her professor and Michelle. With *Ave Maria* she gave the maximum of her voice, as well as her soul. Then she went on with *Carmen* and seemed so relaxed that she even adjusted her body movements to a light dance.

There her mom bursted, gave in and her tears came down her face. Philip's mom helped her organize and dry her face to keep her looking decent in front of the rest of the audience. The husband did not interfere because he knew that it would only make the situation worse.

Melody after melody followed, and the audience enjoyed it more and more. Men began to relax their stiff bodies, and women allowed themselves to dance silently with their hands to the rhythm.

Little by little, the loud end of the concert took place. Michelle got up, took Patricia's hand, both came together in front of the audience, pointing with his other hand, smiling and admiring his colleague, turning his head in her direction. He achieved his goal and the applause became even louder. There was even a whistling sound, and Patricia's dad had allowed himself to do it twice, between the enthusiastic clapping.

Patricia looked happier than ever, and it wasn't just Philip who noticed. At that moment, he was even more glad for her.

Her mother grabbed the flowers, and put the other one into Philip's mother's hands and making a movement with her head, he invited her to follow her to her daughter. Philip's mother turned to him. He was clapping his hands beside her, looking very handsome. She offered him the flowers, but he didn't allow him to get confused, so he gently took her hand and pushed her towards Patricia's mother.

- It is a job for women,- he smiled at his mother and continued to applaud.

Even though she wanted to control herself and remain classy, Patricia's mother hugged her daughter with one hand, forgetting not to mess her hair. She hugged Patricia for a few moments, then kissed her juicy on the cheek, then backed away against her will, letting Philip's mother give her daughter-in-law the flowers. The next bouquet was from the proud professor, then from her friends Magda and Jasmina, and then the proud mother no longer counted or watched them. She kept her eyes on the most beautiful flower of them all - her beloved daughter.

The applause from the audience did not subside even when the two young people disappeared from the podium. They came back for another deep adoration in front of the satisfied and loud audience, and then they disappeared.

Little by little, people began to leave the room and stay in the hall in front. Philip and his mother set out in that direction, hoping that Patricia's parents would catch up with them after her mother talked to the fans saying:

- We, we are her parents... Thank you, thank you from the bottom of my heart, on our behalf and on behalf of our daughter!

A small banquet had already been set up in the hall, and people were gathering around the plastic cups full of refreshing drinks. Philip and his mother were not thirsty, so they stood alone, anonymous, waiting to see what they should do next. Nearby, among the other noises, they could hear a loud female voice teasing the interlocutor with a smile, with the intention of being heard by a couple of their friends:

- My brother loves Carmen anyway, but this time I think he was very impressed by the singer's light dance. I watched him and I laughed like crazy.

- Come on, you're exaggerating,- the young man defended himself.

- Admit it, you passionate lover of dark haired women - his sister continued to tease him.

Philip wandered around the room, this time deliberately looking around to see how many black-haired women were present tonight. It could be said that there were many of them, but the sister teased his brother about the singer. What makes her different, except that she is Philip's wife, her husband wondered if the young man near him did not know any of them personally. For Philip, the answer would most likely be - by no means, except that she was the only one who was on the podium, looking more beautiful than usual. And she was the only one to be heard while everyone else, along with the other black-haired women, were silent. Was Patricia's supremacy attracting this young man?

However, the conversation that took place near him explained to Philip a little more about his wife's irreconcilable desire to make her dreams come true and singing at her own concert. This is what she wanted, and what Philip never wanted for himself - everyone to look at her, to listen to her, to be at peace with her, to be dependent on her, to admire her and want more from her. For the first time since they had been together, he understood that part of Patricia's nature and he didn't agree with it. But she doesn't need to know that.

His mother held her purse in front of her and smiled kindly at the strangers passing by. Two females in the aisle talked about the union of pianist and the singer:

- So are they a married couple or not?- one of them was thinking loud.

The other one raised herself on her toes, swaying from left to right, so that among the people covering it, she could look at the poster in front of the door. When she finally succeeded, she said to her friend:

- Their last names are not the same, but who knows!

His mom looked at Philip, trying to find traces of insult on his face, but she was relieved when she didn't see any.

Patricia's mother finally came out of the hall talking to one lady and flailing her arms in all directions. From behind, they were accompanied by Patricia's dad and one older and one very young gentleman.

- Here they are, Patricia's mother quickened her pace, sternly trying not to lose her company in an attempt to bring them to Philip and his mother, and then cheerfully exclaimed, - These are Michelle's parents and his brother! Our Michelle, their wonderful child, how he only followed our Patricia, dear God! They are made to do this together, they are the best combination, they sounded like angels in heaven!

The woman did not stop talking while the people she brought together got to know each other.

- Don't you play music? - Asked Mr. Dvornik, Michelle's father.

- No, music and I are not such close friends - said Phillip

- Nice of you to support your wife. And what do you do?

The man stood in front of Philip, and he answered without a hint of embarrassment:

- I am a janitor in Trakoscan. I guard and maintain the castle. I show it and present it to tourists, and I enjoy its beauty and the spirit of the past while staying in it.

While Patricia's dad felt a little embarrassed, the younger Mr. Dvornik burst out in front of Philip's face with delight:

- I'm the only one in our family that has never visited the castle. I no longer believe that anyone in my family will work on it, but I sincerely hope that next month I will have my driver's license, and then I will only show them the pictures after I develop them.

The group around him, and especially his parents, laughed sweetly.

- I will be very glad,- said Philip, and winked at him. - Make sure to look for me there, you will have a special treatment, one that those who have already visited could not boast of.

The group laughed out loud again, and Mrs. Dvornik

hurried to clarify:

- Our younger son loves history. He is an irreconcilable seeker of antiquities and we can really be ashamed of our failure.

- Mom, I will have no problem forgiving you if you lend me your car for a weekend in a month - young Dvornik offered a hand of reconciliation.

A laughter on his account erupted again, and his dad hugged him, patting him on the back.

- Here they are, here they are- Patricia's mom almost jumped out of her shoes. -They are so beautiful!

In the hall, people were already crowding around the two musicians who appeared accompanied by their professor. Patricia was shining like a star, and it seemed that all the admiration and all the questions were addressed to her and that the only thing the professor and pianist did was nod their heads to confirm and approve everything she said.

- Let's stay here, let's not go over there. Let's leave them to their audience tonight, - Mr. Dvornik suggested.

The others agreed in silence.

However, not long after that, Patricia, letting go of her friends and colleagues, pushed her way through the people and jumped into her mother's arms.

- Oh my dear, my daughter, my child! -Her mother could not stop.

When she managed to free herself from her mother's embrace, Patricia greeted all the people of that small gathering. She kindly shook hands with Mischel's family and kissed her own. She kissed Philip on both cheeks and stood between her parents.

- Congratulations, my dear, you were great, said Mrs. Dvornik enthusiastically.

-Thank you - said Patricia with a gentle bow -I'm glad you already met.

- You have a wonderful family, said Mr. Dvornik, - and everyone supports you very much.

- Of course, Patricia confirmed with a smile.

Shortly afterwards, the professor and the pianist joined them, and the group began to chat happily, splitting into smaller groups. Philip didn't even want to take Patricia's time, and that would still be perfectly normal if they lived under the same roof to this day and returned to the same bedroom tonight. Since they weren't, it was more than normal that Patricia did not find a moment to talk to her husband, but he honestly liked it a little. Otherwise, he would even feel like a traitor, and only he would know why.

At the dinner organized for the occasion by the professor, however, they were placed next to each other, and then Philip was in charge of nodding his head in approving everything Patricia said and received from the others. He did that when he really couldn't avoid it. Most of the people at the table didn't really know him and the only thing they knew was that he was the husband of the star of the evening. Patricia's parents, as well as the singer herself, were too busy to deal with him. But his mother noticed her son's silence. On several occasions she tried to put it to her son's exhaustion, but she knew her child too well to believe in her own deceptions.

On the way out, however, Philip and Patricia managed to exchange a few words. There was no way to avoid that because everyone left them alone so the couple could say goodbye. After briefly exchanging a few words, after they parted, he knew that she really enjoyed her concert. And she knew that he liked it and that he intended to visit her in the next few days, because she was not planning to go back to Krapina soon, but she didn't want to ask him exactly when. They will talk on the phone and make arrangements when it suits them both.

After kissing each other on the cheeks again, they hurried to those who were waiting for them.

When she gathered her group, Patricia told them:

- I plan to move soon to an apartment I am about to rent!

Some of them were surprised because she made that decision without asking anyone for their opinion. Only her mother approved of that, as well as everything else:

- Do what you think is best for you, honey! We will support you in everything - she stroked her daughter's cheek.

10

A faded light illuminated Elena's face. Philip, leaning on his elbow, was looking at her sleeping beauty. He was trying to relive her life in his head to find the reasons for her strange behavior. He had never thought secretly to go to a psychiatrist, but he allowed himself to dig through the library and look for an answer in the psychology department. He was at peace with himself for a long time now, but he did it for her, because he wanted to help her, not himself. He accepted her as she was and he knew that even if the whole world stood up against him, he would love Elena no matter what. But he was not happy that she was living there because of her physical health. He feared that the conditions were good enough for him as a man, but not for her as a gentle young woman. He especially panicked that morning when her cough woke them up. She assured him that saliva had gotten into her throat, and he wanted to believe it, but he loved her so much that he couldn't look at it without any concern. If that happened again, he would make sure that she sees a doctor.

As for her mental and emotional health, she was in the right place to flourish. She put him in the middle of her fairy tale, so he rarely went home, and when he did, he did it only because he wanted to know that his mother was ok. He would then call Patricia and talk to her briefly. For the most part, their conversations revolved around the fact that he would come to Zagreb so they could talk longer. The rest of his free time, he enjoyed spending around the lake, in the castle or, to be more specific, underground, in Elena's secret hiding place. His Elena.

His...That word melted him. There was no more fear of her leaving, and yet, he did not want to let his senses fall asleep and be unaware of her every touch, look, word... They gave and received and they were both aware that they couldn't do that with nobody else. The more they received from each other, the more they wanted to give. The more they gave, the more they had to give.

Elena took a deep breath, then turned her sleeping head to the other side. Shortly after, she repeated the same thing, but this time she turned her head toward Philip. She remained calm for a moment, then yawned and raised her hands to her closed eyes. She rubbed them gently, then half-opened one after the other. She looked like a child when she smiled softly at Philip and stroked his cheek with her palm.

- Thank God, she said, looking him in the eyes.

Philip took her hand, brought it to his lips and kissed it long and tenderly, and then he said:

- I agree!
- With what?
- With you. Waking up alive is the greatest blessing in one day.
- You are right! But it is not just that! Waking up next to you is almost like waking up alive!

Philip bowed his head and laid his cheek on hers. This woman knew how to arouse so many emotions in him early in the morning that some people have not felt in their entire lives. He didn't think she was doing it because she had to, he knew she was doing it because she wanted and out of love, and he was very grateful to her for that. For what he experienced and lived with and next to her, he was ready to give his life for her.

Feeling his skin on hers, his face on hers, anything his on her, she could never have enough of that, so she was moving her cheek under his so their faces could touch more and more. Kissing him, she would regret to the point of pain that there was no opening under her breast where she could put him inside her and carry him with her always! Like when a woman carries a child in her womb!

The more their half-naked warm bodies touched, the more they needed that. Elena stretched her neck and looked for Philip's mouth, and started kissing him passionately. In moments like that Philip testified that the consequences of life do not come out of a person quickly or easily, because a slight inconvenience would always pass through his being. In three years of living together, Patricia never kissed him before she was convinced that he had washed and brushed his teeth. When she wasn't sure, she would ask him directly, until she realized that she had raised him on her own and that he would never allow himself to do that. She didn't do a lot of things with him. He realized now how much! That is why with his Elena, like the first time and now too, they functioned together as if they were on their own. But when they were separated, it was much worse for them than being alone, it was as if they were only half human.

After all the sheets had ended up on the floor, and after there was complete silence in the room again, and their bodies were still lying intertwined on the bed, Elena was the first to talk:

- Do you have a special wish for breakfast or should I decide? You can't go upstairs after having only me for breakfast, it's not too much and it makes you even hungrier!

- Maybe it would be okay if I have a double dose?

She laughed as he tickled her and didn't stop until she ran out of the bed, grabbed the sheets from the floor and put them back in the corner of the bed, then ran to make a hot drink and breakfast for her sweetheart and herself. He came quietly after her, hugging her from behind and kissing her neck as her hands shook and spilled the food, but she didn't mind. She didn't mind eating together, although they often ate restlessly and made a mess when they were laughing together. Eating together was a ritual worthy of their gratitude. After that, he would help her clean up, but she always took his hands, thinking it was a waste of time. It was good for her to deal with it when he went upstairs, but while he was there, there was nothing worth wasting their time on.

- You're right, - he whispered in her ear as he kissed her - I can't stay today here anyway so let's make the most of the time we have!

- No? - she stared into his eyes.

Her small mouth opened and the holes in her cheeks disappeared.

- I have something to take care of, love! I'm sorry, but I don't know how everything will go, so I took a day off just in case!

She hugged him, trying to keep all the sadness inside. It is clear, he has a life beside what they have and she threw him into it, with her stupid decision that was eating her inside. As much as he suffered for her then, she suffered that much now knowing where he is when he is not with her. She accepted what she got without discussion because she knew she was to blame for everything she didn't get. She bowed her head and hugged him in silence so tight as if she wanted him to feel her grip even when he was away from her.

- We'll say goodbye when I'm done upstairs. Please come up to the castle when I'm done, I have to hurry after work and I don't have time to come back here!

Of course she would go upstairs. Serious but upright and straight she stood in front of him. As soon as he approached her, she surrendered as if she had turned into a liquid.

- I will miss you, I will miss you very, very much, - she repeated, as if afraid he would forget her words when he leaves.

- I will miss you too, I'm sorry, but this time I have to go for us!

A glimmer of light shone in her eyes, but she didn't ask. She just squeezed him harder on her chest and said:

- Please take care of yourself!

After he was gone, she was left with countless questions. "He has to go because of them." She was very afraid of that, but she was aware that she would not be able to avoid the hoop tightening around them and someone looking for an answer for his frequent home absence. They were honored by heaven when his wife wanted a career that kept her in Zagreb, but the truth is that it is not so imperceptible that he does not spend the night at home or with his mother. If his non-return tonight is due to a phone call he has to trick his wife into being home, then it's easy to bear. But if she is coming from Zagreb today, then it hurts! It hurts a lot. But the truth is, he has a wife! How many times should she repeat to herself that he has a wife? As much as it hurts, that is the truth. And the fact that Elena has him, and honestly, more and more often lately, she should only be grateful, keep quiet and ask nothing!

She headed to the library to try to find a hobby to help her cope with his absence, but she could not stop thinking about him and the jealousy was eating her soul. Since there was no one to comfort her, she tried to make it easier for herself and was taken by the fact that it was very unlikely that his wife would visit him on Wednesday.

If she could only fall asleep and sleep through the time when he's gone. Because while he's gone, she's gone too. Only her emotions are there. Her love and her suffering crucify her.

And he was driving, trying to concentrate on what awaited him in the hours ahead. More determined than ever, he looked ahead, often unknowingly grabbing miles toward Zagreb, after greeting his mother and told her he was traveling.

When he arrived, Jasmina kindly invited him into the house because Patricia was not there. She told him that she usually comes around nine in the evening, but it was not for sure either. She invited him to go inside and make himself comfortable if he wanted to.

But he didn't. He drove to a nearby park and spent some time there. He felt hungry, so, seeing that he had time until nine o'clock, he looked for a restaurant to have dinner.

He chose a table in the corner of the restaurant where it seemed to him that it would be quietest and that he would be able to think while eating. However, it seemed to him that he had already thought about everything enough and that he just wanted to kill time and eat. He wanted to have dinner with his wife, but her returning at nine o'clock in the evening seemed too late for him. Part of the plan had already failed, and he sincerely hoped that it would stay that way, and that everything else would be as planned. He missed Elena 's warm hand, but some things in life we have to do alone and we bring good or bad news to the other part and either we have their support or not.

He ordered pasta and water for himself, and took the psychology book from his car to learn something new and useful. He swallowed the pages between which he found his Elena, but himself also. On a piece of paper, he wrote down the things he wanted to read and think about again. Around him other people were having conversations and the plates and the cutlery were rattling. But he didn't react, he was alone with his book and his thoughts.

He was pretty hungry and he emptied his plate. He still hadn't solved what he had come for, but the very idea of resolving it soon made it easier for him and whetted his appetite. He knew that hiding things under the carpet would not do any good to anyone, so he was hoping that even though the process may hurt certain people, things would be different from tomorrow.

For who knows how many times he questioned his intention, trying to recognize and admit to himself if there was selfishness in it. Then he would think of his mother, who had shown her utter selflessness all his life, but she taught him one thing:

- In your life, YOU are the most important!

It is not selfishness, it is self-esteem. Because only when you have yourself and you are satisfied with yourself, then you are good for the others too. On the other hand, his mother begged him to be honest. And his dad was a brutal example of that. Even when he had to endure it, he followed that rule, so the consequences were more pleasant than with people pretending until the last minute.

Determined to obey his parents, he waited for nine o'clock. He then paid his bill and, leaving the restaurant, headed towards the house where Patricia was still living, until she found an apartment to move for greater comfort and freedom. She was already close to moving out, so Philip carefully chose the last days she spent with them for the conversation he was about to have with her tonight. He wanted her to have someone there and not to be alone, as any well-mannered and selfless man would do.

His car slid through the night to its destination, but as soon as it stopped, it became clear to him that not only had Patricia not returned yet, but her friends were not in the house either. Total darkness was covering their home. When he was convinced of this, he continued driving around and looked for a parking space where he could stop and keep an eye on the house. He had already gotten close enough without finding a place to stop. That was the reason he stepped on the gas and drove to the end of that one-way street. Just a few minutes later, his car slid slowly again from the beginning of the street, toward the house where Patricia was supposed to arrive at any moment. Before approaching the finish line, he parked between two other cars and turned off the engine. Left in the dark, Philip pushed the seat back, then, making himself comfortable, turned on the reading lamp and placed the book in his lap. He read patiently as if it were his only obligation for today, and every now and then he glanced at the house looking for a light, especially when another car or pedestrian passed him.

The night was calm, and if he had nothing to read, he knew it would be terribly boring to wait. Boredom would create pressure, and the pressure would have a bad effect on the calmness of the conversation. Then everything would go in the wrong direction, so he turned the pages and was grateful to have the book to shorten his wait, and also for leading his mind into a direction to understand Elena more and to understand her even better than before. For the first time in his life, he regretted not studying psychology, especially because he met Elena when he was young enough to take that road. However, he remembered very well that his parents could not afford it anyway and that they needed help, so he had to find a job, instead of opening another bill with his studies.

Patricia never agreed with that truth. Her opinion was that they were obliged to continue his education and she never forgave him for accepting the frivolity of his parents and remaining only with secondary education. She kept telling him that there would be days in his life when he would regret it. And those days came. But his regret was very different from what she had shown him. The only reason why Philip regrets that he did not study psychology is because he considers himself not educated enough to help his Elena live a better life. That is the only reason!

On the other hand, he was willing to invest himself in her living better. All of him, as he is. Regardless of his level of education, he could love her and make her happy with all his might. He didn't need school for that, it was enough to ask himself what would make him the happiest, and then do the same for her. She gave the same all back to him, and she certainly didn't learn it while studying history.

- Oh, you scared me! - he heard an unfamiliar voice.

A middle-aged lady was standing near his car, pressing both hands to her chest. He quickly opened the door and went outside to show the woman that there was nothing scary or unusual about him.

- I'm so sorry - he tried to apologize.

The woman was breathing fast, still holding her hands in the same position, but she began to laugh at her own expense. Philip was embarrassed and didn't know if it was better to get close to her or to stay away. However, there would be no harm in that, so he asked:

- Are you okay?

The woman laughed even harder, and seeing that she had embarrassed him, she tried to correct it and calm him down:

- Yes, yes, forgive me! I just wasn't expecting you, so I stood as if buried when you moved inside the car and I was too close!

- I am so sorry...

- You have nothing to be sorry about, everything is ok, you didn't do anything bad, only I was walking alone with my thoughts, so when I suddenly saw that we had company.... Ah -she waved her hand - forget about it. It's not your fault. I'm all on needles because I have some bugs of my own, so you were enough for me to get out of my skin. But it is certainly not your fault. You have every right to do what you want in your car. I'm sorry to upset you.

Philip smiled kindly and walked slowly back to his car.

- All right, ma'am, he said, - anything can happen to any of us. I wish you all the best!

Before he returned to his old position, the woman managed to gather herself, so she clearly wanted to know:

- Are you waiting for someone? - she asks quickly.

- Yes, - Philip replied shortly.

- Someone from there? - The lady pointed to the houses on the other side of the street .

- Yes, someone who lives there!

- I live here too, maybe I can help you!

- No need, ma'am, everything is under control. I'm waiting for a woman who hasn't returned home yet, and she should at any moment!

- And that's not me?

- No - Philip smiled.

- Then who is it?

Philip was embarrassed not to answer, but he had no reason to answer.

- Someone…I need - he said vaguely.

- If I can help you in any way…

- No need, thank you!

He went in and slammed the door behind him. That this meeting was a finished story for him was shown by the fact that he grabbed his book and continued reading without paying attention to his surroundings. As the woman progressed, he felt better. If Patricia hurried, he thought, she would save him from things like this. However, she was still not there, and it was close to ten o'clock in the evening. Hand in hand, the two sisters returned to the house and turned on the lights, but there was no sign of Patricia.

In order not to find himself in a similar situation like this with this lady and to avoid people suspecting him sitting in the car and observing, Philip decided to knock on Magda and Jasmina's door.

- Hey, look at you! - Magda greeted him with a smile.

She looked behind him, and the smile disappeared from her face when she asked:

- Are you alone? Patricia is not with you?

By the time he briefly told her about his adventure, he was on his way to Patricia's room. The sisters asked him if he was hungry and then told him that they had to go to bed because they had a lot of obligations tomorrow, but he can wait for Patricia in her room.

When he was left alone, he felt a little bit uncomfortable. He saw his wife's room as her intimacy to which he had no right, so he was careful not to touch things and to be as calm as possible until the owner showed up. He was feeling a little bit sleepy, but it never crossed his mind, to lay in Patricia's bed, dressed like this, without pajamas and without taking a shower. He just sat in the armchair by the window and was looking out into the night. So much he could afford to do there.

He could not remember exactly when, but against his will he surrendered and fell asleep. Nor did he have an accurate idea of what time it had been when the sound of the brakes in front of the house woke him from his sleep. Philip straightens his head like a child caught in the act. He was totally awake for the next second, as if he hadn't fallen asleep. Moving the curtain from the window just a little, he was relieved to recognize Mischel's car in front of the house. Patricia finally arrived.

Mischel parked aside and turned off the car. When Philip saw Patricia not coming out, he rolled his eyes. He had been waiting for so long, so he could wait for her last conversation with the pianist, and just today, as if she knew what awaited her, she postponed their conversation as long as she could. But now she's here. She's finally here.

He repeated in his head the beginning of the conversation. He could not foresee the further course, but the opening line he knew He was unsure whether to stay to wait for her, or to go out anyway, greet Michelle, and take Patricia inside. The books he had been reading lately also benefited Patricia. He had learned that talks like this one between them tonight should be on neutral ground. By no means where people often stay and have to stay after that, because it will cause them pain. They should be away from the places they use every day, so that the bad memory would not be around so often. That's why he wanted to have dinner at a restaurant where Patricia has never been before. But it was so late that midnight had passed, and all hope of talking in the restaurant was dashed. There are only two options left - her room or his car.

Well, Patricia was moving out of this room very soon, so the memory of the conversation will remain there. But he wanted her to remember where and with whom she lived when she began her career, without feeling the pain she had experienced a few days before she left. For these reasons, the decision fell on his car and Philip decided to go out. Nothing could stop him and ask him to understand that it was too late to accomplish his intention. He was sorry, but he also felt sorry for himself, so he wanted to get rid of his burden as soon as possible, for all of them, as he had thought many times before.

He left her room quietly and walked down the hall in the dim light. Watching out not to make the smallest noise that would disturb the sisters' sleep, he came to the front door of the house. He opened it as carefully as if a baby was sleeping a meter away from him, and after taking both feet out of the house, he closed the door behind him carefully. He turned around with relief and took a few steps down the street. He straightened the sleeves of his shirt to meet the pianist and the opera singer, and walked quietly toward the car they were in. He approached from Patricia's side, making sure that he was visible enough to be noticed before he came too close and surprised them, because one surprised and frightened lady for today was enough.

He expected that as soon as they saw him, they would end the conversation, greet him and Patricia would go with him. He was already quite close to Mischel's car, but the two inside showed no sign of noticing him. When he got as close as he could to approaching someone else's car a little after midnight, Philip stopped and, looking inside just a few feet away, waved to his wife and Michelle. In the dim street light, he could see that neither of them saw him and they could not notice that someone was watching them kissing.

He stepped aside, tucked his hands in his pockets, and almost as if was waiting for them to congratulate each other for the successful concert, stood with his head turned to the side. He did not want to do anything, nor did he want to force himself to do so. All he could do was start thinking with a total reversal in his head. He came, although it was too difficult for him, to put all the cards on the table in front of Patricia, to tell her honestly that since they had lost the baby, he doesn't see a bright future for themselves. In all this, he came to the conclusion that the love between them was not even that deep when such an earthquake could separate them, instead of uniting them even more, and when it was enough for him to see his old love again and understood that, although he thought he had the best of intentions, he fled in their marriage to save the memory of her. He was convinced he was wrong as soon as he looked into her eyes again. And that he was sorry that he had to admit to her that their renewed love had been going on between him and Elena for some time, but that all this time he was happy to see that Patricia was also following her dreams, but there was no place for him there...

At this point, he was convinced that her dreams were coming through even better than he expected.

Of course, he was surprised. But that had nothing to do with Mischel. He was surprised that Patricia was no better than him, but the difference was that he intended to tell her the truth. And he didn't really care if she intended to tell him either.

He took a breath because he felt relieved against his will. He felt he was right when he did everything the way he did it. He was relieved that he didn't have to say or explain anything. Because all his preparations, thank God, were unnecessary. Because he knew he wouldn't hurt Patricia the way he thought. He was relieved because everything went in his favor, her favor and Elena's too.

A hint of feeling that someone had betrayed him like a man tried to climb into his throat, but he swallowed it. In his relationship with Patricia, he was never treated as a man. If he ever felt like a man, it wasn't next to Patricia. That was before, as well as after, so he knew very well what it looked like, because he would never learn next to her. He didn't blame her. He was honest with himself, so he also admitted that he did not make her a woman in the real sense of the word. Only Elena, in his arms, could feel what a real woman is.

Without any expression on his face, he stood in front of Mischel's car, honestly not knowing what he was supposed to say or do. After the initial surprise, at least he could look at them again. They were already sitting next to each other, staring ahead. Nervously, Patricia turned to Michelle, said something briefly, and made an expression full of anticipation. The pianist pulled his head back, shook his head, and looked outside. Patricia got angry in his face, so he turned to her, squeezing the first three fingers on both hands and lifting them toward her face. She angrily threw herself back into her seat, while Mischel was still trying to explain something.

Philip could not hear what it was about. They had their windows up, and apparently they knew what time of night it was and how far away Philip was from them. He was not even interested in their discussion, the only thing he wanted to know was what he should do and how to proceed in the next moments. He was not hurt from what he saw, that was one thing, but that caught him unprepared and that was something else, and that upset him. He took his hands out of his pockets and just waited, having no idea how to cut it short, or how to continue the story. He was looking at the house he had just come out of because he didn't want to look at them. With the corner of his eye, he could see Mischel touching Patricia's shoulder with one hand and telling her something. As if annoyed even more, she pushed his hand away, reached out to the back seat, and reached for her purse and opened the car door. Before the door slammed back, Mischel called her:

- Patricia!

Then he turned on the car and headed in the same direction as the woman, who was walking fast in small steps. He caught up with her and drove past, driving along the street. Philip was ready to greet him, but Mischel kept his eyes on the road ahead.

After freeing himself from that first possible rush, Philip faced the second one. Patricia was walking toward the house with a serious face and not slowing down. When she passed him and left him behind to stare at her, all she had to say to Philip was:

- I don't want to talk about anything right now!

He watched her get lost behind the door of the house, so he stayed for a moment just in case she changed her mind and came back. Seeing that this would not happen, he searched his pocket for the key to his car. He started it calmly and drove along the street, in the direction Mischel just left. But there was no sign of him anywhere.

Leaving town, Philip stopped at a gas station. He got out of his car, headed for the trunk, and pulled out something quite large that he had to carry with both hands. He put it on the seat next to him, he locked the car from the inside, and lowered his seat. He took off his shoes, reached for the blanket and covered himself even over his head, so that the nearby light would not hit his tired eyes, then he closed them and fell asleep.

11

After Marko Dvornik walked around the castle for a long time, he admitted to himself that he was not done with it, but today he would take a short walk around. His sneakers raced down the trail as the young man enjoyed the enchanting surroundings.

He was wearing a white T-shirt and denim pants. His hair had grown back, and as it was thick and curly, it spread around his face like a black halo. He had better features than his brother and combined with his dark eyes, made him older than he was.

In his twenties he didn't have many opportunities to be out of Zagreb due to his parents' obligations, but since enrolling in history school and getting his driver's license, he has promised himself that he will travel a little more. Trakoschan was among the first things on his list, but his arrival here was delayed by everything that happened after his brother got involved with the married opera singer. Knowing that her husband works here, Marko waited for things to calm down, and after the divorce he heard that her husband accepted everything very calmly and gave her the most dignified divorce Dvornik's parents had ever heard of. He hoped that that was true, not just a mere attempt by older Dvorniks' to dignify the husband over the mezzo-soprano singer they didn't really like since the beginning of their relationship with their son. The changes she made in Mischel were against the way his parents raised him and they were disappointed, but they put up with everything and believed that Mischel would not just betray what they had planted in him for years. They believed that they should let him go and not force him to do anything, so if the way they raised him was successful, their child will wake up sooner or later when he gets fed up with the singer. And maybe she will change with him. However, they should be patient and not do things by force, making enemies that they don't need.

When the uneasiness after the divorce, that his brother caused had calmed, Marko had the courage to visit Trakoscan, although it was very likely that he would meet Partici's ex-husband there. But after the first visit to the castle, he was pleased because that didn't happen.

Marko made a full circle around the lake and at no point did he feel he had had enough. His artistic soul enjoyed that and was very satisfied. No one, no matter who he came with, would be so patient, so Marko once again felt the pleasure of coming alone. He just wanted to rest briefly on the bench and then move on, whatever that meant. When he came close to the bench, he seemed a little deceived. The bench didn't look as unoccupied from up close as it seemed from afar. A book had been left there, most likely from someone who planned to return there. Feeling slightly defeated, he reconciled with the fact that he had to walk a little further to the next bench.

However, first of all, he decided to make sure that the one who reserved the bench really intends to return quickly. But because he was not staying too long, maybe this privacy violation wouldn't be noticed.

Turning in all directions, he saw several scenes. On the one hand, cyclists passed by and he rejected them as potential vacationers right away, because it seemed that they were not very interested in stopping because they rode their bikes along the trail at very high speed. On the other side was a family, parents with two small children. Although he knew little about the possibilities of a young family, it was not difficult for Marko to come to the conclusion that with such active children, these people could be happy if they read something at home after the children are asleep, but not here in the park. The last people nearby were two friends who were loudly discussing the game and didn't seem to stop even if someone called them by name, let alone voluntarily interrupted their more than interesting story and sat on the bench to read.

So he decided that he will take his short break right here, and if the owner of the book comes, oh my God, there is always the possibility of an apology. His slightly tired legs gave way and his knees bent, so Marko sat down on the bench.

He propped his elbows on the top of the bench and raised his face to the sky and its blueness. He closed his eyes and listened only to his breathing and the chirping of birds. He already knew that he had been deceived, that he liked it, and that he would stay a little longer with these wonderful sounds and thoughtless mind.

Yes, he had heard about it, although it was hard to believe, especially if you were young and if the only woman whose presence you knew was always your mother. But judging by his mother, the story will be true. So there are claims that a woman's brain is always doing something. That there are several centers in it and that there are always some of them, and often more than one on duty. And that as long as she is awake, the woman is thinking of something.

On the other hand, thank God it is not the same with men, because if it was, the question is who could survive it. The male brain is believed not to use more than one compartment, and to have a "center for nothing" between them, which is a very positive thing. That is more than a blessing for men. While a woman watches a man from the side and makes dozens of films in her head about what he thinks about and the truth is that he doesn't really think about anything. He is awake, but somehow he is not. He is there, but somehow he is not present. His brain is resting and it is put on "nothing" mode.

That was exactly what Marko's brain was doing at that moment and he felt like he was floating. He was just looking in front of him but he was not seeing anything. He was a little tired, but that didn't bother him. He had a lot of plans, but he couldn't remember any of them at the moment. He was finally in Trakoscan, the place where he wanted to be so much, but he was not aware of it.

So it is no wonder that when a man returns from this state, he very often asks what time it is, because the truth is that he does not know how long he has been away. When Marko finally shut down the "center for nothing", he asked himself the same question. He turned his head toward his watch and was pleased. There was plenty of time to enjoy this day. His face remained with a satisfied expression. When Marko looked away from his watch, his eyes were drawn to the very strange cover of the book that was patiently waiting on the bench. He loved hanging out with books and many passed through his hands, but this cover was somehow quite different from what he was used to seeing. Its appearance looked special because it looked somehow...... historical.

He looked in all directions , but there was no one watching what was going on on the bench, so quickly he reached out his hand and gently but resolutely grabbed the book. Before lowering it into his lap, without raising his head, he looked again around him. Nothing has changed and that encouraged him to open the book. The title of the book was written in very strange letters, in a way he was sure he had never seen before, but he managed to read, Tristan and Isolde. A pleasant feeling overwhelmed his body.

He couldn't help himself, so he turned the pages carefully and peeked inside. Not only the writing, but the paper itself was strange to him. So he gently took one page between his fingers and rubbed it, and he was even more surprised. It looked like someone wanted to invest a little bit more in this issue and made everything about the book a little bit more unusual, except, Marko was sincerely hoping, the content. He tried to read where he opened it, but quickly gave up. The content was not written in a familiar language. If he did not know history, he would not even know that it was an old national language of European nations. Unfortunately, he did not understand that language.

It was very unlikely that anyone understood it. Holding the book on his lap, Marko asked himself if the owner only had this book just because it looks like it was printed a long time ago, and that made it a special piece that has no price. Since he did not want to get into trouble, he returned the book with light movements to the same place from which he had picked it up, trying to leave it in the same position as it was before.

He stayed on the bench for a little bit longer, returning to the " nothing" state of mind and when he turned on the other, the more conscious part again, he realized that a group of people were gathering near the chapel. Most of them looked young and that attracted his attention even more. An irreconcilable desire took over him to want to see what was so interesting about the chapel.

So he stood up and glanced a little sadly at the book. It would be a real treasure to him personally, and someone carelessly left it on a bench in the woods where anyone could take it. He looked sadly at the book again and a quick thought ran through his mind to take the book, but he immediately chased that thought away because that would be a theft. Standing up, he glanced again, hoping to see someone coming to get this treasure and when he didn't notice anyone, with a heavy heart he decided to go to the chapel, but to return later to see what had happened to the book.

In front of the chapel he now saw something that he could not see from the bench. It was true that there were young people present, although there were not many of them, but one couple between them was a couple waiting to be wed there. Two young girls made sure that the bride's wedding dress looked exactly as it should, so they were fixing it. But the only thing that the bride was interested in was her groom's face. She stared at him, her eyes shining with happiness and excitement. Mark would love to see these two happy people here sealing their love. They remind him of his parents. To this day they looked at each other in a similar way, especially the way his mom would look at his dad when he was telling something. Marko was not one of those young people who were skeptical and did not believe that love could last long. Of course, they thought so because of the experience they had. All his life he watched in his home how his parents loved, respected and fought for each other with the same intensity, but also for their children. Although young, he envisioned his marriage like the one his parents had .

That's why he enjoyed looking at these two young people. Then he notices an older couple coming along the path and looking excitedly at the young couple. After looking at each other and smiling, they managed to reach an agreement, and they approached the group. Marko realized that they were not guests, but that they had decided to attend this wedding, so he made the same decision. The chapel is a place open to everyone, he thought to himself with pleasure.

He could not see who had invited the people inside, but they all walked inside one by one. In front of everyone, of course, were the newlyweds. Marko went inside and stood opposite the older couple near the door, waiting for the ceremony to begin. The eyes of all present, including his, were fixed on the newlyweds. He couldn't see their faces all the time, but when they turned to look at each other, they seemed to glow with happiness. That is why everyone present felt the love in the air.

He could not follow the priest's words because it was more interesting for him to look inside the chapel. It's not that he's been to places like that often, so the details were interesting to him.

At one point, Marko saw a shadow of the person entering in front of him. It seemed that the person was a little bit late for the wedding. She walked silently past him, so he could see that it was a woman. She took a place appropriate to watch the wedding, but she did not forget that she had passed someone, so, without attracting attention, she turned slightly and looked over her shoulder. Mark's dark eyes met hers after she measured the distance between them and made sure that he can watch the wedding and her not being in his way. That eye contact brought a smile to their faces. With a nod of her head, she asked him if he didn't mind if she stayed there, and he replied with a quick nod too that it was ok. Then she looked in front of her and didn't turn her head back again.

Marko tried to concentrate on the newlyweds. The married couple near him had big smiles on their faces, and he could not help but notice. He was glad for them, and they remind him of his parents a little.

Later, his gaze fell on the woman in front of him. Of all those present here, though there were not too many, she somehow stood out, and it wasn't just because he had to look almost over her shoulders at the newlyweds. It wasn't even that surprising eye contact between them. There was something about her and Marko, keeping everyone present under control being behind everyone, decided to investigate her. He let the newlyweds and the priest and the chapel go for a moment, so he began to analyze this woman. Her hair was the color like his mother's hair, but not the same length. This woman's hair was longer and shone like silk in the daylight. It ended in delicate curls just above the belt on her narrow waist. Then he got it. He had never seen a similar dress, nor a cut or material. Trakoscan is a place where tourists come all the time, so maybe this woman or girl bought her clothes in a different place then all the other women he knew. So he accepted that as not that important and continued to concentrate on the event that brought him there without planning.

All of a sudden the silence in the chapel was replaced with a laughter and loud shouts:

- Repeat, repeat, we can't hear here!
- Oh, how sweet, I'll cry!

Marko caught himself unconcentrated and felt a little bit ashamed about it. His thoughts had even wandered out trying to find out if the book was still on the bench, but there was no way to figure that out.

Fortunately, he was there completely alone and there was no need for him to justify himself to anyone that he did not understand what had just happened. The couple wiped the corners of their eyes as laughter brought tears to their eyes. Only the woman in front of him stood with her arms in front of her as she had been since she got there and she didn't seem to be laughing or intending to move. But that's why her head was bowed a little bit more, he could notice.

Soon the peace and order in the chapel were restored and the wedding process continued. Then Marko noticed another unusual detail on the woman in front of him. The shoes she was wearing...he had never seen shoes like that in his life.

- Isolde .... he thought.

The book was still in his mind, so he could only imagine that those shoes were inspired by the Middle Ages. If he ever thought that he knew something about a stranger, then today, in this place he allowed himself to think of the lady in front of him that he must love history. But there was also the possibility that we look at people through our prism in an attempt to find the ones similar to us.

He decided to stop thinking about her and her appearance and he looked again at the newlyweds, hoping that the most interesting part is yet to come, and felt a desire to see that part. But only a few moments after he decides not to look at the golden - haired woman, her movement makes him look back at her. Namely, she bends a little too far forward like it was completely normal and stays in that position, still holding her hands in front of her. Marko wanted to think that it seemed unusual only to him, or that the woman was praying, but the serious faces of the married couple, who also looked at the golden-haired man, upset him.

Ready to do anything, but having no idea what to do, he remained stiff. But the moment the golden-haired woman turned abruptly and strode toward the exit, he ran after her, and then, afraid to touch her or ask anything, he strode out with her outside the chapel.

When she went outside, she tried to lift her head up, but her head fell down again. She even tried to force it up with one hand, but when she failed, she put her hand back in the other, in front of her, bent down again and staggered over the cut grass. Marko stood on the edge, still not condemning himself to get too close to her, but when he saw her falling on her knees in the grass, he surrendered and with only a few steps he was next to her. He knelt right next to her and quickly asked her:

- Are you okay?

Turning her head to the side she looked at him with her dim eyes and only nodded with her head. Then she felt all the way on the grass and sat, almost folded in half.

- You don't look good, - Marko said. - You're not ok! How can I help you?

She couldn't even turn her head this time. She remained

motionless and silent.

Marko reached out and touched her shoulder with his palm. She didn't react. Then, with his other hand, still kneeling in front of her, he pulled her hair away from her face, because the strands seemed to be interfering with her breathing. She managed to look at him and thank him with a slight smile.

It was nice of her, but he just wanted to see that she was feeling better and that was not happening yet. He gathered her hair in one place and, holding it in one hand, tried to cool the woman's face with the other. It seemed to suit her, so she tried again and managed not only to raise her head, but to keep it in that position this time. She sighed, and after that, she seemed to be breathing normally. The color on her face became normal again and she smiled.

- I'm sorry, - she managed to whisper.

Thinking that she was indignant because he was holding her hair in his hands, Marko let her go lightly and said quickly:

- I'm sorry!

She could not speak right away. Only after inhaling and exhaling for a few seconds was she able to add:

- It is OK! I'm sorry I scared you. I'm fine, and I'll be even better, please go back to the wedding!

But he couldn't do that

- It's ok, I was an intruder there anyway. I just wanted to see, otherwise I'm not a guest, I'm just a tourist.

She laughed. Two cute little holes appeared on her cheeks.

- Me too. Now I see that it was not a good idea! I almost caused those people trouble. Luckily, I noticed quickly and went outside. Thank you for coming after me!

- Are you sick?

She nodded.

- Does this happen often? - he asked anxiously.

- No. So far it has only happened when I... ..

All of a sudden she became silent. What she said seemed to shock her. He couldn't understand exactly why she kept quiet or why she changed her expression, but he didn't want to give up.

- Maybe because of the enclosed space? Although the chapel is open and there is enough air inside.

- No, no, - she defended herself confusedly.
- Then what is it?

She was still silent. Then he realized that he was bothering her and that instead he should take her thoughts away from what just happened. Asking an unknown woman about her health was not wise at all and she did well not to answer his question. Admitting his mistake, he changed the subject.

- Let me help you get up - he stood up and offered his hand to her.

But she was still not thrilled. She looked like she wanted to stay down for a while longer, so he quickly added:

- If you can, if not, as far as I'm concerned, it's okay!

Turning her head, she looked toward the chapel. Understanding her thoughts, Marko whispered with a smile:

- It's gonna take a while! Stay as long as you need!

The holes in her cheeks reappeared, and she pulled one hand from under her chest and took his hand. He lifted her carefully as he was lifting something very fragile, and as soon as he placed her on her feet, his gaze remained under her chest where she was still clutching one of her hands.

- Is that your book? - he asked, surprised.
- Yes - she said briefly.
- I saw it on the bench.
- Alright!

Raising an eyebrow, Marko added:

- Is it okay that I touched it?

As if hearing nothing new, with a serious expression on her face she said:

- It's ok! If it weren't, I would have interrupted you on purpose!
- But you weren't there!

Walking close to him, concentrating more on how she was feeling than on the conversation with him, she said softly:

- That doesn't mean I didn't see you!

He was glad he didn't make a single move that would a make the book's owner angry.

- I peeked inside, - he said.
- That is ok, too!

- I didn't understand anything, - Marko whispered a little shyly.

It brought a smile to her face.

- I'm sorry, - she told him honestly.
- Don't tell me you understand?
- Ok, I won't tell you then!

Marko stood in place. He put his arms around his waist, tilted his head and pretended to be jealous, and he said defeated:

- You are lucky! I can't say the same thing for me!

She smiled in support.

- You seem to like medieval novels, letters, clothes and shoes....

A sad shadow crossed her face, but she didn't let him notice.

- It seems so! - she said.

Walking side by side, they reached the bench. It was not questionable whether they would sit down because the situation required it.

- Thank you,- she said.
- You don't have to thank me! But I still wonder if you are really ok?
- Ah, thank you for caring, but it's over now! That's how it is, only I didn't know it would be the first time today, so it caught me off guard!

He sat next to her and nodded, looking at her face and trying to understand what does it mean "that's how it is", and today it happened "for the first time". It didn't say that on her face. He could not read anything from her face. But that he had been trying for a long time, he realized when she changed her expression from the discomfort of him looking at her for a long time, explaining some things to himself. He knew he had to cover that somehow, and anyway, it is her life and it is none of his business to get involved there.

- I love history, - he said abruptly.

To his surprise, her eyes lit up, and he quickly thought that he was right about what he had thought when he was looking at her in front of him in the chapel.

- Me too, - she said, opening her eyes wide.

- Really?
- Really! I graduated history!

This struck him for several reasons. First, she did not look at all like someone who had already completed her studies. Second, she had already graduated, and he was only at the end of his first year. Third, even if they did go to the same college, they would not have met there because she had already graduated.

- In Zagreb? - he didn't even know why he asked that question.
- Oh, no! In America.
- You studied in America?
- And lived there!

"Yeah. A tourist. That's why her wardrobe and shoes are a bit unusual for this area. But wait, he still speaks Croatian..."

- And you still live there?
- No.
- Have you been here long?
- Depends on what "long" means!

He agreed.

- I asked because you speak really good Croatian!
- Thanks to my parents who taught me.
- So you grew up here and studied there? Sorry if I ask a lot!

She smiled understandingly.

- It is OK! No, I have always lived there, but my late parents taught me Croatian as a mandatory subject. We always spoke Croatian at home. And they made sure I read well and I know the grammar.
-Smart! I'm sorry for your parents!

Barely noticeably, she bowed her head at her tragedy.

- You've always lived here, I guess?
- Yes, in Zagreb!
- Nice.
- With my parents and my older brother. I'm just finishing my first year in history - he laughed at his own expense.
- It'll go so fast! If you have chosen what you love, you will not even notice how quickly it will be over!
- I love it, I really love history!

She smiled contentedly. She herself uttered that sentence too many times in her life, but she never came across a person who loves history for the same reasons as she did. And it's better that way. Because it won't be easy. To get entangled between the living and the dead is anything but easy.

- I'm very glad to hear that, - she encouraged him.
- Thank you, - said Marko. - I am very glad to visit this castle. I've wanted that for a long time. I almost made it last year, but something happened to my family that delayed the visit again.
- I hope nothing terrible happened!
- Terrible, no! It's a little unusual, but it's under control now. I am glad that I am finally here!
- Have you been inside yet? -she hurried to hear his delight.
- Yes, yes! Extraordinary!

She smiled. Of course, she expected a little bit more excitement, but it is true that not all men talk that much!

- Have you been inside?

"Have I been inside... Oh, young man...."

- Yes, yes! Many times! It's never enough for me. I'm getting lost in those rooms, inhaling them in silence, and all I want in the end is to come back.
- Who is patiently waiting for you to do this? I came alone because no one I know would allow me to do exactly what you do.

It's the one who, although he does not believe in her story, fully understands her soul. But she certainly wouldn't share that with a stranger.

- Then it's best when we enjoy it alone, - she smiled sympathetically.

Without thinking too much he just said:

- We can come together tomorrow! Are you staying here or are you leaving, actually? I'm staying.

She looked at him fondly as she composed words in her head to reject him without offending him.

- I'm afraid I won't be able to, - she said.
- Oh - he felt ashamed - I apologize!
- It is OK!
- I'm staying until Sunday afternoon, just so you know!

- Okay!
- How do you feel now?
- Much better, thank you!

Just then a group of people came out of the chapel, much happier than when they entered. They were led by the newlyweds bouncing in front of them. With a smile and honestly from his heart, Marko said:

- I wish them luck!
- Until death do them part, - the historian added.

They just watched them as they walked away, all laughing for the same reason. And then Marko suddenly thought of something.

- Last year I met a gentleman who worked at the castle. It seems to me that he doesn't work there anymore, because I haven't seen him.

And that he was glad he didn't meet him, he wanted to keep that to himself.

- Oh really? - and to mention someone who works in the castle in front of this woman would not go unnoticed.
- Yes, at a concert in Zagreb. My brother is a pianist. He was at one of his concerts and he said he worked here. Then I told him I could not wait to visit the castle.
- Nice, you are here now!.
- Maybe he is working tomorrow, - Marko said quietly.

"No, his interlocutor knew. He will use the three days of his vacation to dedicate himself to his mother and her high blood pressure, so there is no hope that he will stop by at night."

- Maybe,- she said softly.

The mention of Philip, as well as what happened today in the chapel, required peace, rest and reflection. She was grateful to the young man for his care, but suddenly she felt she had to go.

- I have to go now. Thank you....
- I'll walk you, - he interrupted.
- There is no need, thank you!
- Please, you were very weak, so I don't want to leave you alone!
- I believe you don't want to, but I assure you you can. I know how to take care of myself and I know what I need now.

Nice to talk to you, colleague - she laughed.
- Don't do this, please, let me walk you to your place!
The holes in her cheeks begged him too!
- Trust me, everything's fine!
The look on his face showed disappointment, but he didn't want to bother her. So he surrendered.
- Okay, he said, if you still need...
- I won't, thank you!
- Good. Just so you know, I enjoyed everything except that you got sick. I hope that you will be ok and that we will hang out again. My name is Marko - he said and put his hand out.
I know, she thought to herself.
- Elena, - she accepted his hand.
- I am wishing you all the best, Elena! Please rest!
- I will! Thank you, Marko!
"Dvornik. Marko Dvornik. Brother of Mischel, may both of you be well."
He watched her go in a direction he hadn't expected, but she had already won in the knowledge of the castle, so it wasn't even a wonder that she had chosen to go there. He watched her walk in her strange shoes as the dress, an alluring cut for a man who loved history, spread behind her. Her long hair bounced on her back as she carried her medieval novel in one hand close to her body.

He was thinking.... There are a few strange things about her. Strange in a positive way. It would be nice to see her again, if she manages to recover by Sunday afternoon.

12

- Mrs. Ana Dolezal! - the nurse called her.
- Here! - sais Philip.
- The doctor is waiting for you!

Philip took his mother by the arm, helping her to get up from her seat in the cardiology waiting room in Zagreb. His mother looked at him lovingly, and said:

- I can do it myself, honey, you worry a little too much!

True, he was worried. For two women in the world he did care a little bit too much. Both were irreplaceable to him and he could handle everything except them being sick. When she saw them together in front of the door, the nurse asked:

- Sir, are you coming too?
- I would be very grateful if I could, very grateful. I was there the first time, it would be nice to be there now too.
- I didn't say you couldn't, I'm just asking, - said the nurse,

and moved aside to let the mother and son through the door.

An older man, holding the results in his hands, stood near the room and waved towards the nurse. He leaned and told her something. She nodded, giving him hope.

- Here, just let the doctor finish with the lady. Sit still, it won't take long!

Her last words reassured Philip's mother as well. She and her son came in and greeted the doctor.

- You are back again - the doctor greeted them - I've got your results.

The mother was silently looking at the papers in front of the doctor, while her son's uneasiness was felt in the office.

- What is going on? - Philip asked impatiently.

- Sit down, sir, - the doctor pointed to a chair next to Philip's mother, - there is nothing to be afraid of. It is nothing serious!

These words were enough to reassure his mother, but not Philip. He looked the doctor straight in the eyes, begging him to finally say something concrete. Aware of this, the doctor did not want to procrastinate.

- You see, - he said with a calm tone, - high blood pressure can be very insidious because it's very hard to feel. Most people don't even know they have it at all, until they measure it, so in medicine we call it "the silent killer."

The doctor was silent for a moment, and Philip said:

- As in my mom's case. If she hadn't visited the doctor for that headache that hadn't subsided for a few days, and if the doctor hadn't checked her pressure, among the other things, God knows when we would have noticed!

- That's right. Is your headache better? - the doctor looked the patient straight in the eye.

- It was sinusitis. I keep the area warm with a red lamp, it will take a few days, and since then I wear my hat not only over my eyes, but down all over my forehead, all the way to the eyebrows and the frame of the glasses - Ana laughed at her own expense pressing her eyebrows with her fist - Like this! - she added.

- I'm glad, - said the doctor, - now that we've done these tests, because we don't make a diagnosis based on a single blood pressure measurement, we've confirmed that your blood pressure is not ok. The amount of resistance your blood vessels have while your heart is pumping blood has increased. It results in more load on the heart trying to pump blood, as well as damage to blood vessels under that pressure. Narrow arteries increase resistance. The narrower they are, the higher the blood pressure is. This can damage your other vital organs. The good news is that it's not that serious. But we can't just leave it like that.

- How sure are you that it's not serious? - Philip was worried.

- Sir,- said the doctor calmly, - I know you are worried, but you have to trust our profession, too. I am not saying that it is harmless, but there is no reason to panic. Your mother will only have to follow our instructions and everything will be fine.

At the same time, the doctor and Philip looked at Ana and she understood why.

- Yes, yes, yes, of course! - she answered.
- What do you recommend? - Philip continued.
- First and most important, if you already don't have one, you need to get a device for blood pressure measurement as soon as possible.

- We don't have one! But we will get one today,- said Filip.
- That's right - the doctor was satisfied- As soon as you get it, immediately and without delay, learn to use it, especially you ma'am, because you have to control your blood pressure constantly, even when no one is around you, and I guess there are moments like that.

She nodded.

- And then? - Philip absorbed the doctor's words.
- Then, repeat the measurement several times a day. In case the pressure is high, you will take one of these pills, ma'am. Without any delays! I will write down the dosages and it will depend on the pressure level. Sometimes you will take half, sometimes the whole pill. After taking it, you will measure it again until it is in the normal limits.

Ana looked the doctor in the eyes like an obedient child.
- Is that all? - she asked.
- No. You will go to your doctor for regular check-ups and,

if necessary, she will send you here again. If you are obedient and stick to the agreement we have just made, this wonderful son will have nothing to fear when it comes to his mother.

Philip didn't have time to feel uncomfortable, so he said:
- Thank you, doctor! May I ask you, why did this happen?
The doctor smiled kindly.
- Life, - he said. - The organism ages day by day, and if there are greater earthquakes in life, they accelerate that aging, some of them relentlessly. The least we can protect ourselves from is the loss of loved ones, which I have no doubt you have experienced so far.

Philip's mother bowed her head before saying,
- Several times. I was also an orphan, and now I am a widow. My son's child was also born dead recently, so ....

The doctor looked at her with pity, then tried to insert a glimmer of hope:
- As far as I can see, he is still young, and I guess your daughter-in-law is too. And you're not as sick as your son thought. You will have grandchildren, and you will be able to take care of them without any problems, only if you adhere to everything we have agreed on today.
- Of course - she nodded, having neither the desire nor the intention to mention her son's divorce.
- Of course, - Philip confirmed.
- Keep a healthy diet, be moderately physically active, rest as much as your body asks you and something else, very important - don't get upset about everything in life, because sooner or later everything comes to its place.

On the way home, they were silent for most of the trip, but they were relieved after hearing the good news from the doctor. Here and there, Philip held the steering wheel with one hand and with the other he was holding his mother's hand. She held his hand the same way she did when he was a child falling asleep, and she wanted to tell him that she was there for him.
- You have to take care of yourself, please, - he repeated, wanting to hear her promise as many times as he could.
- I will, honey, when we've already lost dad, I want you to have me for as long as possible. When I join him, I want to tell

him how wonderful grandchildren we have and how wonderful father and husband you are. He will be surprised by some things, but he will also be very happy to hear that Elena is back with us.

Philip said nothing. He just smiled and squeezed his mother's hand even harder. Ana was silent for a while, and then, aware that Philip had to follow the road and that he could not look her in the eye, she had the courage to ask:

- What's your plan, honey?

He got serious. Not because he didn't expect a question like this, but because he can't tell his dearest mother about the details. The fact that Elena will not leave the castle for any reason, that he no longer even condemned himself to ask such a thing. His mother can't even hear about the little room under the castle, about Elena's madness, about her driving him crazy in some way. All that madness drove him crazy because at first he was full of fear and stress, and as time went on, he got rid of it and looked more and more at her crazy life as a normal course of events in a person who he loves immensely. How much madness can a man who loves do? Philip doesn't recognize himself anymore, compared to the first time he was in love with Elena. To the extent that he tolerated not only not reporting to the police and psychiatry, but also hiding in the underground with her, using centuries-old furniture, passages, dishes and way of life, he just couldn't believe it. At first his suit, slung over the chair in their nest, aroused confusion in his head, and he was aware that it had been made in the twentieth century and mixed in an incompatible way, they were not even treated like made in this or that century. They were just "their things".

But to talk with his mother about it...He wasn't that crazy yet. As much as he got out of control, he didn't want his mom to go crazy with them. He wanted to save her from that, to keep her in the illusion she had created for herself, that Elena lived somewhere outside their city and that was it. He stays with her, there's nothing strange about that. Just let her keep thinking that, for her own good.

- Mom, why do we always have to worry about plans?

She felt uneasy.

- No, honey, I didn't mean to bother. Please don't think

I want to put any pressure on you. I am here to support you in everything, even if the whole world turns its back on you, and I would never want to force you to do anything. I'm sorry, but I love you. And you know how much I love Elena too. It's not that I didn't love Patricia and I still love her and wish her all the best, but of all the people in this world, you are still mine.

Philip smiled lovingly and said to his mother:
- Don't worry about anything except regulating your blood pressure, if you want, and I know that you want me to be happy.

Ana managed to loosen her seatbelt just a little, grab her son's face and, while driving, carefully kiss him.

Philip then sank into contemplation of what was to come. They were already carrying the blood pressure measuring device home with them. At the pharmacy, the woman was thoughtful and a little absent, and yet she made an effort to train both of them how to use it. They appreciated her efforts precisely because they were aware that it was not easy for her to do that and yet she gave her best. However, Filip insisted that he visit his mother's doctor on Monday and check if they were trained right. Because, he thought, there is no room for mistakes.

Until then, he didn't want to leave his mother alone but he couldn't come to terms with not seeing Elena until then. The kilometers were passing under his car as he tried to set in his head everything he wanted and needed to do. His thoughts revolved around the Trakoscan. He saw his dearest Elena sitting by the lake, calmly holding her hands on her lap or holding the book she was reading. He admired her every time he saw her in those positions. He also admired her when she was sleeping, talking, not talking, crying and laughing. He always admired her. She was the source of his happiness and joy of life. And the way she was, as no one in the world might accept her like that, she was the reason for him to keep going on with his life.

At the same time, and it must have happened countless times, she thought of him, too. She didn't imagine him in the car, but she knew he had a worried look on his face. Although he bravely and resolutely nurtured the love for the woman who, according to him, was a little bit crazy, he was extremely weak for her, Elena, as well as for his mother and everything that was happening to them. That day, he was not far from the truth. She was sitting by the lake, but neither read nor kept her hands on her lap. With her head down, she had something in her hands, concentrating as much as possible.

- Bu! - she heard behind her and jumped.

A little angry, a little scared, she turned and behind her, near the bench, she saw Marko squirming with laughter that he had frightened her. The fear was gone, and the anger in her grew.

- It's not interesting at all - she told him in a very serious voice.

- Why? - Marco asked, still laughing.

He jumped like a deer on the bench she was sitting on and sat down next to her without asking permission.

- Why? - he repeated his question.

- Because - she looked him in the eyes seriously - when you know too little about someone, you know nothing about his fears, nor about his health, you shouldn't be playing like this. The worst thing you can do then is look at it through yourself, because we are not all the same, we do not love, we do not suffer, we do not enjoy, we do not get angry in the same way. If someone had asked me five minutes ago, I would have bet your parents taught you that.

Mark's mood changed immediately. He wanted immediately to get up and leave. But it wasn't true that his parents hadn't taught him anything. He remembered what his father had always advised him: "You have to overcome the anger. It will never benefit you but it will not spare you either."

Gritting his teeth, looking at the grass, the young man allowed himself to say:

- I'm sorry!

There was silence. Elena followed her rapid heartbeat. She wanted to stop being angry and reluctantly accept the apology, but she couldn't right away. Overwhelmed, she stared ahead as her nostrils fluttered.

It was extremely embarrassing for Marko, but it didn't occur to him to do anything smarter.

- Come on, don't be mad at your colleague - he tried again.

With a laugh, she blew out all the air she was holding in

her lungs, but after refilling her body with a new dose of oxygen, she made a serious face again.

- You deserved it! Big time! - she told him sternly.
- I apologized! What else should I do?
- Promise not to do it again....
- Okay, I promise!
- To anyone!

Raising his right palm in the air, Marko solemnly repeated:
- I promise!

Elena silently checked the functions of her body. She focused on breathing, heartbeat, palm and knee stability, and touched her neck under her hair, looking for sweat.

- Did I really scare you that much? And I just wanted to have fun!

She looked at him reproachfully.

- In a very childish way - she said - If you were a kid, maybe I would understand. But the fact that you, like an adult, don't think about the consequences on other people, worries me.
- Oh, you are taking a simple joke very seriously!
- That was not a joke! You saw yesterday that I got sick, I am still feeling the consequences! I came here to breathe some fresh air and enjoy the sun, and you still sneak up on me and scare me! I'm sorry, but it's not much fun for me!

That's where she hit him. When she mentioned her situation from yesterday, he no longer used the apology mechanically, but he really felt sorry for her. He remembered her kneeling and then sitting in the grass the day before and he was ashamed of his reckless jokes. Maybe the woman, though young, is really sick and it really wouldn't be right to make her condition worse.

- I'm so sorry - he whispered.
- And you should be!

He was silent for a moment, then offered:
- If I can redeem myself in any way, please tell me!

She looked him in the eyes and rebuked him with a look telling him that she was aware that he was trying to soften her, but that she was not a child, if she had already emphasized that. Then she thought of something, grabbed the ball of beige natural wool from her lap and pushed it into his hand.

- Untangle it - she told him sternly.

He took the ball and bowed his head over it, turning it around in his arms. He turned it to one side, then the other. Then, under his eye, he tried to see if she was watching him, and again he tried to figure out how to do that, but he had no idea.

- And how do I do that? - he dared to ask her.

She didn't even look at him when she answered in a monotone voice.

- It should be untangled and arranged in a ball, without getting tangled again. Wrap it nicely, so it can unwind easily while working.

- But I don't know how to do that!

- That is not my problem! Figure it out! It's not like the only thing you know is how to scare people around! Or???

Ugh, she did it. She provoked him just as much as she wanted to.

He threw himself into the work, unwinding the threads, but then the unwinding stopped and it wouldn't go forward nor backward. His eyes were fixed on trying to understand how it was going. And then he had no choice but to pull hard to help himself to untangle the thread.

- Noo! Don't do that! - she yelled almost in his ear - I said untangle, not tear it! Wool is natural and despite how much it costs, it is even more important that it is not so easy and simple to get it. While getting it in that form, I guess you don't even know how much work it takes, so forget about tearing it up. Because someone, and not only because he had nothing else to do, took it from an animal, washed it, and if you only knew how much water it takes, and then knitted it so it would get this shape....

- Then what should I do with it?

- Well, you know what, I don't care at all about your assessment of quality and the assumption of what and how much it took for this to be made. Just untangle it!

-But how ?!

She sighed. What she already had in her hands, she put down on her lap again and took the ball from his hands.

- Well, like this - she said, looking him in the eyes to see if he was following her.

Holding the ball with one hand, she pulled more rounds of thread out of it.

- Are you crazy?

If only he could know how much he hurt her with that question. It hurt somewhere in her chest, and then, in the shortest amount of time she could, she managed to think about what she had been convincing herself of for years - no matter what people thought of her, she will remain the one who will not change herself.

- Even if I was, it's none of your business! But if we are for real, I am not the one that came to you yesterday or today, I'm not forcing you into my company, you have complete freedom to leave if you don't like me, without having to turn around!

He blushed, so he tried to justify himself:

- I didn't mean that, sorry! I'm just... I was just surprised by the way you are trying to do that! It wouldn't cross my mind to do it that way! In fact, I wanted to ask if you were sure it was the right way to do it! That's exactly what I wanted to ask! I apologize if Croatian students have a different vocabulary and if it is a little strange for you, girls returning from America!

- Don't you think it's better to cut down on the appologies, huh, colleague?

- Maybe you're right!

- Maybe it's up to you to check it out! And maybe I did a good thing when I did this with the ball, although it doesn't look like that yet! Well, look!

Scattered between the circles on her lap, she began to pull the ball. After every two, she would release a longer thread. When it became too long for her, she wrapped the thread around the ball, then repeated the same procedure. And then she got stuck. He looked a little pleased when she came to the knot and rejoiced within himself that now she would have no choice but to tear the thread, just as he had tried a moment before.

Well, it was a miracle! She patiently lowered everything to her lap, lifting only the thread and the knot towards her. With movements that didn't even make any sense to him, she touched the knot with her fingernails. And it went on and on. He felt like yawning, but he followed her advice, so he avoided another opportunity to apologize and, acting patiently, allegedly watched what she was doing, but saw nothing. All his concentration was on her clean fingernails, her long fingers, her seemingly fragile wrists, the delicate skin of her hands. Then his gaze wandered to the curls of her golden hair, to the nose protruding behind the strands, to her lowered lashes…

- Here it is! - she exclaimed triumphantly, yet modestly.
- How is it even possible?
- It is! Everything is possible for the one who believes!

He laughed, and she laughed at him, then she told him:
- Now go ahead, wrap it up! You can do that at least!

He looked at her, pretending to be angry, and said to her:
- Don't create situations for which you will have to apologize!

He accepted the hoop and, looking at it as if it were of the thinnest glass, slowly and steadily, began to wind it up. Just inches from the ball, she straightened the thread to keep it straight so he wouldn't tangle it again, since his experience was at zero.

- Can you go a little bit faster? - she provoked.
- I'm sorry! No!
- Ok then! Don't hesitate, I have time!

He could feel her thorns, but if he told her anything, he was afraid it would sound like he was talking to her as a friend again, and that would throw her back into that mood he didn't like. . She was so sweet to him, so serious and maximally concentrated on her part of the job, until she shouted out loud:
- Watch out!

He jumped as if she had thrown a nettle, not a woolen thread, at him. The ball fell out of his hands, which was already a shock immediately after the first shock, and he threw himself into the grass to pick it up, intending to hold it.

- What is it? - he asked, scared, when he grabbed the ball.
- I don't know what happened to you! I just wanted to announce the victory and that we have come to the end, happily throwing you the end of the thread as proof!

Returning to the bench next to her, he looked at her a little reproachfully.

- Well, you scared me!

- Oh really? What a coincidence! Someone did the same to me too, a little while ago, you know, just because he didn't know that not everyone communicates his way, just as I did now and didn't think that not everyone works my way! Sorry!

She lowered her head to her lap and touched her fingernails as if embarrassed. They were silent for a moment, then he began to laugh out loud, and she followed him.

- Thanks for the lesson, colleague!
- You're welcome! But as for those lessons, that's enough!
- Agreed - he couldn't stop laughing.

She was the first to return to her original state, so she squeezed the long metal needles with her hands and began to wrap the wool around them.

- What are you doing? - he was curious.
- I'll try to make socks!
- From wool?
- They're the warmest!
- I know that! I just didn't know that they were created by graduate historians!
- Not all socks are that lucky! Just some of them!

They smiled at each other. He had never seen it before, so he was tempted. At first it all seemed pointless to him. But when he saw the thread turn into a knit with loops the same as soldiers, it became even more interesting to him.

- Look at this miracle! - he exclaimed.
- A kind of art! To me, handcrafts are a kind of art!
- Where did you learn that?

He wouldn't want to hear the answer to that question.

- If you want, you can do anything - she told him.

Her thoughts wandered for a moment, and she saw the women around her with whom she had spent time constantly centuries before. Then, no one was surprised that a woman knew how to knit socks. It would be a miracle if she didn't know how to use wool and needles for various purposes, but she doesn't remember a woman or a girl who could do it. As if she had taken them off yesterday, she could still feel things made of wool scratching their skin. They were not overused in her family, but they were used in cold, long winters, especially if they traveled with the mules somewhere.

- I agree - Mark's voice came back. Immediately he changed the subject from the socks to the beds. - Did you see, up in the castle, how strange the beds are? I thought they were cribs, but then I saw there were no beds for the adults, so I think everyone seems to have had short beds like that.

- Yes - she replied, sure of what she was saying - they slept in a semi-sitting position.

- They didn't! So can a man really rest like that?

- Um, it's all a matter of habit. I have no doubt that they were successfully resting because they were still doing very important work. Several bans, counts, and even cardinals came out of the Drashkovich family.

- Yes, that's true!

Although she was happy she didn't have to get used to it. Before the Drashkovich began to use shorter beds, those from her time had larger ones. And she and Philip have it to this day.

- Good thing at least they breathed normally while they slept. Unlike Louis XIV, who always had those heavy curtains around his bed in the palace and in Versailles, which were drawn in the evening, closing the air - said Marko, and Elena added:

- Still, he woke up well rested! Several people worked on his morning rituals and dressing, in the presence of other people. From his morning routines, they did plays, in a way!

- I just hope that all the thousands of people who lived in the castle he deliberately built, didn't attend, because his intention was to put all the people he needed under one roof so he wouldn't have to go to Paris, because he hated Paris.

- Yes, after what happened to him in Paris when he was a child!

They seemed to find a topic that suited them and was on the same level. They talked and talked about Louis XIV, enjoying their knowledge and the opportunity to repeat the material. Then they switched to the second king, then to the third. She had already graduated, unlike him, and had studied in America, whose education, Marko assumed, was a little more advanced than theirs there. That's why he noticed that even when they talked about the same things, she seemed to know things a little more and a little better. At one point she even said:

- That is not exactly true, although as such it has been going on for centuries!

- And how were you taught in America? How do they know it's not true? - he asked.

- It has nothing to do with America, I'm telling you it's not true and I'm sorry it hasn't been discovered yet.

She bit her tongue because she realized she had said too much, so the sooner the better, she changed the subject and switched to Napoleon.

- He achieved everything he believed in, but almost the strangest thing for me is that people will worship him even after his death.

- Not really! Even if he had died only twenty years ago, his admirers would have turned to someone else!

- But there's a little truth in all that, you know?

- My God, here and there maybe!

- No, no! I don't mean that! In a home for disabled in Paris, where his grave is located, because of a wall, visitors cannot see very well, so they have to bow their heads...

- Really?

- That's what I heard!

- What else did you hear?

He absorbed her stories and enjoyed telling her his. On these topics, the pleasure was mutual. They lost track of time, and then, to his disappointment, she announced her departure. He tried to keep her in several ways. Among other things, he suggested that she knit another sock, when she had finished the first one. But he didn't convince her. Thanking him for his company, she got up, picked up her things, and after showing him the sock with a smile, greeted him and left.

He refrained from falling into a conflict again, but he could bet that, although it started well, she would fit in that sock.

Until his departure, he never saw her again.

13

On Tuesday morning, Elena was suddenly awakened by the sound of a water container she had forgotten to put aside last night. She jumped abruptly and the question just popped out of her throat:
- Who is there?
- It's me, love! - almost at the same time, Philip answered and ran towards her.

Squeezing her tightly in his arms and pressing her head to his shoulder, he kissed her without hesitation and also apologized:
- Forgive me, forgive me, please forgive me, forgive me my love.... But I don't understand, what was that?
- That old plate in which we used to bring water, forgive me, I fell asleep, I was tired and I forgot about it...
- We bring water? I don't remember!

She hugged him even tighter.
- It doesn't matter - it was smarter to say that, than to explain that she wasn't saying that about them now, but the way they brought water in the old times - Just hug me. I missed you so much, I was so sad and scared when you didn't come yesterday.

Is everything okay with your mom?

- Yes! She'll be fine - he touched her hair with his lips - Thank you for asking and forgive me, but I had to stay with her yesterday, I'll tell you everything!

- Are you sure she's okay?

- I am, I am, one of these days I will take you to see her and make sure. She can't wait to see you - Filip told her everything that happened those past few days, finally saying - that's why I had to stay yesterday because we had to go twice until we found her doctor. Forgive me, I'm so sorry!

She tightened her grip on him, showing him that everything was fine, now that she was convinced that everything was fine with him. Then she asked him:

- Do you have to go home fast after work?

He sighed, stroking her back.

- It's not like I'm in such a hurry, but I'm definitely taking you with me!

Satisfied, she kissed his neck harder and harder. It took her a long time to restrain herself, and then she collected herself, moving only far away from him so that, after she had tamed her hair and removed it from her glittering eyes, she could look into his, and using all the tenderness of this world, say:

- Happy birthday, love!

He hugged her again and brought her to his chest. He kissed her hair and face, barely whispering:

- When I have you, every day is happy! Thank you for being in my life! That you receive my love and that you selflessly give me yours!

He kept thanking her as she kept repeating:

- You too.....

After a while, sharing the same pillow, they absorbed each other's eyes and wished that he didn't have to go upstairs and that they could stay here forever. And as a rule, she was the first to become aware of time that does not stand still, so she said:

- You need to eat!

- Not now!

She looked at him disapprovingly.

- Some new rules have taken place in our house. Frightened

about her own, my mother was even more panicking about my health, so she swore to me that I would not leave the house in the morning without milk or tea and at least a small pastry.

- I agree!

- And I like to eat breakfast from your hand, so I hope that we will quickly ignore the new rule, as it usually happens when people are afraid for their health, and when they feel a little better, they forget again.

The holes in her cheeks showed her satisfaction about what he said.

- Then - she said - we have time for your birthday present!

- I already got you!

- Not me! I am already an old, shabby gift that loses its value if it is not upgraded!

- That is not true!

- Okay, I exaggerated a little. It loses value if it becomes routine. Things need to circulate and change. That way I'll be fresh longer.

- Fresh or not, I want just you!

She rolled her eyes and the holes in her cheeks appeared because of the provocative expression on her face.

- Now you're just provoking me to convince you that you're wrong!

- Come on, please try!

He leaned to the headboard of the bed, crossed his legs and arms, and waited. She went to the closet and reached for a wooden box on the top shelf. She brought it close to her and stroked it with her face, then sat across the bed next to Philip and handed it to him. Taking it from her hands, he laid it over his legs with a smile, opening it with a lack of curiosity.

Under the wooden lid, there was something he had to pull out to figure out what it was. He held woolen socks in his fingers. Each was as small as his index finger, and he noticed that they certainly looked old-fashioned or, more precisely, medieval. He figured that out by the small horn they had that curled up.

- Cute! But did you really think they could compete with you? - he asked.

- Even if I made them and spent a lot of time making them?

- That incredibly raises their value in my eyes. I am also proud of you and your effort. And I admit, you surprised me! I didn't know you could do it!

A little dissatisfied, she looked at him.

Of course he noticed!

- Come on, love, please! - he hugged her - Of course I appreciate them, as well as your efforts, but there is no thing that can be compared to the smallest strand of your hair! Thank you! It means so much to me! I will keep them in my car and enjoy their beauty every day. They're great, I really can't believe how you made them! The material is rougher because it's natural, I believe!

- Wool - she interrupted.

- I assumed. But the way they are made is amazing. They are perfect and both are the same as if they were made in a mold.

Still with a sad face, she whispered:

- That's not the point! What hurts me is that you always understood me, even when I'm not saying anything......

- No way! - he yelled and before she could look at him, scared, he grabbed her with all his might and squeezed her so she had to fight for air - I mean, sorry my love, I didn't want to say that, I wanted to say, in fact to ask you, I mean... to say....

He pulled her away, squeezing her upper arms as if she was gonna run away from him.

- Elena! Please don't tell me......no, please tell me love, are you sure?

She didn't blink, just looked at him innocently.

And that was that moment when he understood her without words. He covered his mouth with his fists and screamed. Then he jumped off the bed letting her and her holes in her cheeks alone, running around the room, then through the narrow hallway, all through the wooden door he had left open when he came to the end of the stairs, and back and at the same speed and for the first time since she entered his life not caring too much that he will hurt her, jumped on the bed next to her, kissed her briefly, but juicy than grabbed the pillow, pressed his mouth on it to muffle his yelling, and yelled in a loud voice:

- We are gonna be parents! Thank you, God!

14

- I swear to you, Elena, everything will be as you wish. I would not do anything to hurt you and make you unhappy, but my love, this time I beg you with all my heart to come to your senses - in the room below the castle, Philip cried in front of his beloved woman.
- I'm more reasonable than it looks. If you listen to me, you will protect our child from much suffering, and I know you want to!
- Of course I want to, but Elena dear, have you ever put yourself in my place?
- Many times - she bowed her head sadly.
- And?
- And I can only congratulate you on your courage - she gently touched his face - Sincerely and with all my heart. You are so brave that sometimes it seems a pity that you were not part of the Drashkovich family. What you go through and suffer because

of me, rarely a man in the world could. And allegedly you have no noble blood. It's hard for me to believe that.

- Elena, you don't have noble blood either, my darling, admit it! You have the same last name by sheer coincidence and you love history in the way I admire you, but my love, that's all!

She glared at him.

- Keep that opinion to yourself - she told him, you are gonna tell our child what I asked you to or you will destroy all the good you are doing now. The child deserves to know the truth!

He pressed his fingers to his temples and did his best not to raise his voice at her, even though a train was passing through his head.

- My love, you know that I would never want to offend you? You know that?

When she nodded, he continued:

- Then forgive me if it sounds like I am doing that, but first and foremost, I beg you, don't tell me to talk to our child because you will tell him everything yourself!

- My love, I won't!

- Okay, don't you have the courage to tell me if you plan to leave again?

- I will never tell you because I never plan to leave again. But love, I know I'm going to die!

- Yeah, me too! Maybe tomorrow! Or today!

Although it was the most horrible topic, Elena managed to laugh and pull him into her arms. She wiped away his tears and stared at his soul through his blue eyes.

- So - she said then - as far as the names are concerned, no matter what we agreed on, you can always change it. Don't take it too seriously, please. When I said "always," I meant until he was born. After that it's over.

- I am still thinking that we should choose a girl name just in case!

- For whom, love?

- Okay, I don't want to argue with you about that! It will be just funny if a girl surprises you. If only you had given yourself a little encouragement that this is still possible!

- No! The child I am carrying is a boy! And you know

pretty well how I know that and have the courage to claim that for sure and I know that you will never agree with that, but it is ok, we don't have to repeat that. We repeated the material, and it's really not difficult for me to put everything on paper.

- Don't! - he raised his voice at her. - Please stop, neither your demands nor any postmortem letters will make me let you believe in your imminent death. Forget it!

- Ok! Just don't forget to bury me where I told you!

- God please help me - he whispered softly - I really don't know how I didn't go crazy with you, either from the happiness you are bringing me or from the craziness you are talking about sometimes .

- That's true! I admire you, my love!

- Thanks Elena, but please help me! Promise me that you will live with me, or in any other place with me, give birth to a child in the way that women give birth for yours and his good, and that you will, for his sake , stop doing this to all of us.

- I understand you don't understand love, trust me. That's why I pleased you and came to the doctor, just to calm your heart. Now that you are convinced that everything is as I told you until then, please let me do everything to the end. He must be born here or I am afraid that something else will go wrong, and we do not want that!

- Elena! Nothing can go wrong if a child is born in a hospital!

- Like you've convinced yourself once before!

- It doesn't matter! My daughter died before Patricia arrived at the hospital. If you care, and I know you do, then don't play with our child's life. I have already lost one and I can tell you, God forbid, you will pull your hair out if we lose this child by your fault.

- We won't - she said quietly and firmly.

Philip had no more patience, but he knew that today's dose of reasoning would have to end quickly, or it wouldn't end well.

- Love - he tried calmer - In less than a month your body will start to change. My dear, you will not always be able to get out of here in the same way. You can forget about pushing the closet, and you certainly won't be able to crawl there anymore.

- Just say it, I'll get fat!
- Yes, you will!
- Come with me, please!

She took his hand and pulled him toward her improvised kitchen. She pushed a piece of furniture with her foot. Beneath it, the floor was not the same as everywhere else. It was wooden. She knelt down and pulled the handle out with her finger. Then she pulled it like the lid of an empty box beneath her.

- It is not difficult at all, try it - she offered him.

He stared at her in astonishment. He accepted the lid and set it aside, not thinking of its weight at all.

- Bring a candle, please! And light it!

He did it obediently.

- Walk behind me! Just be careful! You are in unfamiliar terrain!

He walked without a word. She held the candle in one hand and his hand in the other one. They descended a wooden ladder. The space downstairs was really low. Even she bowed her head a little, and he bowed hers even more. She led him, but not for too long. The smell of earth followed them. Then she turned to face him. At first he didn't care why her expression was like that. He was too surprised to think about it. But when daylight shone through the cracks in the wall, he came to his senses. Then he realized she was pushing the wall with her back.

She blew out the candle and put it on the ground next to the match and another almost burned out candle. Then she leaned her hands against the wall. Now he saw that the wall was made of wood. As a trained criminal, she observed the situation outside with one eye, and immediately afterwards, she pulled a small mirror out of the wall and, using it, trained and professional, looked at the other side. Then she put the mirror back in place and pulled the shocked Philip behind her.

- It is ok, we can go out - she said.

In the next second he was blinded by the daylight and Elena's hand called him out onto the path beside the castle.

- Come on, love, this should be done very quickly, especially during the day - she said as she pushed back the door, which was an inconspicuous part of the stone wall.

He looked at her as if was seeing her for the first time. She gave him a questioning look, then tried to encourage him.

- I know, but that's the last secret, I promise!

He tried to talk, stammering:

- I... I can't.....believe it! Why have you been hiding this so far?

- Because I wasn't carrying your baby, so you couldn't swear in him. I was afraid of you, you know. Not always, but sometimes. Not you, but the possibility for you to give in. I have used this way out many times, but I couldn't tell you because it was hard for me to believe that one day you will not give in mentally and betray me. If anyone came for me, this would be my way out. And, yes, you're right! For me, I would be able to live in the castle anymore, but at least I would fight for my freedom. I wouldn't just give up that easily!

- This is so crazy......

- We've been hearing that for eight years, love!

- And it never stops being crazy!

She was already dragging his hand along the path to the lake, when she said sadly:

- It will, that's what I'm talking about. But like everything else, you can't and don't want to accept!

- Sorry, but - he tried.

- I know everything. Unfortunately, I have no other evidence than what I already have. And that is not enough for you and I'm so sorry, it hurts my soul, but I love you. Very. You helped me find myself, and you keep helping me.

- I think all the time that, contrary to your opinion, I helped you lose yourself. Why I kept bringing you here! Why?!

- Shhh, my love, you never know who you have beside you. And you will agree, now is not the time to argue. And it would be better to separate now. You have to hurry up anyway. I'm going to get some fresh air for myself and our son. We will not kiss here. See you later!

As he walked, Philip felt weak. The ring of madness around him tightened to the point of pain. In that pain, he felt so alone. He could share everything with his mom, but not this. In everything else, Elena supported him, but she drove him crazy with her story. He did not take his friend Goran into account at all, because he would immediately go to the police and report not only Elena, but him too. Not because he hates him, but only to protect him, of course. And the few people with whom he had a good relationship for years, he avoided now. He was afraid that they would find out everything and with their unbelief they would hurt him and Elena too. He lacked understanding. He needed to dig a hole in the ground, a deep narrow hole, an infinitely deep hole, to bend over it and scream until he lost his voice. To punch his chest until he tears it. Who? Who to turn to for help after she tricked him into swearing in their child. She was only twisting him around her little finger, but he loved her with all his being and he was ready to give his life for her.

Today, too, he was only physically at work, with all the questions and evil thoughts eating him inside. Until he saw the young man's smiling face in front of him.

- Mr. Philip?

Dressed in a linen beige shirt, with embroidered ethno details with brown and black thread on the collar, edges around the buttons and cuffs on the sleeves and dark wool pants, the young man looked at Philip in surprise.

- Yes - he answered, confused, as he tried to place his familiar lines on the right memory in his head. He knows this boy, and he needs so little to remember, only if he manages to put his torment aside for a moment, then he will remember.

- Good afternoon - the young man offered his hand. - Nice to see you.

Philip accepted his hand, but he still struggled to remember how he knew the man in front of him.

- Don't you remember me? - it wasn't hard to guess.

- No, I mean, I remember knowing you from somewhere, but give me a moment.

The young man gave him a moment, and when he saw that it no longer made sense, he shortened the search on his head.

- Marko - said the young man. - Marko Dvornik.

Philip squeezed his forehead with his thumb and forefinger and patted his head lightly.

- Oh yes, yes, that's right! Mr. Dvornik!

Marko already regretted introducing himself, because as far as he understood, Philip might not even recognize him. But then he thought he did the right thing, because it would be more than stupid if he recognized him after all and found out that he didn't said hallo on purpose, and he knows he's working there.

- How are you? - Marko asked Filip.

- I'm fine, thanks, working. You?

- I am good too. I decided to visit the castle again because it is a place that calls you to come back. I was here once, you know, two months ago!

- Yes I know!

- You do? - Marko asked in surprise. This, in addition to surprises, awakened hope in him! - Who told you? - Marko added, as if there were at least seven people who could tell Philip that a young man named Marko had visited the castle and asked for him.

Confused, Philip quickly figured out how to get out.

- Well, you said at the concert that you would come. I'm not here every day, and since it's been a long time since then, I thought you were already here and that we didn't have the chance to meet here.

Disappointed, Marko accepted:

- Yes, I see! I just thought someone told you because I was asking about you that time some gentleman here. But it doesn't matter.

"The gentleman didn't tell me anything, but Elena did, young man," thought Philip in his head.

- I'm at your service today - he said out loud.

- Thank you - accepted Marko.

They set out together to tour the castle. For Marko, this tour was much more interesting than the first one because he learned a lot more about the things that fascinated him. But he struggled with discomfort all the time, so at one point he decided to say:

- Mr. Philip, I have something to tell you!

Philip turned to him because he was sure he was going to talk about some castle.

- You know, that situation, with the woman?

Philip felt his palms sweat. Wasn't it nice enough to talk

about the castle, why mention Elena now and force Philip to act and pretend.

- For which woman are we talking about? -Philip asked, feigning disinterest and looking away.

- About yours - said Marko, looking at Philip.

Those words startled Philip. No, no and no, he was sure Elena hadn't mentioned their relationship. She would tell him if she has. However, there was a chance that Marko saw them together a little earlier that day. It is not a tragedy. But it would be if he saw from where they came out.

"Trouble over trouble," thought Philip.

- OK? - Philip signaled that he was ready to listen to the sequel no matter what.

- I'm so sorry, you know!

"Yeah... He seems to know more than I think he knows."

- Please spare me - upright in front of him, said Philip firmly.

- I'm glad you think that way! I sincerely hope that what happened did not do you much harm!

- Sometimes we are stronger than we look, Mr. Dvornik. So strong that even we surprise ourselves. Because in some things, we have no choice but to be strong.

Mark liked Philip's way of thinking.

- I'm glad you're dealing with it that way. They say what doesn't kill us, makes us stronger. Yet you take two strong blows in a row and I really admire you standing here today, continuing to live and not feeling sorry for yourself!

- There is no use in feeling sorry for yourself! Instead, fighting is the only cure!

- I agree! I was raised that way too, you know - Marko admired him - but I wouldn't want to be in your shoes going through all this. But you are young, capable, and as everyone says - she is not the only woman in the world.

"What do you mean!? Not in the world, but she is the only one in my world! Stop making me think with your brain, look with your eyes and say already what you really want!"

Mark was less embarrassed now, so he said more freely:

- I felt obligated to talk to you about it. More precisely,

I apologize. Sorry to bother you. You know, even people in the family don't always think the same, even though they try to live by some rules they've established together. But we are each an individual for ourselves and we make our own decisions. We, as a family, were glad that my brother found for himself a woman who suits him professionally and that he will have even greater pleasure in working, but that this woman was married to another man, that we didn't like at all. Our parents even tried to dissuade him, but things had already gone too far before we noticed. He then admitted the whole truth, but had already made up his mind. I'm sorry, you know, and my parents are too, believe me, but he's family, and we finally justified his reasons and gave him our support. We are aware that this hurt you, it happened not so long after you lost your child. But life has many more pleasant surprises for a person like you. I sincerely wish you all the best.

Philip wanted to grab him and give him a friendly hug. His palms were sweating but this time of pleasure and relief. He was making great effort to remain calm and without emotion in his voice, said:

- Thank you, Mr. Dvornik. Say hello to your parents. I sincerely wish Patricia and Mischel all the best.

Marko smiled in gratitude.

"As for happiness, you would be the only one to feel it if you knew how it has been since they were together. Their characters stand out from each other like stone upon stone, but that doesn't even interest me. I'm interested to know, old man, do you know about Elena. "

- I will! I will greet my parents, thank you very much. And thank you for your effort to show me the castle and make my time in it interesting. I love everything that is old. I love and study history, among other things. When I was here two months ago, I met a colleague, a historian. She studied in America. She was then visiting the castle. She had long golden hair, when she laughed she had holes in her cheeks. And yes, she told me her name was Elena. She looks differently from the other girls, which was very interesting. Her clothes and shoes were a little strange for what we are used to in our country, I would say!

"If after all this he doesn't say he knows her, then he really doesn't know her. Make the shortest description for yourself, if I go beyond that, I'm afraid I'll sound obsessed with her. And that is not true. The only thing I feel is the desire to see her again. Great desire, in fact… "

- Trakoscan is a beautiful castle - said Filip calmly - our rich cultural heritage which with its beauty leaves no one indifferent. That is why it is constantly visited, every day, people from all over the world come to enjoy its beauty and originality. Your colleague, I have no doubt, was one of the visitors.

"And that's all?! Ah, what could I expect? This is my life lesson! I left the most important questions for the last day, like she will be there forever waiting for me. How could I just hope that if I came again, I would find her or hear something about her."

- Yes - Marko whispered.

The rest of the time spent in Philip's company he struggled without thinking that his intention had failed. That was not even a realistic intention. But well, life goes on. The pain after the defeat will pass quickly, like any similar pain so far in his life, and he can enjoy at least the castle and the lake, only not in the company of the beautiful Elena.

When they greeted each other, Philip asked Mark:

- Are you staying tomorrow?
- No! Some other time, maybe!
- Then have a safe trip!
- Thanks, good luck to you too!

But before the trip, Marko wanted to relax by the lake. It was one of the smartest decisions he made in his life. After almost an hour's walk between the greenery and enjoying the chirping of a bird, Marko happens to be close to a young family with a three-year-old girl. The little girl, dressed in a pink dress and a pink bow in her hair, hesitated briefly, and then through the game, she carried her basket of flowers closer and closer to the young man who was alone sitting with his arms wrapped around his knees on the grass by the water. She came close to him for the first time, and when he looked her straight in the eyes, she pretended she didn't see him. On the second approach, she looked at him. He didn't want to make her turn around again and leave if he looked at her, so deciding to let the child enjoy herself, he remained motionless looking in front of him.

- Milena- he heard a woman's voice -Come here, honey!
- I'm here, mom - said the girl.

After a while, she went back to her parents, but not for long. This time much braver than in the first two attempts, she came closer to Marko. She bent down picking flowers and putting them in her basket, but she seemed to be losing concentration and her gaze stayed on the young man in front of her.

With his mind deep in his thoughts, Mark didn't mind. However, since her parents were not that far away, he felt obliged to greet the child in some way when she came so close and showed interest in his appearance.

He smiled at the little girl, waving at her.

- Milena come here! -this time a male voice called -Don't bother the man!

Marko turned, waved to her parents, and yells:

- I don't mind, it's okay!

Milena thought she had tried hard enough to finally conquer the field, so she decided to get down to business.

- When I grow up, I will live in a castle like this - she pointed to the castle, and then removed the hair from her eyes and innocently, but confidently added - I will be a princess!

Marko remained open-mouthed. He glanced at the little girl and at the castle, before exclaiming enthusiastically.

- Oh, my God!
- Honey! - her mom from behind tried to get involved and ruin their conversation.

Marko turned and kindly, with his finger on his mouth, gave the woman a sign to let her daughter talk.

Not understanding his reaction very clearly, the little girl opened her eyes even wider, absorbing Marko's eyes.

- Please don't tell me - said Marko with a serious face.

He crawled on his knees to the girl, then got down again and sat in the grass saying:

- Don't tell me I'm sitting here in front of a princess to be!

She got encouraged. He accepted her plans more easily than her grandmother, which put a smile on her face and even more self-confidence.

- Yes! - she said firmly.

Marko took her hand, brought it to his mouth, kissed it, and bowing his head in front of the future princess, he said obediently:

- I'm so glad to meet you, Your Highness!

She was smiling for a while, and her parents were laughing in the background. Then she asked, though she knew the answer, but she wanted to hear a confirmation from him.

- Are you a Prince from this castle?

Marko made a face like when a child is caught scratching the wall with a pen. Thinking how not to ruin the girl's ideals, he counterattacked with the question:

- Why does your smart head think that, princess?

Satisfied almost as if she had received a positive answer, she said:

- Everything! I recognized you! Dads who are not princes do not dress like you!

She stared at his shirt. Ah, yes, Marko realizes that, intending to please his colleague, in case he finds her here, he has trapped this little one.

- Oh, yes, my shirt! That's how we dress, my lady, here, in our village.....

Her parents from behind couldn't suppress their laughter. Looking him straight in the eyes, everything that went through her head came out on the girl's tongue, as it usually does with all children her age, as soon as they relax a little.

- My mother told me that she would take me to the castle because I went to kindergarten and I didn't cry every day. I was still so good and ate all the food they gave me there because I want to grow up and become a princess. You don't become a princess if you stay young, mom says, and you don't grow up if you don't eat fruits and vegetables. They can be awful, but grandma said it's not easy to grow up to be a princess. That's why I try to be obedient every day. Dad also said that to such an obedient girl, the prince would certainly appear. Dad! He is a prince! He showed up! - she shouted.

Her dad covered his face with laughter, but also with embarrassment because an unknown man had witnessed his deceptions. Marko didn't think about it, all of that was interesting and sweet to him.

- Yeah - Marco nodded in approval, with a serious expression on his face.

- Where's your room in the castle? -she was gathering information.

Marko decided to accept the challenge and make the happy girl even happier.

- There, that window! Do you see it?

She stared at the castle with her eyes wide open and her mouth slightly open.

- Where? - she asked.

- There, you see, right where my finger is!

Him pointing his finger didn't help her much. She still looked questioningly at the castle, but she looked at his finger twice, too, and she quickly thought she understood.

- I see, yes! Can I see your room? - she asked him.

- You can, of course! Anyone who visits the castle can see my room!

- And when you sleep?

- Then no! But I sleep at night like all the other people, and they don't visit the castle at night.

- And when do you sleep after lunch?

Ah, he had forgotten that people sleep after lunch too, but he quickly remembered and managed to answer quickly:

- No one is allowed in my room at that time. And those who stay in the castle at that time must be really quiet. Because it's not okay to wake up the prince. I don't have to grow up, but I have to have the strength to go hunting.

- And where's your white horse?

He made a sad face.

- He's a little sick - he said quietly - so they had to take him to the vet. But he will be ok very soon. Strong and fast again.

- How fast?

- So fast, that one time my crown fell off my head.

- Did you find it? - she was visibly disappointed now.

- Never. So I ordered another one to be made for me. But since then, my mom doesn't allow me to carry it when I go out.

He bowed his head sadly. The good-hearted girl tried to comfort him:

- My mother also won't let me wear the shoes she bought me for my cousin's wedding to kindergarten. He says I can't wear them because I'll destroy them. It's not true, but I can't convince her!
- You're going to a wedding, how beautiful?
- Yes I am! And you know what, I'll throw petals when the bride walks down the aisle.

Marko gave her an enthusiastic look and covered his heart with his hands, saying:

- My God, how beautiful!
- Yes! When I become a princess, they will throw a lot of petals at me. And then they will put a crown on my head. Everything will be made of gold and pink precious stones.
- Pink....
- Yes, pink is my favorite color.
- Yes, I can see that - Marko confirmed.

From behind, her mom called again:

- Milena, honey, I think that's enough!
- But Mom - said the little girl - I haven't asked everything I wanted yet.

Marko defended her. Her mom relented, and quickly repented, but also laughed sweetly at what followed.

- So, you don't have a wife?
- Not yet and if you were hoping to meet a princess here today, I'm sorry, I'm not married yet.

Without any hesitation, the little one offers a solution.

- When I grow up, can I be your wife?

The couple behind them burst out laughing, and Marko remained serious, honored by the offer.

- Are you asking me to marry you? - he asked.
- No. I want to be your wife when I grow up. And you to be my husband.

The young "just made" prince grimaced as if thinking, and pointed to the problem:

- Apparently, when you grow up, you will be a beautiful girl. And I'll be old. And, I'm not sure you'll want me for a husband then.

- Don't worry, princes don't grow old!
- That's true - he hit his forehead with his hand - how could I forget that!

When he removed his hand from his face, Marko couldn't believe his eyes. Elena was walking down the path with her hair, dress, shoes ...

"God, am I dreaming?"

Everything inside him moved like hot water was poured on him. He jumped to his feet. His spirit and soul were already walking beside Elena, but he gathered himself and thought that the little girl did not deserve a different departure, so he tried to prepare a decent one for her.

- I have to go to eat now, then I have to sleep, you know? Princes do this that every day at the same time.
- The children too.
- And the future princesses?

She smiled. He bent down, picked a saffron flower, and handed it to her gently, saying:

- It's not pink, but it's a beautiful color. Take it, I give it to you from the heart. You can dry it and keep it as you grow. And then we will meet again. Ok?

He didn't have time for her thoughts and emotions. When he ran after Elena, he waved to the little girl and her parents, shouting:

- Bye Milena! Come here again soon!
- Oh, you shouldn't have said that - said her father.
- Thank you - said her mom.

Walking behind Elena, he deliberately coughed several times, but failed to interest her in turning around. He felt a little stupid and wished he could approach her from the opposite side and be "surprised" when he met her. This way he had been running after her for some time and he was already embarrassed not to call her right away, because he knew she was aware that someone had been walking behind her for some time and any delay in calling her, will make the situation even more uncomfortable. So he immediately shortened the story and invited her:

- Elena!

His voice surprised her. Even more than that, it scared her. She quickly thought of how to react. And in the end, she didn't have much of a choice. The one who calls her knows who she is. Even if he came from her greatest fears, which appear every now and then because of the shaky trust in Philip, she has to either run away or stop and accept what follows with her head held high and dignity as real Drashkovich.

The voice called her name again, a little bit louder this time:

- Elena!

She stopped. Her face froze with a dignified expression and she turned resolutely with her arms beside her body.

- Ah - Marko smiled - for a moment I thought you hadn't told me your real name.

Now that everything was far safer than she had imagined, she could let her hands shake with relief.

- Marko - she tried to sound natural.

- To my great pleasure, in front of you - said the young man.

She wasn't really happy with this meeting. She wasn't happy with many things lately except that she still had Philip and his child growing inside her. It was the pressure he was making on her, ever since she told him she was carrying his child, that took her joy into simple, everyday things. Once, as a little girl, she used to take off her shoes and run barefoot in the grass, lie down in it, letting the sun caress her face, sing along with the birds because she felt she was on her own. All those small things that she thought made her life great, she stopped noticing now that she began to believe that the end of her life was approaching, but that the rest of the time she had, unfortunately, would not be spent in peace to which she was accustomed.

She had already seen everything. She had once managed to give birth to her son on her own, with a quick and short delivery two weeks before the midwife claimed that the child would be born. Then she had to fight for him because they had taken him away from her because of her lack of breast milk and because of the upbringing they thought they should have subjected him to even though he was unaware of anything around him. When her health deteriorated, opinions were divided. One of them cheered for her and claimed that the child's closeness could only heal her, making her happy and giving her the will to live. The second one, was strict and determined to distance her child from her, because no one could prove to them that the disease was not contagious. However, she doesn't remember the last few days were easy for her. She only remembered her tears and prayers, which were her best friends when she was left alone.

Being the saddest person in the world because she had to leave the two beings she loved more than her life, and yet happy that they loved her too and that that hasn't changed until the end, she left her body that night. She never knew what to call it, and then she called for sure — the last twitches of her body as it separated from her soul, weren't strong enough, they were too weak, powerless, and maybe full of emotion. Maybe they felt sorry for her, maybe they wanted to leave her there, repent and leave without her. Or maybe they just underestimated her, thought they had overpowered her, and had no idea how much strength the love she felt had given her and that she slipped from their hands and stayed half there and half here...

To this day she still stands in the same place. She hasn't moved. She was given the opportunity, 8 years ago, to make everything right. And she gambled on that opportunity. She thought she could fool it. But she hasn't. Ever since heaven had been merciful and revealed her secret, it had reminded her of everything and offered her to try again, to close her story this time. Everything that has happened to her since she met Philip, who was given the opportunity to bring her back to her past life and try to correct her mistakes in this one, has led her to believe that nothing new will happen. Whatever she did, things just kept coming back. She knew everything in advance, because someone from heaven was merciful enough to let her remember everything.

The only thing she was wrong about was that she thought Philip knew what it was all about. She quickly realized that he didn't know and even worse, he had no intention of accepting it. And so she loved him so much, just as she loved her husband the first time.

She had no choice but to surrender and escape the game

that heaven is trying to play. But she hasn't found her peace in America either. On the contrary, she felt as if demons were dragging her until she was picked up and returned to Croatia. Since then, she has been playing by the rules, because you can fight the heavens. And maybe this time it will have mercy on her and reward her by really taking her soul this time, where the rest of Drashkovich were waiting for her.

Marko noticed that she was looking at him as if looking through him.

- Elena, are you ok? - he put her back on the path around the lake.

- My colleague - she said rather coldly.

Marko stood in front of her, still unable to control his emotions with excitement. He really believed, so with that intention and his clothes he prepared himself in case he saw her, but on the other hand he was also aware that he was looking at the almost impossible from life. Therefore, he was quite calm when he accepted that he would only see the castle and Philip, but everything in him stirred when she appeared and made him infinitely happy. And why? He didn't even know!

- Nice to see you, Elena! I am very glad to see you!

Lies were never her choice, so she didn't repeat what people usually do, meaning it or not. She just laughed silently. The holes in her cheeks aroused in him even greater pleasure than he had felt a little while ago while enjoying the role of prince.

- I'd like to stay with you for a while, if you don't mind! I was so angry last time because we didn't even say goodbye and it was my fault, so I would like to play a little better now.

- You didn't have to greet me in a special way. Nor should you feel guilty about it.

- Could you help me forgive myself? Because I will only incur more anger if I don't tell you the details I have learned about King Arthur in the meantime, and I know you will be interested.

-King Brit?

-The most famous figure of Celtic mythology of the twelfth century.

Ah that love for history among all other loves! She tried to pretend she was not interested, but she consciously begged him to "catch me cheating, please!" When he understood what she was trying to say silently, they both laughed out loud.

- Ok, ok -she said - you have my attention!

Satisfied, he reached out and, taking her hand, led her to the bench and walking along he offered:

- We can go somewhere else if you want! To a restaurant for lunch!

- Oh, no! - she refused firmly.

- I swear you can trust me!

- I know, but thank you anyway! Although I believe when one swears, I have no idea how sincere you are in saying them.

Lowering his body beside her on the bench, he opened his man's soul:

- I also strongly believe in curses! -He exclaimed contentedly -I don't know where it came from in my life, but it has been relevant since I can remember myself. None of my parents taught me, nor any of my grandmothers. But from an early age, I was in a strange way, connected with spirituality. Being a child of intellectuals, my father, as a former supporter of communism, among other things, was indignant when it became apparent to me. I remember our long conversations, in fact, his conversations with me, while all I did was look at him with open eyes. And he talked, and talked and talked, presenting me various theses and proofs that I was wrong. The more he spoke, the more I was disgusted by what I listened to and the more he pushed me in the opposite direction than what he intended.

She looked at him feeling sorry for him. If anyone knows what it's like when your loved ones don't support you and don't trust you to see what they don't see, it's her. So she told him sympathetically:

- It wasn't easy for you. And how are things today?

- I can more skillfully avoid talking about it with my father. But I'm still convinced that there are supernatural things.

- Are you superstitious?

Squeezing his mouth, Marko said:

- Yes, but I'm not ashamed of it. And I think that sooner or later, even those who fight with all their might will bow to higher powers.

Marko was full of personal examples and he believed they were sent to him to confirm his beliefs. Elena managed to find another passion of his and she even seemed to like it. He told her about the times when he tried to ignore all of that and check if maybe it wasn't as serious as it seemed, and then things turned out to be even more serious than he thought, and they confirmed themselves even more in his life. With her mouth open, she listened to his story about the neighbor.

- Our older neighbors, Mirko and Nada, lived in the house next to ours and they hung out with my grandparents when I was a child. My grandfather died when I was very young, and my grandmother much later. Before her death, I had a supernatural experience again... But let me tell you first about the neighbor. I was little and they used to send me to the nearby store to buy them groceries. They had three daughters. I knew the one who lived in Germany because, whenever she came to visit, my parents would hang out with them because my dad knew German, so her husband could talk to him. I didn't really know their second daughter, she didn't often come from Belgrade, but when they did, I remember playing with her son.

I knew the third one as a student and she would visit them often. Then she married in Varazdin. The old people were left alone. At that time, I didn't even think that they were old but sick too. The only thing I could notice was that the woman would still walk along the street, but her husband was not going beyond their balcony in the garden. . I say this on purpose, so that you know that it never occurred to me that a man was going to die soon.

I was starting high school and one morning, I still clearly remember the details, I had a dream. In that dream, I was playing in our garden, and playing that game I went into their garden. Otherwise, they never told me not to play there, they were even glad to catch me playing in their garden and defended me in front of my mom if she scolded me for it. They had a two-storey house, and the first floor was very low, partly even below the level of the woodshed. Their living room window was quite low, and even a child needed to bend down to look inside.

In my dream, I went to that window, knelt down, and peered inside. On the table in the middle of the room, there were open suitcases. My neighbor Mirko was packing his things. But he didn't look happy. I just stared at him. When he saw me, he looked up and asked sternly:

- What are you doing here?

Being a regular visitor to their garden, I didn't feel offended, so I calmly said:

- I am watching you. Mr. Mirko, are you traveling?

- Yes - he said, lowering his gaze.

Without hesitation, I asked directly:

- I would like to go with you! I want to go where you are going!

I have never seen Mr. Mirko angry in my life, especially not angry at me. He surprised me when he looked at me angrily and yelled at the same time:

- Come with me?!?! What!?!?! You want to come with me?

- Yes - I felt a little embarrassed, though I didn't understand why he was mad at me.

He probably saw my confusion, so he tried to calm down, and thus calm me down. He let go of his things for a moment, approached the window from the inside, and said much more calmly:

- Dear child. You can't come with me. Not now. But! When needed, I promise I will come and personally take you away with me.

I was still not happy, but I knew that what Mr. Mirko promised, he fulfilled.

- Go home now, please - he told me.

After the last words, I woke up. I saw that it was still dark around me. I looked at the digital clock and saw 5:31. Thinking that even today I would not make my mother happy that I woke up on my own, and happy that I still had time to sleep, I turned to the other side and fell asleep again.

My mother came to my room because I woke up at the same time every time. She shook my shoulder, then said:

- Wake up, Marko, it's six and a half!

I didn't jump right away, so she had to work harder:

- Come on, baby, wake up, I'm in a hurry today, and I have to tell you something!

We always wake up faster when someone has something to tell us, so I looked at my mother questioningly and whispered:
- What is it, mom?
- Take your time getting up and after you're done, come downstairs as always to get your breakfast. But there is something you need to know. Aunt Nada is in the living room. Don't be surprised.
- So early?
- Yes, honey, I have to tell you that she came to ask me to call her daughter Suzana in Varazdin. You know Marko, Mr. Mirko died.

Elena froze!
- I was startled - Marko continued - and asked her:
- What? When?
- An hour ago. Aunt Nada didn't want to wake us up so early, so she came just now and please be as quiet as possible for her sake. Because it's not easy for her, the woman is crying, you know what it's like.
- No way!!!!! - Elena moved away from Marko on the bench - What are you talking about!
- It's the truth,my dear colleague! Since that day, I have never dreamed of my neighbor Mirko again. And God forbid I dream of him. I hope you understand why I say that!
- Yes, yes, I understand. Oh, I got chills!
- And I cringe whenever I think of it. I can tell you that, although it wasn't that long ago, I completely forgot what my neighbor Mirko looked like. The only thing I remember is that he was a skinny man who walked terribly slowly. And that he was a good man. Which gives me hope that he won't come to take me on that trip soon - Marko tried to laugh.
- Oh, my God - Elena stared at Marko. - This is morbid. What did your mom say about that? Did you tell her?
- Yes, and I wish I hadn't. She wasn't compassionate, of course!
- She was only acting! Although I don't know the woman, I can assure you of that. Because I am convinced that she couldn't remain indifferent, but that she didn't want to add salt to your wound. Jesus....

- I saw Jesus twice in a dream! We talked - he said not thinking if she was scared enough.

Contrary to his expectations, she was no longer frightened, but returned to the place on the bench from which she had just escaped. She stared deep into his eyes and almost begged him.

- Tell me, please...
- Are you sure?
- More than sure.

He laughed.

- OK... My grandma was sick. For days, my parents took her to the doctor and called the doctors to see her. But my brother and I were not told much. One night I dreamed that I was in the garden with my grandmother and she was lying down because she was not feeling well again. In the sky above us I saw him to the waist. His arms were outstretched, he was wearing a brown shirt made of some sort of antique material. Frightened, I asked him what he wanted.

- From you, nothing - he told me, pointing to my grandmother.

Everything was clear to me.

- Did she die shortly after that? - Elena thought she knew what was coming.

- I was surprised too, but she didn't. Still, she lived a year or so longer. He must have really wanted her, butI guess he wasn't in a hurry.

- Creepy - she said.
- And I saw him one more time in a dream.

Elena held her hands calmly on her lap and stared at him.

- I'm listening - she said.

- A group of men were gathered and they were sitting in a circle. He was sitting at the head. Everyone was facing him, sitting in their seats, but they strongly condemned him, throwing various accusations at him. My dad was among them. He called him a liar... ..I thought I could die of shame. Jesus was sitting in a low, three-legged chair with his arms folded and his head bowed, but completely still. When I thought that was enough, I bravely ran between the circle of people, knelt right at his feet, put my head on his lap and said in front of everyone:

"I believe you"
I felt his hand on my head. As he stroked my hair, he said:
"I know"
Tears of emotion filled Elena's eyes.
- You are blessed, Marko! - she whispered.

The longer he talked to this woman, the more he wanted to talk. Time passed quickly, the thought that she would want to leave scared him. Not once did she interrupt him, not once did she roll her eyes, not once did she laugh ironically as they talked about this subject. Everyone he met on the path of his life has done it so far. But she didn't. But he didn't return to look for her again because of that. He didn't even know that until now. Even before he found out now, he had an irreconcilable desire to return here in an attempt to find her again. It was true that he was looking for her in Zagreb and at his faculty. He looked for her silently, trying to hide even from himself that he is looking for her and that she is always on his mind. Although it seemed to him that he would easily get over it if he didn't find her, he was still glad that she was there next to him, looking more beautiful than the first time.

The sun rose high above the castle, showing all its beauty and whiteness. Today it looked even more beautiful to Marko than the first time, and he thought to himself that he was somehow smarter today. This time, he can afford everything except to fall asleep and dream of his neighbor Mirko, but also to let Elena go while he sleeps, without telling him anything more about herself. And he wanted, he had to admit it to himself, he wanted to keep meeting this woman again and again.

- You lied to me - he heard a serious voice coming from behind his back.

He turned and laughed when he saw a little pink girl right next to the bench. She stood looking at him angrily, clutching the flower he had picked for her before he went a little farther away from her and her parents.

Elena looked at Marko questioningly, and kindly at the little girl, not understanding anything.

- Hey Milena ... -Marko smiled at the little one.
- You lied to me - she repeated the accusation.

He admired her freedom to approach him and told him something like that with that look and tone, but he still didn't understand what it was about. Before asking her for details, he decided to introduce her to the lady who was in his company.

- Elena, this is Milena, we met a little while ago. Milena, this is Elena.

Milena looked at him seriously, and he was lucky to be in the company of this lady, so she wouldn't be hard on him even more. Pulling her dress aside with her hand, putting one foot behind the other, she bowed to Elena.

- Hi, honey! - Elena smiled -Can I help you somehow to punish my naughty friend who lied to you, and I still don't know what!

- I will be happy to receive that punishment, but it would be much easier for me if I knew how I deserved it, too - Marko admitted his surprise.

Still serious, the girl, her voice confirming how betrayed she felt, she said to Elena:

- Your prince told me that you didn't exist!

Elena's eyes absorbed the cute little girl, but now she was even more confused.

- Look honey, first of all tell me who are you here with?

Everything was already clear to Marko. He hid his smile with one hand so as not to offend the girl, and said to Elena:

- Everything is fine, she is with her parents - he pointed to them and briefly told Elena Milena's story.

The girl kept an eye on him in case he made a mistake, and every now and then she glanced at Elena because she was keenly interested in how she experienced this little princess. As Marko talked, Milena proudly spread her dress, stretching her legs one after the other so that Elena could see her shoes better.

Deep down, Elena loathed the lies in which this innocent child was forced to live. But she didn't want to react instinctively not to hurt the child further, so she gently tried to get closer to her little head.

- So - Elena pursed her lips, - but you see, honey, Marko didn't lie to you that he didn't have a wife.

The little face cheered, and Marko proudly straightened up

in a sitting position on the bench.
- I don't - he nodded at the child.
"That's the only thing you didn't lie about" Elena thought sadly.
- She is not your wife ? - Milena asked innocently.
Elena leaned over and said:
- No! I am not his wife, and as far as I know, there is no other woman in his life!
- Then will he be my husband when I grow up? - the little child wanted to reassure herself one more time.
- We've already agreed on that - Marko confirmed.
Elena looked at him sternly! He understood that he was against his lies, but it seemed to him that she did not understand that he wanted to help the child and keep his dreams alive.
She understood, she just didn't agree with that way. Not lying!
- Then you're his sister? - the little one was full of imagination.
- No, honey - Elena replied.
- But you have hair like a princess! And a dress! And shoes! And hands and eyes! Whose princess are you?
Squeezing his mouth to keep him from laughing, Marko looked at the castle.
Elena didn't care how small the child was, she didn't want to lie to her, even if it would make her happy, which she sincerely wanted. She insisted that a painful truth was better than a lie that tickles the ears, and later hurts much more.
- I'm not a princess, sweetheart - Elena said honestly.
Disappointment and disbelief appeared on the little girl's face at the same time.
- Yes, you are - the little girl decided to fight for her beliefs.
Elena reached out and gently took the girl's hand, then said:
- I'm not, honey! I'm sorry! Not everyone you see near the castle is a princess or a prince - she glanced angrily at Marko again.
- That's right - Marko intervenes to save the situation from Elena's attempts to destroy everything - Some of them are

kings, queens, some court fools, others nannies for little princes and princesses, some just servants, cooks, women that comb the princesses' hair!

At the last word, Milena stared at the strands of Elena's hair and unknowingly began to touch hers. She wondered what it was like to have a maid in charge of combing your hair every morning. She certainly shouldn't do it the way her mom usually does. Her mother always combs her hair when they need to go somewhere, and it is not uncommon for Milena to suffer pain in those moments. Mom would hurry, so she would pull her hair, and if by chance Milena wanted to look away, Mom would quickly grab her, return her head to its original position, and angrily tell her not to move, because they are in a hurry. With mom they are always in a hurry.

Dad and a hair comb are a much more bearable combination. That is not happening only when they go out. It happens just like that, when, for example, everyone sits in front of the TV in the evening. Then Dad asks first, unlike Mom, and when Milena agrees, she brings him her comb. He put his daughter in his lap and began to comb her hair gently and slowly. It seems to her that the comb barely touches her hair. It can take much longer than with mom, but it never hurts. Mom should learn from Dad, and Milena is sure that maid does it the same as Dad. She must not allow herself to comb the way her mother does, otherwise Milena would let her sleep with the pigs.

- Then you're the queen? - she asked hesitatingly, because she couldn't imagine a queen without a crown.
- Wow! - Marco exclaimed.
- I'm not, honey - Elena ignored him.
- Then what are you?

Marko secretly enjoyed this pressure on Elena. He waited and waited for his colleague to accept the game.

- I'm a Countess - Elena said.

Marko barely restrained himself from bursting out laughing.

- What is a Countess? - The little head was eager for knowledge.

Marko didn't hide from Elena that he found all that very

interesting, but she explained to the child in the same tone in her voice:

- It's a noble name, honey! In some cases it is hereditary, you know, when the parents are Counts, then the child is too. And sometimes it is a service assigned by the king himself!

Although small, Milena understood that Elena was not what she was looking for, but she was still interesting to her, even though not more than her prince. She therefore endeavored to strengthen her relationship with him, and said to him:

- I don't know when I'll be back! But if another princess comes and asks you to be her husband, tell her you already have me!

- Of course! - Marko said seriously - don't worry about it, my princess!

He took her small hand from Elena's hand and kissed it. He watched to see if his parents saw him, and with a smile signaled that he was delighted with their smart child.

The little girl revolved calmly around them for a while, picking flowers, and then her parents picked her up and drove her away, after they greeted Marko and Elena up close and asked them if something was happening in the castle today and they were not informed. They based their suspicions on the fact that they were both dressed a little differently than everyone else there. Surprised that there was no event, and it was only spontaneously like that, they took their smart child to lunch and rest. The little girl waved as she, already sleepy, left Elena and Marko.

They have already talked about the history of military uniforms in the Middle Ages. Elena felt slightly tired, but not Marko, so he tried to keep her with provocative, for both of them, topics of conversation. By the way, he dared to ask Elena where she lives and if she plans to return to America soon.

She told him it was over with America, and where she lived was none of his business.

- I am interested because you are my colleague, and you are a very interesting woman!

- We're not close friends after all!

- But no one said we couldn't become close friends!

She stuck to her original decision to his great disappointment.

He even tried to tease her with the fact that the meeting with the little girl probably reminded her of how her mother taught her when she was little - not to give information to strangers and not to go with them. But he hoped that he was no longer a stranger

And that attempt was unsuccessful. It only reminded her of the little girl, and since she was gone, she could openly talk about it now:

- A gentle child, and yet the ones she trusted the most get to lie to her the most. And you only laugh, colleague! It's a tragedy for me!

- Come on!

- Yes! Because one day she will be big enough to "know" that they lied to her! It seems by the way they are doing it, they are lying about a lot of other things. Thank God he shut my mouth so I wouldn't throw it in their faces when they approached us. Because I know how they would defend themselves, that is not my concern how they raise their own child. And I'm so sorry for the little one. What will happen to her when she grows up and when she wants to share things with them, and she won't be able to!

- Maybe she would!.

- Only if they fix it right away! If they stay this way, she won't. Neither she nor the children who are served lies like that Santa Claus exists and stuff like that!

- Dear Colleague, don't get mad, they are just children!

- Only children? - she was visibly angry.

In an angry tone she said to him:

- Because they are "just children", we shouldn't treat them like they are stupid, because they are not!

And then she spoke with such fervor in defense of the children that he saw that she could not be distracted from the already established opinion.

- Never even think of having a child until you change your mind, Mr. Marko, because it will cost you, sooner or later - she got up from the bench.

- I respect your opinion Elena, and maybe I'd better keep quiet, but my long tongue doesn't rest, so I'll just remind you - we're human. Well, you told the little one yourself that you were a countess.

After he said that, he learned one more thing about the woman standing in front of him - when she loses, she loses with dignity. Even though he attacked her with something she didn't mind, so she didn't say anything in her defense, she remained calm. No blush, no twitching on her face, and he wanted to see that so bad. Upright body position, unchanged voice and she said calmly:

- Have a nice afternoon, Mr. Dvornik!
- You too, Elena! Hope to see you again — he kissed her hand before she turned and left him alone.

That evening, wrapped in a sheet, she told everything to Philip, who confirmed her suspicions that her relationship with Mark was not so harmless when he told her that he had asked him about her.

- I'll try to stay inside tomorrow and not go out. Maybe it's better not to meet him again. Although what we are talking about is very interesting to me, I don't like the way he looks at me - she said.

- I don't even like the way he thinks about you. I saw his eyes and was furious, but from the outside, I remained calm. I hoped that was only my male jealousy. But don't worry! He's leaving today. You are free to go outside. Our child needs air!

- He's leaving? He told me he was staying....

Philip gritted his teeth, then strained.

- Maybe he changed his mind....

Jealousy consumed Philip's body. Like an attacked animal, he pulled Elena to his chest and sank into his thoughts. All the time she was gone, he felt this way, but he could comfort himself that she had left him, rejected him, and was no longer his. Still, the thought of another man looking at her with interest hurt him. But now that she is completely his and is carrying his child, the thought of her even talking to another man, and that she admits to him, the father of her child, that these conversations are interesting to her, was like she was scratching him with her nails on the face.

Philip tried to control himself because he was afraid that Elena would react to his jealousy if he showed her exactly as it was. It was eating him inside and this time everything roared inside him like a lion. He handed over his wife to one Dvornik without a word, but they can forget about the other one! Because Elena is not only his wife! She is his... ..everything....

Cold sweat broke out on his forehead and palms. Not all men in the world seem to be guided by logic like Philip. In Elena's short stories, he would not believe that the whole world would stand across from him and laugh at him. But he had never thought before that it might be worth believing. Yes, ever since she came back to him he thought they were alone in the world. He barely let his mother into his life, Elena noone, but why did he believe so much that it would really stay that way?

He felt a buzzing in his ears. The young Dvornik could trust her! He has the potential to believe in her stories!

Philip felt more defeated in his life only when she secretly left him. But, he thought, in this case, defeat had not yet taken place. He must stop it with all his might. No matter what the price is. Today he takes Elena home. He must get her out of here no matter how hard it will be. Thank God, she said she didn't want to see Dvornik tomorrow. However, in case he sees her in the morning preparing to return to the castle with him, Filip will knowingly lie to her for the first time, and to other people, that his car is broken and that he will not be able to go to work tomorrow. Okay, it sounds like he is the biggest coward, but is there another choice?

He had never felt so pressed against a wall like this before. He might have been when he found out she was planning to leave him when she did, but he didn't know. Then it was a finished act. Now the danger looks face to face with him. And he can say that she looks like the most cruel beast. Yes, and it can be said that he is afraid of the beast! Really afraid! If someone took Elena away from him now, after more than a year since she returned to him, he would die! He can say that for sure. And yet, in a way, he pushed himself into that danger when he never gave her what was so important to her - to believe her and support her in her, unfortunately really unbelievable story. But what could he do when he never wanted to lie to his beloved wife? Now, for the first time, he thinks he can. Yes, he really means it. While the sweat is cold on him, while she is lying on his chest without a word, while he is not sure where her thoughts are wandering, he comes to a conclusion that surprises him, but it is more than justified - if ever, today, tomorrow or anytime in her life, she approaches a danger of this kind and becomes very serious, Philip will forget who she is, trample on herself and lie that he believes her. He will act it out as he knows and can and will support her and be with her in it and he will stay and live with it, he will do everything, just so he doesn't lose her! Just so he doesn't lose her one more time....

She got up silently, letting go of the sheet she had been wrapped in to stay behind. She wore a long linen dress with a hood from which the laces fell to her waist, intertwining with her hair. She rolled up her sleeves to below the elbows, tying them neatly with a ribbon sewn for that purpose, and tied a string around her waist.

She took a basket made of reeds and put chestnuts in it, then walnuts, and stored the cleaned almonds in a jar. From the vase on her chair, she pulled out a bouquet of flowers she had picked today, wiped the dripping water with a cloth, and freshened it with a rope, lowering it to the top of the basket. Covering everything with a white cloth, Elena set the basket down on the table, returned to Philip, who was watching her silently, and kissing his forehead, she said softly:

- When you are ready, love! I look forward to talking to Ana tonight and tomorrow!

It was the first time Philip had seen the sun and heard the birds in this little room below the castle.

15

Six months after Filip feared that the younger Dvornik had gotten too close to Elena, he still shivered on the thought of the danger of losing her again, in any way. His love, though he thought it impossible, grew along with her belly, more and more each day. He became much more lenient with her, but also much more frightened as far as she was concerned. He felt torn as if on a cross, and only his mother could notice it and be wisely silent in front of them and talk about it only with God, begging him most sincerely to save the life of her grandson this time.

Philip fulfilled Elena's every wish, taking her to the castle whenever she wanted and staying there with her at night. Deep down, he hated himself for doing that. He hated that he was not brave enough to rebel against it, because the truth was, he was afraid for both the child and her. He was very afraid. As much as she approved of the room and the corridors that led to it, the truth was that they were unventilated and there was no light. He hid it from his mother the best he could. He was letting her think what she already thinks, that they have another apartment that Elena rented and that they are staying there, because if she knew where they spend their time, she would be very disappointed with both of them.

But, as they say, three things can never be hidden from anyone - misery, love and coughing.

The coughing.... The word that Philip was afraid of. The sound he fainted from.

After months of not having it, Elena's cough has returned recently. It always remained the same length and depth, but it's more frequent occurrence froze the blood in Philip's veins. Even before she was pregnant, he promised himself that he would not tolerate things about her health, and since she was pregnant, even more so. But after struggling with the fear of losing her again, he sometimes even had to pretend not to hear her cough, suddenly attacking her again in the morning and waking her up rudely. She would cover her mouth with her hand, then get out of bed and walk away not to wake Philip.

Tired of arguing, he let her think she had succeeded. But not always. He knew to follow her sometimes, and as he watched her bend sadly, he would hold her body from collapsing from the strength and depth of her cough. After calming down, she would tell him:

- All right, it's ok!
- Elena, it is not ok!
- Love, you know that was it and that it will not happen again today. And maybe not tomorrow or the day after tomorrow. If I'm sick the way you think, it doesn't work that way! If I cough, then I will cough the whole time!
- That's not a reason to ignore it! Especially when you are pregnant!
- Everything is fine with the baby! I beg you, this has nothing to do with the baby and please don't think that you will lose your child again. I assure you you won't. This time your son will be born alive and well.

That was really encouraging and he loved to hear such encouraging words, but still....

- It's not just about the baby, love!

She would look him in the eyes as if she wanted to remember him well. As if she wanted to see in them whether he is hiding from her that he believes just a little bit in her story. And then, unable and unwilling to enter into discussions with him again, she would say quietly:
- Okay, if it happens again...
- It is happening again and again!
- Then if it intensifies....
- It is intensifying!
Shrugging, she would let him know that the conversation was over for her, saying just:
- Then it will start to calm down again!
The heavier her belly became, the harder it was for her to argue with him about the same things, so she finally began to show understanding for people who used to lie a little bit. She was ashamed, but she still didn't justify lying as a way of life. After all, she told the whole truth to Philip. He didn't like it. So maybe she'd rather just throw in a few lies here and there. She is ready to do anything, just to have him by her side.

Fortunately, she managed to wake up that day without a cough, so she said to Philip:
- I'm going with you today! Please!
Ah, if only he could be in the loneliest place in the world and scream and say whatever he wanted to say! She was always unreasonable and will always stay that way!
- My love, look at yourself! I don't think that's a good idea - he said calmly.
She stroked her big belly gently, puffed out her mouth and, pretending to be angry, said to Philip:
- Don't insult us in the first place! Secondly, today we really want to go and that's why I'm begging you...
"Only two more weeks," he gritted his teeth and threatened her in his head, "and you and I will talk differently, my dear. I have no other choice, I have to reason with you, I have to set boundaries for you, I have to stop you from destroying yourself. May God give me the strength to endure this little time until the baby comes!"

They separated in front of the castle. Filip hurried to pick up a group of primary school children who had to visit the castle today, and Elena headed for the lake with a reed basket under her arm. Whenever she moved away from him, Philip felt that all the organs in his body were not working properly. It was becoming an addiction, and not just love and he was aware of it. But he couldn't help himself.

There were quite a lot of children, but they were dear visitors. They were not tiring, they did not take more time than they were supposed to. They opened their eyes and twisted their necks around the castle, absorbing every word. It was not the first time he had taken a group of children through the castle, but he thought they were never as sweet as today. He saw his child in each one of them. He looked for similarities with Elena in the girls and with boys in himself. The more he listened to their voices, the closer they became to him.

And then the castle fell silent and Philip remained silent with his thoughts. Those thoughts attacked him, they were asking everything, and today he was passive and unwilling to think of answers to all these questions. He needed a break. Of the whole situation, he needed a turnaround as far as Elena was concerned and everything would be fine for everyone. Unfortunately, he was already sure that the pregnancy hadn't changed her much. God willing, he hoped that the baby would at least change something.

The baby... He would freeze every time he thought of him. To people like him, everyone around him can talk and talk all day long. This is not what they imagine. He knows better than all of them that the same thing would not happen like with the first baby, but no one could know how difficult it is and impossible not to think about it. No one but, perhaps, Patricia.

For the first time since he had looked at and touched Elena again, he wished he could sit next to Patricia and be silent. She would be silent, too, he was sure of that. And even if she spoke, he could bet on everything that she would never say - don't think about it. For she would be the only one to look at him with the same gaze and understand the fear in his eyes. The only one. The only time he wanted her was close after realizing that he was only trying to comfort himself with her and deceive the pain for Elena, in short, to survive. He succeeded in this and will be forever grateful to Patricia. He was so afraid that after what she did to him, he would hurt her and make her regret for the rest of her life that she had met him at all. But life was on her side and Philip was sincerely glad that she found Mischelle next to whom she could not feel the pain of divorcing him. Philip also owes him more than he has ever had time to think about.

But his brother! His disgusting little brother!

Fillip stood looking out over the crown at the lake. Everything in him started screaming, shouting, smoking and exploding again when he saw Elena sitting next to the young Dvornik on the bench! Philip almost felt his horns grow out of his skull and he was ready to stab this young man!

Stiff with fear and jealousy at the same time, he remained staring at them, struggling to decide if he should go there and disperse their company, or try to stay calm until he came up with something smarter. But one thing he knew, this has to be the last time he sees this young man near Elena or he will go crazy!

Out of his body with rage, he grabbed a piece of his hair with his sweaty palms and squeezed and pulled it out to keep the physical pain away from the real, emotional pain. With his eyes on the two of them on the bench, he wanted to scream from the top of the castle!

And then his life took pity on him once more, without being aware of how he deserved it. Without taking his eyes off the scene in front of him, he saw Elena get up, stand in front of Marko, raise her finger on him and yes, she threatened him! She leaned toward him, raising her finger even higher, then pointing at the castle and then again near Marko's face. He crossed his arms over his chest, then lowered them to his lap in an attempt to stand up in front of her, then gave up again, crossed his arms again, and crossed one leg over the other, holding it with his hands. He kept his chin so that his head wouldn't fall, so he spread his arms again, saying something shortly, and she took control again and placed him in the corner of the bench. She deceived him that she was done and that she wanted to turn around and leave, but then she attacked him with even greater fervor.

Then Marko folded his arms as if begging her for something, so he pointed to her belly. She shook her head even harder, her hair falling all over her face. With nervous movements she pulled it away and continued to bend towards him, from which he pressed more and more into the corner of the bench. He held out both palms to her as if to show her that he had washed his hands today, trying to tell her to calm down for the sake of the child, but it only made her more enraged.

Philip saw too much to be able to think about the consequences. In the blink of an eye, he was running down the castle and was already out taking big steps toward the bench where Elena was and squeezing his palms. There was no force to stop him from flying there and protecting his beloved wife, and breaking Marko into pieces if necessary. For the first time in his life, he ran into a physical confrontation with someone, but he had neither the time nor the will to be surprised. Nor did he have time to think about how a pregnant woman would react.

Therefore, only heaven could protect the pregnant woman and her child. When he could see the bench he was running toward like the wind again, Philip noticed that Elena was already leaving, taking big steps away. Marko remained on the bench with his back turned to her, then got up abruptly and ran in the opposite direction. That image gave Philip the strength to bury himself in place. He watched silently, aware that they had not noticed him, and the only thing he could consciously think about was that it was better to stay that way.

Already sure that Marko would not follow her, and aware of where Elena was headed, Philip wanted to run after her, but not the same way, over the outside exit, but over the castle. As he came back to life, his reasoning came back too, so he was aware that if it came to her now, he would not be able to pretend that he had not seen them. So he decided to wait until the end of his shift and wait for her to tell him what it was all about.

But he was sure that there was something between Elena and Marko that he had yet to find out. He breathed deeply, trying to dispel any suspicion that his beloved wife was hiding something from him. He forced himself to remember that it was impossible and that she had always told him everything. All he had to do was calm down, work his way to the end of the day, and then go downstairs without panic, find her resting or reading, and wait anxiously for her to tell him, and for him to understand cold headed.

Beneath the castle, Elena entered her space with an ever harder step. Her hands were shaking, she was sweating and breathing hard. The conflict with Marko will not pass for her without the consequences he hopes. She threw herself into her bed and cried in fear. She thought she was ready for it. She thought she was brave enough. Now that she was so close, she seemed to be wrong, too, and though she knew how things would end, her steps toward them weren't quite as sure as she'd imagined.

After about two and a half hours, she heard Philip approaching her bed, entering from the side of the castle. Weak, but she wanted to be able to gather the strength to smile at him. The closer he was, the quieter he was. The last few feet he walked really quietly. His eyes had not yet adjusted to the dim light of this space, but, though with difficulty, he saw her in bed, with her back turned to him. He was glad she was asleep. She's been sleeping a lot lately. She would turn to one side to rest a little, then close her eyes a little, and in a short time she would fall asleep again.

His mother warned her of low iron in the blood, a situation that affects most pregnant women. Elena accepted her remarks with a smile and added that it was easy to get tired now. Even when she does the simplest thing, it requires a lot more effort than before pregnancy, so she is constantly tired and sleepy.

Philip loved watching her sleep. This time he had the same plan.

First he would make sure she is really asleep, and then he would pull up a chair or just sit on the other side of the bed and watch her sleep. It happened to him that he also fell asleep watching her, although rarely. For the past few months, in complete silence and peace, he had been able to feel the movements taking place in her belly. They were a little stronger than Patricia's, until the day they stopped forever.

Ah, the same thoughts again! It occurred to him to swing his arms over his head to chase those thoughts away!

He closed his eyes and tried to remind himself of all the promises he had made to himself and Elena.

When he opened his eyes again, he leaned over her a little. He wanted to see her face, her eyes, but he had to wait for his vision to adjust a little more to the darkness in this space. Her quiet voice eased him:

- I am not sleeping, my love!

A gentle smile spread across his face. He could not see it, but his eyes shone as they always do when they see and hear her after a while.

He reached out and stroked her bare shoulder, then put a long kiss on the same spot. She managed to reach out and stroke his cheek with her other hand. Not that it left him, but the desire to quickly find out what was going on with Marko wasn't that important at that moment. When it is time for their tenderness, everything else must wait. He rested his cheek on her bare shoulder, resting his body on his elbows against the bed. He remained perfectly still for a moment, his eyes closed. The very next moment, their angel appeared. His movement was felt by both Elena and Philip, certainly it was him, not one of them. Like always that warmed his soul and he sighs:

"Thank God," he thought.

And then again.

The same reaction from Philip.

- Schhhhh....-quietly said Elena.

Philip smiled. Of course! Of course, they will remain silent for as long as they need and wait for the next movement, clinging more and more to each other in an attempt to explain this happiness. At Elena's warning, barely noticeable, but nodded obediently.

She remained calm for a while, then turned her head toward Philip. He greeted her with a kiss, ready to give her more. She was always happy to receive those kisses, but this time after the first one, Elena shook her head and refused the next.

- My love, I need to introduce you to someone - she whispered.

She didn't give him time to wonder who she would introduce him to because she hardly knows anyone here in this place. Turning away from him, with a gentle and slow movement of her hand, she shifted the soft white cotton sheet that was crumpled in front of her chest. A small pink hand appeared in the air, and then another one.

After that, Philip literally jumped up and sat on the floor like Elena poured cold water on him.

- What? Why are you pouring water on me? - he asked in surprise.

- Oh, go to hell! - Elena said those words she would normally never say to him.

Immediately afterwards, with one hand resting on her chest and the other still holding a container of water, Elena laid wearily on the bed. Only now he could see that she was very pale. And now he realized - she had given birth, and when she tried to introduce him to the child, Philip fainted. Embarrassed, he lowered his head to her knees. It took them a few moments to come to their senses again.

And then the joy followed - the baby cried because it is in their nature to cry when they meet the outside world. Philip and Elena cried because they felt that they had the whole world in front of them in only about 3 kilograms of pink crumpled flesh with arms and legs.

- Is he alive and well? - Philip asked frantically.

Elena pursed her lips and scolded him:

- Don't you think that only a living baby can cry, my love?

He was unaware of her rebuke. He was short of air, and he had an overflow of emotion.

- Let me see him! - he jumped toward the baby.

- That's what I was trying to do when you slid down and rolled your eyes! You scared me to death! I don't know how I managed to get up and get water. What happened to you? You've never seen a baby before?

- But this is our baby! - Philip's eyes shone like stars in the night. -Love, is it a boy or a girl?

It seemed to her that he really intended to make her angry today.

-What did I tell you before? I said that it is going to be a boy! Arthur! You can change the name in the next five minutes or never!

- I don't want to change it - he looked at the child as if

dazed. - Is he all right? It seems somehow....
She looked at him questioningly.
- Somehow what? - she asked.
He would have kept quiet about it in any other situation, but he was so impressed that at this point he was not thinking what to say and what not to say. That is why he said innocently as a child:
- Somehow colorful!
She wanted to get mad at him, she really wanted to, but instead she started laughing. She didn't have the strength to do it, but she couldn't stop herself. At first he scared her, now he makes her laugh. Only he can do this in such a short time, the only man she loved and with whom she had a child that now was moving and crying in front of her.
- He's not bathed, my love! He came out of me just a short time before you came in here. I thought I wouldn't be able to get up until at least tomorrow, and then you fainted in front of my eyes, so I had to drag myself out of bed to get some water.
He regained his composure and embraced her with both hands, kissing her frantically. Tears were falling down his face as he spoke:
- My Elena, my love, you gave birth to our child here alone. You struggled so hard and I had no idea. You cried here while I was bored upstairs! How can I ever thank you? You gave birth to our child and he is alive!
- Hey! - she felt provoked by those words. -We said it wasn't Patricia's fault!
Aware that the words came wrong out of his mouth, he immediately jumped to his defense:
- And I will always say that! And I will never say the opposite!
Reassured, she rested her head on his chest. She could hear his heart beating really fast, so she asked:
- How do you feel now?
- Me? How do I feel? You just gave birth, and you ask me how I feel!
- My love, you fainted!
- I'm sorry - he whispered, pressing her head to his chest.

- I'm fine now, thank God!

She raised her head and stared into his eyes.

- Do you want to take the "colorful" in your arms now? He really wants to meet you!

She placed the baby in Philip's trembling hands with great effort, warning him to calm down or the baby will feel his restlessness. When he managed to calm himself, the baby stopped crying. So Dad kept shedding tears of joy.

- He is so small - he whispered through his tears.

- It wasn't easy to push him out, though! Fortunately, he was obedient, so we did it quickly!

Philip looked at Elena, then the baby.

- But how? The doctor said two more weeks!

- The doctor was right! But someone was in a hurry - Elena looked at the baby.

- What does that mean? Will everything be fine?

- Don worry, my love! He is a strong boy! He will be your pride and joy!

- And yours, too!

She inhaled. Yes, and hers, but not nearly as long as Philip.

- And mine - she didn't want to talk about it now. - Say hello to Daddy, Arthur!

The new dad was expecting a greeting, though he didn't know how the baby would greet him, so he looked into his face and then asked Elena anxiously again:

- Why are his eyes closed?

She inhaled, then smiled.

- Love, all babies have their eyes closed when they are born. After eight and a half months of darkness in my stomach, even this light you despise is too much for him.

- Ohh...

Funny. Elena thought Filip was really funny today. She would probably have laughed at him even more if she hadn't been too tired and scared her when he fell. Watching him holding the bundle she put in his hands, she melted with joy, though she has always knwn that he was the best man she'll ever meet.

All the happiness of this world lived under the castle that September day, in a secret hiding place that Elena discovered and made it her home. The happiness was so great that it pushed all other feelings out of the room. Perhaps it was the last one, but the fear left the room too, so Philip got up and carried his son in his arms from one side to the other without shaking his hands, fearing that his child would fall out without explanation. When his son stopped moving in his arms, it turned out again that there was no sign of fear left, otherwise he would have asked in a panic what had happened to him. But this time he said calmly to Elena:

- I think he fell asleep!
- You are thinking good!

They didn't let him sleep on the bed. He was sleeping in their arms, little bit in hers and little bit in his.

Along with the fear, the doubt also flew through the small opening of the room. It filled Philip's chests for hours and made him ask countless questions. This time it left the room and even when he thought Elena was asleep after he entered, the doubt tried to persuade him to wake her up and wait for her to explain to him what happened with Marko, and if that didn't happen quickly, then he would start asking her, at first not so much, and then directly. But now that happiness had taken up all the empty space in the room, nothing mattered to Philip about the young man named Marko, and another day, there would be time to clarify with Elena why she was arguing with him. And then he'll have time to think about how to put that kid where he belongs. But not today, today he will be happy.

He was in a hurry to tell his mother that the child had arrived, that his brave woman had brought him into the world on her own. But even if Elena told him to do it, he would ask her to understand that he can't do it today. All he wants on this day is to stay with these two beings who aroused so much love in him that it seemed to him that he could die if he leaves even for a moment.

When the baby woke up, Philip had to get a little more active. He gladly did everything he needed to do and in a short time he had a clean wife and son by his side. He was positively surprised by Elena's dexterity, which seemed to be happening behind his back all this time. While he had a plan for Elena to give birth like all other women, she carried diapers, bottles, baby baths and various things for the baby from the city to the reed basket in front of his eyes. There were far fewer of them than in the baby room they had prepared with Patricia, but they were so practical and useful that Philip was once again amazed how smart and resourceful woman Elena was.

After he took care of her and put her back into the clean bed, she asked him if she could sleep a little. He promised her that he would be the one to take care of their son and that she can rest as long as she wants. Such treatment was to be expected, it was Philip, her beloved Philip. She fell asleep with a smile on her face.

Shortly afterwards a strong, merciless cough woke her. Philip jumped up and held her as she bent over, looking at the baby and to his surprise, he didn't react and was sleeping peacefully.

- As soon as you recover from the childbirth, my love, we will go to see a doctor - he whispered.

She nodded, slipped out of his arms, sank down on the pillow, and continued to sleep peacefully.

He knew Elena so well that he knew she couldn't close her eyes for days now that their child was there. She wouldn't let herself fall asleep, but she would just look at him and look and look, just like he is looking at him now. Since sleep was all she could do, Philip could only imagine the agony of childbirth she had to endure on her own. And he got everything organized. He had prepared everything, even his vacation. But these little pink cheeks suddenly came two weeks early and prevented any plan, torturing his mother here today and there were even no butterflies to brighten her eyes!

But can he be angry? For God's sake, never!

The day went by, and Philip lit a candle and continued to stare at his two angels.

16

In the months that followed, Philip saw another Elena, not only because she was a mother this time, but because motherhood changed her and, thank God, reduced her stubbornness. She was more obedient than ever. Here and there she would tell him that she misses the castle, but a week after the birth of her child she admitted that Philip was right and brought the baby to the city, so she no longer spent nights with him underground in the castle.

With her being that kind, Philip was even more open to give her back with kindness, so sometimes he would say to her:

- We can sleep there whenever you want, but without Arthur, please! We will leave him with my mother and rest in peace knowing that he will be alright!

- I'm not tired of him! I didn't even say I was tired at all!

He was so careful not to offend her, and he was just a human being who has feelings like everyone else, so he quickly tried to make things right:

- I didn't say you were tired of him! I just wanted to say... My love, you know what I mean! I don't want him to spend time there and you know why! And I know you love him, maybe as everyone says about moms, even more than I do, so I ask you to be careful! You know very well that I don't want you to be there either, considering the cough that bothers you, but I love you too much to be against going there sometimes. I'm sure it means a lot to you, you've proven it to me a million times! But Arthur...

- Don't bother! I won't take him there overnight! But thank you for allowing me to take him there during the day and spend some time with him there. I can never explain to you how much that means to me. I understand your fear, but please get rid of it! Arthur will live a long and happy life!

He never liked when she told things like she knew from the future, but he was glad when she said that about their son. Finally, he could find some satisfaction in her crazy stories.

- Thank God - he approved of her statement.

Anna was really happy with her grandson. She did not impose herself and as a grandmother she was moderate in everything, but when she shared the care of a child, she was irreplaceable. Never, but honestly, has Philip ever seen his mother so fulfilled, talkative and happy.

Little Arthur slept more on his family member's chest than in his crib. But he didn't complain, and he was always in the mood to take another nap. He ate well, so he met all the criteria for his age. So in a short time he doubled his weight and got chubby cheeks. And when he started to smile, he had his mother's cute holes in his cheeks.

- He looks just like you - Philip and Anna would often say to Elena.

If Philip was looking at her, she would smile. If not, sadness would fill her eyes as she thought to herself:

"You will be grateful to him for that, my love. At least he will remind you of me."

Elena used every second to hold her son in her arms. No one blamed her for that, but she didn't tell anyone what her real reasons were. Even before he was born, she told Philip everything. She even presented her last wishes to him and made him swear that he would fulfill them. But he never believed her. Then why spoil this little time they had left together?! That is why she changed into the kind woman he always wanted her to be. But even though she wanted to leave him happy, she never gave up on her truth. That was the only thing she couldn't do, not even for Philip. But she could keep her mouth shut. And for the things that are coming. She wanted peace in the days ahead of them no matter what.

Sometimes she felt guilt for hiding things from her beloved. Sometimes she reminded herself that she had already told him everything. There was nothing new, and there was no point in repeating it.

But she was hiding something from him. The consolation was that she did it out of love and the desire to protect him and let him live in peace. Because she knows him. He will live in anticipation of something that most likely will never happen. And if it really happened, he is a smart man, he will face it bravely. And if it doesn't, he will live in peace and at least he will never expect it.

So, not long after giving birth, when he asked her about her last meeting with Marko, whom he had seen from the castle, without giving too much importance to the story, she said coldly:

- Marko Dvornik? Ah, love, I don't know how to explain it to you, but I'll try. Our conversations revolved around history. Not for the first time that day, I knew things that he didn't learn the way I know them, if you know what I mean!

He looked her in the eyes, but he couldn't get to what she was thinking, so he said:

- You studied differently in America?

"Ah, you don't understand, my dear, but I promised myself I would save you as much as I can" she thought to herself.

- However, our information differs. Sometimes he and sometimes I was stubborn to defend my thesis. That day we both wanted to be right.

- And you argued!

- Well, we did! Although it feels stupid to admit that now!

"And I, my dear, would like to hear that."

- And? - Philip wanted to make sure he heard everything - Was he attacking you? Insulting you?

- Do you think I'd let him?

- The argument seemed serious!
- It was, but decent too!
- Are you sure?
- I am that sure so you don't have to ask about it ever again!

He calmed down. He was satisfied with her answers. He trusted her. Even now that he trusted her, she was happy about it, though deep down she was ashamed.

That time, as well as who knows how many times after that, she was ashamed. But she did as she chose things to be done.

- Look at his legs - Philip admired his child. - Can you believe that one day he will wear my size 42 shoes?"
- Love, I'm sorry, but I sincerely hope he wears forty-three!
- Why?
- No reason, only to have bigger feet than yours! -she teased him.
- Well, we'll see!- Philip's eyes lit up.
- We'll see - she insisted.

And she was ashamed again. She was ashamed because she lied. Because she knew only Philip would see that. She won't.

She was ashamed because she felt weaker and weaker with every passing day, and whatever she did made it difficult for her to breathe and she began to feel chest pain. She was ashamed because she couldn't stay. And she wanted to. More than anything, she wanted to stay with Philip and Arthur.

One evening she was sitting in an armchair with Arthur on her chest. The little one rested after his meal, and she enjoyed his warmth and his scent. Philip was napping on the couch watching a documentary about World War II. Elena watched him too, admiring how beautiful he was when he relaxed. His head was resting on the pillow, and smooth strands of light brown hair fell backwards, revealing his forehead, which she loved so much. He is the man who gave her all the happiness in the world. How could she just be so crazy and secretly leave him? In his place, she wouldn't forgive herself either. And he forgave her and loved her again as if it had never happened. Only Philip can do that. The most beautiful man she met had the most kind heart in the world. She was inexplicably glad that he would raise her child. May God protect him and give him strength.

She hated that her body did this without an announcement, especially when she had Arthur in her arms, but she started coughing and she jumped up squeezing the baby. Philip was beside them at the same moment, and she could only signal to him to take the child out of her arms as soon as possible. He took the baby and she ran to the bathroom. Her tears came from her cough, and it seemed to her that it had never lasted so long. After it finally stopped, for no reason she stayed a little bit longer in the bathroom and then returned without saying a word, ready to avoid the subject and asked Philip:

- Do you want something to eat , my love?

When she dared to meet his gaze, she repented. Holding the child gently with one hand, he extended the index finger of the other hand toward her. His blue eyes were bloodshot. She had never seen them like that before. Glancing at her, he addressed her in the most serious tone:

- Elena! Look!

She approached and froze in front of him. He had a red stain on his finger, and a trace of where he had found it on the child's clothes.

- What is it? -she asked in surprise.
- I'd like to believe it's not, but it seems to be blood, love!
- What? Where did the blood come from? That is impossible! Let me see him!

He moved the child back.

- Elena - if he was ever strict with her, it was now - Since when do you cough up blood?

She froze.

- I'm not coughing blood - she defended herself quietly.
- My love, look at me!

She did not want to. He turned abruptly and disappeared from the room. After hearing the door of Ana's room open, it seemed to her that in the blink of an eye he returned alone without the child.

- Love, sit down - he gently pushed her back into the armchair - I have a serious question - when, why and where you decided that you can not tell me everything?

She remained silent.
- Love, you are not helping by keeping quiet!
She surrendered. In a calm tone she said:
- A week ago, I coughed in the bathroom for the first time. I haven't since, so I thought there was no need to panic. If it really happened again, and it did, I am worried now!

Her eyes were full of tears. And he saw that. He knew that if he didn't react, they could even withdraw. However, he has never been a supporter of any person's tears withdrawing, whether male or female. He was convinced that this was doing great harm to the organism. He always allowed her to express all her emotions in front of him. So he took a step toward her, hugged her, and let them flow.

She cried like a child in his arms. He thought he knew why and understood everything, while she knew it wasn't like that. She cried for reasons he never would have accepted. But he always let her cry as much as she needed to. When she began to calm down, he kissed her forehead, stroked her hair and whispered:
- We're going to the doctor tomorrow morning!

She nodded and let him know that he could do whatever he wanted with her.

17

Elena stood by the window holding Arthur in her arms. She turned him toward the window. At first the baby murmured in shock at the whiteness of the snow, but the small brown eyes adjusted quickly and wide open stared out.

Little Arthur already had a habit of squeezing his hands tightly and shoving them into his mouth. When he realized that it was impossible to put his whole palm in, he squeezed it even harder and growled at it, and with his gums hoping to bite, but kept losing the battle and he wanted to do that even more. Very rarely, he would accidentally take his hand to his mouth first, then remember to squeeze his palm. In that case, he would be able to grab two or three of his fingers, and by pressing them with his gums like all the sugar in the world was in them, all that was heard was sucking and his contented breathing accompanied by relieving sighs.

Philip enjoyed provoking him.

- Oh my God, they are so sweet - he would tell him.- Let me try a little!

He would pull the little hand from his mouth, carrying it to his face, and at the same time Arthur would fight with his hands, feet, head, all his strength, and his whole little body, and protest loudly. If Dad quickly returned his fingers from where he had taken them, the little outburst would quickly be over. But if he had to fight for it longer, anger would spin out of control and his movements, accompanied by loud crying, would make Philip regret that he had done that.

- He is a little fighter - his grandma Ana would say.

That was no surprise for Elena. In essence, her child had all the qualities of the world. She was glad when someone else noticed, but she had no reason to be surprised. Because her mother's intuition knew exactly that she had given birth to a person that all the people around her would make proud of and those who would be close to him throughout his life, too.

- I know you will raise him just the way I want him to be - she told Philip.

That morning she was enjoying the view of the snow when she heard Philip saying:

- Today we will decorate the Christmas tree. So, do you want to come with me to buy one or would you rather stay at home with the baby?

- I'll come with you! Arthur too! I just hope he will fit into the winter suit we bought for him just two weeks ago, that he hasn't outgrown it already - she laughed.

Arthur answered with his coo, and she turned him to face her and hugged him even tighter.

After they bought the Christmas tree and the decorations, Elena said that they will decorate it right away.

- Are you sure you are not too tired? - Philip asked carefully.

- I would tell you if I was, my love! I'm feeling better today, don't worry!

- I'm glad you're better, but I'd like it to stay that way!

- Please, I'm just going around you and Ana while you're doing everything yourself!

He hugged her and, as he usually did, held her until she was the first to pull herself out of his arms.

Even in the decorating of the tree, you could tell that this family did not enjoy it as everyone else. But there was still a lot of love between them.

- Elena, darling - Ana protested gently - I know how much you love him, but don't let him pull your hair like that! Protect yourself, my dear, lift your hair so he can't reach it!

Elena didn't care about her pain, she was focused on her child's joy. As for her hair, all she cared about was that there was no hair in his palms before Arthur put it in his mouth. Elena didn't care about what Ana was worried about, so she said:

- Don't worry, Ana. I'm ready for the worst. But as we can see, my hair defies chemotherapy. It seems that I am stronger than I look, in some parts at least. And even if this hair weakened to such an extent that Arthur could pull it out, I would be thankful to God that I still had it longer than I expected.

Trying to change the painful subject, not for himself, but for the woman he loved, Philip interrupted them with a statement:

- I organized a photo session with our Christmas tree. Tomorrow evening, I will ask everyone, especially my son Arthur, to dress himself appropriately as it suits a gentleman like him.

Instead of Arthur, Elena replied in a squeaky voice:

- Yes, Dad, I'm wearing the suit you bought me in Zagreb. Because if I'm waiting for another chance, I might miss it, because I'm growing so fast and I'm not planning to stop, and as far as I can see, my clothes aren't growing with me!

The family photo, even before Christmas, was framed and placed above the fireplace. Smiling, the adult members of this family hid their pain. Looking at Elena, one would never say that a young woman was suffering from a third stage lung cancer.

After her being diagnosed, Fillip was depressed for days. First, he took unpaid leave from work until further notice. Luckily in all this Elena still had enough money in her account because she sold her property in America. So he was satisfied, because he would be able to devote his time to her to the maximum, and yet there would be enough money for her treatment and everything that comes with it sooner or later.

And except that, he was a mess. The diagnosis did not surprise him, it threw him to his knees and he thought he would never be able to get up. Elena, his beloved Elena, the woman to whom he dedicated his life and was ready to give his life for her at any moment, was suffering from a vicious disease. If it wasn't for his wonderful mother Ana, he would be depressed and he would never be able to help himself or Elena. Thanks to Ana, he managed to get up to prepare for the fight for Elena's life.

He did not know how strong he could be until being strong became the only way to change the situation. And to change the situation, was the only intention of this family.

The support they gave her and the love with which Philip and Ana fought for her life, knew to provoke even Elena to start believing that things can, if not change, then at least be postponed. Besides, she could afford everything, but not that she had empty hands, at least for a short time in her days. Either she held Arthur, or Philip, and very often Ana too. They knew it was worst for her after all and tried to understand her to the fullest, but Elena was the one leaving, no matter how much they disagreed. That is why she had a well-developed plan for her last days and did not want to deviate from it.

Even when he drove her to Zagreb, Phillip had to do it with her head on his shoulder. As they waited in the hospital, he did not dare to let her hand go. It was never enough of her warmth or her closeness.

And she was obedient. Extremely obedient. If she had known she would postpone her death for a minute, she was ready to do anything about it. She listened to the doctors and did everything they asked of her, and she never refused to drink or eat the strange preparations Ana made for her.

Everyone in the house hid from each other as they struggled with their thoughts, but the purest were Elena's thoughts, because only they knew the end of the story with certainty. And yes, many times, countless times she hugged her child holding him on her chest and covering him with her prayers. She mentioned Philip countless times in her prayers and thanked God a million times for bringing him into her life. Anna, her dear Anna, has had a special place in her heart since she met her, and she was immensely pleased that she, in some way, will take her place in Arthur's life.

When she wanted to make her days as easy as possible,

Elena thought that, no matter what, she would at least die happy.

" To die" - Anna was still not able to believe in that.

To Philip, dying was utterly unbelievable, but also unacceptable. He never dared to think of it as a possibility after surviving the first shock when the doctors told them the diagnosis. On the contrary, he wanted to believe that Elena would not leave again. She can't, because she promised!

But he was aware, and he felt on his skin how fragile life was and how upside down everything could be turned in an instant. His depression was felt in everything he did, but he worked non-stop for the sake of his wife, and thus for the sake of all the others in the family. But the truth was, Christmas was not as happy as before, nor was any other day. On the one hand, little Arthur was a reason for happiness every day. On the other hand, Elena's condition was not as good as he believed and expected it to be.

But he knew it was very important that he stay strong, and willing to keep a balance between what the doctors said and Elena's wishes that he fulfilled before she even said. Because her being happy would help a lot for the drugs to work on her.

He went even that far and promised her things that he didn't want to think about before. She wanted to visit the castle one day, stay with her books for a while, rest her tired body on her old bed, and he, without a word, was already preparing everything he thought was necessary for her and Arthur.

- My love... I didn't mean to take Arthur this time!

He looked at her in surprise.

- Really? - he was confused - I mean, I welcome your decision and I have to praise you for being wise this time, but you surprised me! Are you sure? Don't do it for me, I mean, if you want to take him with you, it's not a problem at all. I will organize everything, it is not difficult for me, I will go one day before, clean and arrange everything nicely, I'll warm the place, you will not miss anything!

- Except maybe some fresh air!

He looked at her seriously.

- Now I don't know what to think! Are you kidding me or are you finally willing to admit that?

The holes in her pale cheeks didn't give him the answer, they only increased his suspicions.

- Both - she said finally.

He could choose to start talking about being happy, but!... And to keep talking about his suspicions about the consequences that space has left on her health, for hours. Or, he could hug her, kiss her forehead and thank her.

He chose the second option, and smiling, he said:

- Let's remember the days when we were still without him, anticipating his arrival.

She got serious. She felt bad at the moment, but she had already swallowed enough embarrassment, so she would this one too.

- My love - she said - will you be mad at me if I tell you I want to be there alone for a while?

The smile faded from his face. He sighed.

- No - he said - but I want to be there with you and take care of you!

- You are taking care of me more than you need to, love! I want to give you a break for those few hours!

He agreed with a heavy heart and asked her when she would like to go.

- It's not urgent, I'll tell you! I just wanted to make sure you still loved me and wanted to please me, and I wanted to know that I had your promise!

- You have it... - he squeezed her hand tightly.

In the days to come the snow melted, then fell again. Winter was still biting with its cold teeth. Elena knew how to spend hours and hours in the swing in front of the fireplace, holding Arthur on her chest and whispering quietly in his ear. Sometimes he would not hear the whispers because he would be asleep and sometimes he laughed looking his mother in the eyes.

Sometimes, when her voice did not betray her, she sang softly to him. And he was trying to sing with her. Then tears would come down her face. If she was alone with him, she would allow the cought to suffocate her. If Philip was there, he would react silently with a sad look, and she would say:

- Sorry love, but I love him so much!

He forgave her. But he didn't really know what he forgave.

One day in February, Ana said in a serious voice:

- Winter tightened its grip again. Quite low temperatures are announced, especially at night. I suggest not turning the fireplace off. But, to be honest, I'm a little worried about the pipes in the bathroom. Unfortunately, Philip, while your dad was still alive, we had planned, but we never solved the problem with those pipes.

- Yes, Mom, you're right! We should fix them in spring. Do you think that everything would be solved if we doubled that wall?

- Dad believed it would, honey. But we could never afford that work, so we regularly had frozen water all over the house in the winter, remember?

He remembered. Dad, and sometimes mom too, would then bring water from the neighbors for a few days to satisfy their need for water in the house. Philip didn't care so much then, because children don't go into the depths of these things. He never lacked for anything, neither washed goods nor clean dishes, and how that was possible was not his concern.

After his father's death, and him already a married man, he wanted to solve this problem for his mother, but again everything dragged on for one reason or another, and it was mostly put aside because of the fact that there were several mild winters in a row.

But this time, in the spring, Philip will surely fix it. They just have to survive these last few bursts of low temperatures.

When Anna left the room, looking at the fire, Elena said like he was talking to herself:

- I would like to go to the castle tomorrow!

Philip came and knelt beside her. He watched her face, but did not comment. He struggled less and less, and he became more and more skilled in his silence. She turned her head toward him and added:

- Please!

- It's not a problem at all - he said calmly. - I just want you to try to eat something today.

She looked back at the fire without answering.

The next morning, as usual, Anna was the first one to

get up and unfortunately saw that her bad prognosis was true. There was no water. But since the same thing happened to Anna many times in her life, she was organized. In several places in the house, as well as in the garage, various bottles and containers full of clean water stood quietly and waited their turn. But this time, unfortunately, the matter was even more serious.

After Filip woke up, she told him the news, and they had to explain it to Elena because she would definitely notice. Elena did not show much interest in that. She looked pretty bad that morning, so, hugging Arthur on her chest and looking into the distance, she said:

- I didn't sleep well last night!

It was to be expected that Philip would beg her to postpone the trip. He would be surprised to know that she wanted it more than he did, but she couldn't.

- You promised me - she reminded him in a serious voice.
- Yes, yes, yes, of course! As you wish, my love!

He was already preparing her things when Anna secretly called him.

- I know - she told him - that you told me you have something to do today and don't worry about the baby, I just wanted to show you something, so you decide.

She led him to the bathroom, lifted the tray in which they kept the towels, and pointed to the wall between this part of the house and her room. Philip's mouth dropped, because the wall was wet and yellow.

- Unbelievable - he commented.

Anna put her hand on her chin.

- What do you think, son?
- I don't know, Mom, I'm not a plumber! But it's pretty much clear. Water is leaking from somewhere. If we do not stop it, no one knows what the consequences will be.
- It will spread!
- I have no doubt... And then the wall will peel off. Did you look on the other side?

She nodded.

- It's a little bit better - she said - but it's not that good.

Philip bit his lip for a while, then said firmly.

- We need to react urgently. Don't worry, Mom, we'll definitely work it out. It is good that it is not on the ceiling, so that there is a danger that part of the wall will fall on our head. But we have to fix it.

He hurried out of the bathroom. After talking briefly to Elena and asking for her to have a little bit of patience, he left the house looking for a plumber. It cost him more time than he imagined because no one is sitting at home waiting for someone else's troubles as we imagine when we go looking for a solution. After a while, he returned home and, finding them all in one place, said:

- The plumber was working. But it won't be long. His wife promised to send him here as soon as possible. You're home anyway, Mom! Dear Elena, I'm driving you according to plan, I'm leaving you there and I have to come back here to see what and how it needs to be repaired. Someone must be with the plumber, preferably a man, but not this one — he bent down and kissed Arthur on the arm.

There are days when everything accumulates, but with good will a person can solve everything. So Philip reassured himself, but he had a feeling that Elena had sabotaged him today, but not on purpose, of course. She was extremely slow. He helped her with everything, but he couldn't help her separate from Arthur faster. She hugged and kissed him and it didn't bother anyone, but it was as if she had forgotten about the time.

- Do you want to take him with you after all, my love?" -Philip asked her once more.

- No! - she replied firmly.

He had no choice but to wait patiently. He enjoyed watching her whisper something in his son's ear, and he grabbed her hair with both hands and tried to bite her cheek. She understood that as him kissing her and started to cry. When she finally decided to go, she carried the child on her chest almost to the exit of the house, and then, already in her coat, she hugged him again while Anna held him, kissing her too.

- Take good care of him, please!

- Of course, sweetheart - Anna calmed her down. - You know I will, don't worry!

As if about to leave, Elena turned again.

- You know- she said to Anna - he likes to sleep on my shoulder.

- I know, honey!

- And let him suck his fingers as much as he wants, he needs that. Just make sure they are clean.

- Of course!

Elena ran towards them again and held them in her arms for the longest time. And then abruptly she turned and went through the door that Philip had opened for her. As he drove her towards Trakoscan, she did not lift her head from his shoulder. At one point he even noticed her crying.

- Elena! - he reacted.

She quickly wiped away her tears and, trying to calm down, said quietly:

- You know I'm not used to leaving him!

He put his hand on her cheek as he spoke:

- Nothing will happen to him. Don't cry, you know he enjoys grandma's company. You know Grandma will take good care of him! My sweet emotional honey! Do you want to come back?

- No!

It was a pleasure for him to fulfill her wishes because that was how he served her. So he fought for her recovery more and more. It is not that he always agreed with her, but he kept silent and suffered, just as he is doing today. He sincerely hoped that her doctor will never find out that he took her to that small underground room to spend a few hours without fresh air

But he did that. He laid her in her bed and covered her up. He put her bag down on the bedside cabinet in case she needed anything. He didn't want to bother her to talk a lot because she was tired enough anyway. He asked short questions that she could answer only with a few words:

- Are you sure you want to stay, love?

She nodded.

- You don't mind me having to go back for the plumber?

She waved with her head.

- I believe, because you already asked me to leave you

alone here. But I wanted to be close to you, I wanted to wait for you at the castle. Now I have to go back home. How everything just got complicated today! I don't really want to be far away from you. On the other hand, and you've seen it too, the situation with the wall is serious. We have to fix it, with you and the little baby at home, that moisture can be dangerous. But I have to be there when the man comes so my mom is not alone with Arthur in her arms.

- Shhh... - she whispered.
- Okay, I know I'm repeating myself!

He was silent for a moment and hugged her.

- Promise me you'll be good and reasonable!

She confirmed with a squeeze.

- Look - he pointed to the table - I brought some books for you.

She glanced at them. On top of all was "Tristan and Isolde." She smiled sweetly at him. She didn't want to scold him and ask if he really thinks she could read today here. She just squeezed his hand in gratitude.

- You're the best - she whispered. - Never forget that.

He grabbed her in his arms. She would repeat that many times, and he never remained indifferent. Everything he did, he did out of love, not for her to praise him, but still, when she did, it warmed his heart.

- Thank you, my love! But you deserve only the best!

Tears streamed down her cheeks again, and she hid them along with her face behind his neck. She has already done the hardest thing today, she released her child from her embrace. So she must do this too. She must let Philip go, but not right away, even though she knows he's in a hurry. She already knew his "never let go first" game, so this time she used it to keep him no matter what, and she used it. She inhaled his scent as every beautiful day spent with him was before her eyes, from the first day she met him on the streets of Krapina until today.

She didn't lie to that little girl Milena, she met her by the lake, when she said that she was a countess. She was a long time ago. But she was supposed to fulfill the child's wish and admit that she was the queen, because Philip made her feel like a queen this time. She was happier than any queen ever, and even happier than anyone she had ever known. All of them together haven't laughed as much as she did next to Philip, they have never felt such tenderness as Philip gave her.

And then he gave her Arthur. Once again, he gave himself to her that way, even though the child looked like her. He gave a child to her and fulfilled her greatest wish and greatest plan. He never believed her in what she wanted the most, but he was the one who reminded her of everything, who helped her live her life again and fulfill it just as it should have been fulfilled. She would never be able to repay him, but at least he has Arthur.

She imagined Arthur growing up. She imagined Philip breaking everything in front of him and fighting only to protect Arthur from all the bad things, just as he had done for her. Her wonderful Philip, the man with a wonderful and brave heart. The man who sacrifices himself for those he loves.

She sobbed.

Philip interrupted the play "Never let go of first" because he couldn't stand her tears:

- My love, please! - he stared into her eyes- I want you to fulfill everything you want, but don't make me think I made a mistake today. I'll take you home with me! Why are you like this today?

- I am being selfish! I left him alone so I can enjoy my time here alone!

- You deserve to rest if that's what you want! I don't want to hear you call yourself selfish because if I've ever met someone who isn't, it's you! You don't even know, my dear, what a selfish woman looks like and behaves. Wipe away those tears and if you will not stay here in peace, trust me you won't stay at all!

That frightened her a little, although she knew that he would not be able to hurt her, but she had to try to calm down, so he could go in peace.

- Forgive me, my love, but you know, considering how much medicine I'm taking, it's no wonder I'm emotionally weak!

- Pssssst...we won't talk about it! And you're not emotionally weak! You never were! You only cheated yourself once when you left me, but you realized you were wrong because you weren't born to be emotionally weak. You are someone who always fights for yourself and for the people you love. And this time will not be any different! We are here with and for you, you are strong and you can do it!

- I can do it, love - she repeated. - I can do it.

She looked him in the eyes and calmed down completely, so she repeated grinding her teeth:

- I can do this!

He kissed her on the face because she was her old self again. He hugged her again, but this time she let him go after only a few minutes. But, she didn't let him get out of that hug quickly. She wanted him to do it slowly and gently, and in the end she squeezed his fingers, looking him in the eyes, and at the end she let them go too. He waved at her, and her pale hand fell beside her on the bed. Before he turned and left, she said once again with a firm voice:

- Thank you for everything, my love!

He smiled at her and let her rest.

Stepping away from his car, he raised his head and looked up at the sky. It was white, it seemed heavy. The castle drowned in its whiteness in a perfect way. And Philip loved the castle, and even more since he fell in love with Elena. He loved it so much that he felt a little sorry that it was so high on the hill now that the cold wind was blowing strong like this.

He lifted the collar of his coat and covered his ears with it, bending his head as far as he could. He held it with one hand and he put the other hand into his pocket. Then he replaced them and so on until he got to his car.

He reminded himself once again that leaving Elena here alone was not right, but that he is only doing it because it makes her happy and is giving her the strength to fight and stay with them. His mother, as a woman who does not talk too much, but when she talks, she is saying smart things only, advised him that doctors are not always right. When a person has love and satisfaction in life, it can heal him before all other medicines, although they should be taken regularly.

Everyone was doing everything as they were supposed to do it and although the doctors were not very optimistic, they hoped for the best.

Philip arrived home, but the plumber was not there yet. He reassured himself that it was not the man's fault and that their situation had suddenly happened, but that, as his wife had promised, he would come and see. Meanwhile, he laid down next to the sleeping Arthur, and when he fell asleep himself, Anna covered him and let him sleep.

The doorbell woke him, and he jumped, hoping the plumber had arrived. He was right. After apologizing that he could not come sooner, he showed his professionalism and in a very short time he offered a resolution for the condition in their bathroom.

- Is it possible that you do it today? Or at least tomorrow? Because you know, we have a baby in the house. We don't have water and that moisture too. And on the other side of that wall is my mom's bedroom , and she has some health issues too.

- I see - the man was thinking. -Look, I can fix it, but you have to buy a new pipe today.

- So can we buy it today?

The man scratched his head.

- Maybe , we should go and check!

- Where? - Philip insisted. - I'll come with you right away.

- Yes, but if we ate too late and they are closed, I really don't have time to come tomorrow. So what bothers me now is ...

- What? - Philip asked in anticipation.

- Look…. Your pipe broke. The water is currently frozen, so there is no flow, but when it starts again, it will start there as well. So to do my job I definitely have to turn off the water, so I don't mind that it is frozen now. But to know what I did, I need to turn the water back on. I think I need to put a heater to defrost it on this wall where I'm sure it's frozen, but if we don't come back with a new pipe? And even without that, it seems that it will snow again, so the temperature will be milder, it can thaw itself at night or tomorrow morning. And I can't come and fix it tomorrow. So I just want to figure out what is the best thing to do… ..

It was too much information for Philip in such a short time.

- Why don't we go get the pipe right now, and we'll know where we're at!

The man seemed phlegmatic because he was still standing

in the same place, looking at the wet wall and scratching his head.

It was only when Philip came to his face and repeated the question that the plumber said:

- Let's go then!

Philip was relieved. He was already leading the man outside, trying to provoke him to speed up his pace, and he kept talking.

- I will tear down the wall only where the problem is. After that, you don't have to hurry, but you need to call a bricklayer who will remove everything that needs to be removed and fix the wall on both sides.

- We will - Philip was obedient.

They were lucky. The store was still open so they got all the necessary things and headed quickly back to the house. Anna had already set lunch on the table and was waiting for them. Philip ate quickly and left his mother with the plumber after he kissed her on the cheek, kissed his son and went to look for his coat, apologizing that he had to hurry somewhere.

- Be careful because it's snowing again -said his mom.

- Really? -he raised his head, then hurried out.

It was true. Everything was white outside, and it was still snowing. He didn't want to panic, but he could not forgive himself for taking Elena to the castle today.

His winter tires struggled with the snow on the road to Trakoscan. At one point, the wipers on his car began to squeak, signaling that it was no longer snowing. He was grateful for that. But just minutes later, he saw a column of cars in front of him.

He slowed down and carefully placed himself last in line. He tried to see what was going on, but he couldn't. He remained calm for a while, and when two cars had already lined up behind him, he got out and headed forward towards the column. In a few cars in front of him, he saw people one or two at a time, just like him before, stretching their necks in an attempt to figure out what had happened. A little ahead, in the direction of the rotating light, he saw people standing outside next to their cars.

He approached a gentleman, and after they had only looked at each other as a greeting, Philip asked:

- What happened?

- Two cars collided. There are two women in one and a man in the other. They say that the damage is only material, no one is injured, but that one of the women, presumably the driver, is in shock.

- I'm sorry! But does that mean we all have to stand here now? Philip asked, scared.

Another, fat gentleman came up to them, pulling his hat over his ears. He heard Philip's question, so he said:

- It seems that we will have to, the police need to proceed with the investigation.

The two men who shared the same fate with Philip talked to each other, and Philip walked away towards his car, because he just didn't want to talk. He had to hurry to pick up Elena, he had to! It was not the first time she would sleep in the castle, but he wished he didn't tell her that he would come and take her home because she doesn't want to be without Arthur. He promised her and he had to get there!

If only God would calm him down when he saw her so that she wouldn't see in his eyes that he still thinks that this was a bad idea. Only if he manages to hide that, to swallow it down.

He kept the car running like most other drivers in front and behind him, to keep it warm. He was pleased to think his Elena was safe and warm.

He tapped his fingers on the steering wheel, and time passed so slowly. They were lucky it wasn't snowing anymore because it would be worse if they all got stuck there in the snow. God forbid!

Elena may have been right. Without regard to the festivities that winter brings with it and in which even she knew how to enjoy for a short time, in principle she did not like winter and did not easily accept it's arrival, and sincerely rejoiced at it's departure. She argued that everything is easier to do without a thick coat and other clothes over clothes that restrict your movement. And not infrequently, it was her opinion, so many clothes are not enough not to be paralyzed by the cold. And then you have to stay inside like a mouse in a hole for so long and really think a few times if you want to go out.

The warmer weather for her meant freedom from the cold

that does not allow a man to live as he wants to live. To some extent, and as far as these things were concerned, the evidence was this evening that did not cooperate with human plans. In the column of the car, through the white silence, there were people coughing, women nervously attempting to give an explanation to the children, as well as children's cries. Several cars pulled out of the convoy and drivers with petrified faces and clenched teeth drove back from where they came before they got stuck.

It never occurred to Philip to turn around and return to the warm house. He would not have forgiven himself if he had not overcome the bad weather and taken Elena to their child at all costs. Nor would he forgive himself for leaving her in the castle, in her condition, too weak to go out for air alone, and even if she could, she would not dare because her exit would leave a mark in the snow. These traces tormented him greatly. But for now he could concentrate only on getting out of this column, and as for the snow around the castle, he hoped the wind would be enough to cover their footsteps.

To keep himself busy, Philip opened the compartment and pulled out a piece of paper that the plumber's wife gave him. As they drove to the store, the man shyly pulled the paper from the inside pocket of his coat, and handing it to Philip, said:

- My wife begs you not to blame her! But she heard about the situation in your family, so she sent this with the best of intentions. People are satisfied with this medicine, so, if you want... you can try...

Philip opened the paper and began to read:

"Asparagus puree, with honey.... Method of preparation:"

He absorbed what was written with his eyes, and then he thought - when is asparagus season? He knew they were seasonal vegetables, but he couldn't remember exactly when they were harvested. He had never been interested in it before, but that's how nature can surprise. He will have to ask her mother for details and help, because she herself has already improvised to Elena some natural remedy she has heard about. His mother did everything in her power in the situation they had, and Philip was infinitely grateful to her for that.

Time passed in the column and the only thing that moved

was the rotating lights of the police vehicles. Staring at their splendor, Philip felt himself fall asleep at one point, but flinched just as his head tried to fall behind the wheel. He yawned and rubbed his hand in an attempt to warm them, but the best warmth was the thought of his son in his mother's arms by the fireplace they made because Elena insisted. It wasn't until it was done that everyone agreed that the idea was extraordinary and that the solution, now that they have a baby, is great.

Elena 's ideas, her desires, her way of life... sometimes from crazy to unacceptable, and sometimes as tempting as she is.

A few hours later, Philip approached the castle at a brisk pace. He was not happy. After struggling in that car column that barely disintegrated, he managed to drive to Trakoscan, and now there is a situation he hoped would bypass. A few inches of snow betrayed every trace. Everyone will be able to see that one person has approached and two people have moved away. How to solve it and whether it is possible to solve it, he will think later. Now he must hurry to hug Elena.

For the first time, he dared to enter through her secret passage, outside the castle. That was the only solution that came to his mind. When he puts Elena in the car, he will return and continue to walk along the wall for a while, until the tracks are mixed up to such an extent that no one will be able to understand who passed, how many of them came and where they stopped and whether they stopped.

At night, using the light of the white snow, Philip tried to find the opening in the wall. Now he understood that it was not enough for Elena to show him just how to get out, but also how to get in, because the opening, and he saw that now, was so camouflaged that even he who knew the opening existed really couldn't see it. . Another thing that began to bother him, even if he found it, how was he supposed to open it from this side?

He took off his hat because this nausea warmed him, and he remembered the plumber's words and believed that the air temperature had risen a little. He tapped on the snow in an insane wish that he could at least tell Elena that he was there and trying to get in. Little by little, nervousness rose in him against his will, and he angrily did with the traces in the snow what he wanted to do later, so he turned abruptly and headed for the entrance to the castle. He will think about the consequences later, now he has to encourage his sweetheart and explain to her that it was not his fault that he was late and that he certainly came to take her to the child.

He strode around the castle, taking off his coat as he walked, and shoving his scarf, gloves, and hat into his pockets. For a moment he was in the closet and pulled it hard and freely, because in the empty castle at this time there is no one to hear the noise except a bird perched in the snow on the crown of the castle.

He pulled out the closet so much that he stepped behind it as if through a door. But when he dragged his body into the hallway, he pulled the closet back in its place because his intention was not to return here with Elena. He felt the candle and the match, and as soon as he turned on the light, he yelled:

- Love, I'm back!

The fact that he was finally so close to Elena drove any thought out of his head of how much effort it took him to find himself in this position today. Everything suddenly lost its meaning, except that he wanted to take her to the car, and come back to get rid of the clues as he thinks it would be the best and hoping that the trip back will go smoothly to return this mother to her child.

- Elena! - he ran down the stairs - I'm here!

Entering her room, which had essentially become "theirs", he immediately realized that Elena had not turned on the light yet. This stopped him abruptly, because in his excitement he didn't think that it was possible that she was asleep. Suddenly, from a person that is running, he turned into a person walking slowly.

- Oh no ... - he thought.

Under the candlelight, he was convinced that Elena was aslccp, but he was suddenly annoyed that she was sleeping naked. Her not-so-big body, that became even smaller in recent months due to her illness, was compressed on the bed. Her knees were close to her chin, her arms wrapped around her. Just as she used to sit by the lake. Her hair fell over her eyes and her head was facing the ceiling.

With quick movements, he grabbed the sheets she had pushed with her feet to the bottom of the bed and pulled them over.

- You bad girl, all you need is to catch a cold now!

He covered her up to her shoulders to warm her up as soon as possible. She didn't move. Then he pulled up a chair and sat down by the bed after finding an apple on the table. He nibbled on the fruit, staring at the thin bundle in front of him. Her breathing had been so weak lately that it was no longer possible to see the bed inflate.

He quietly finished the apple that tasted good after all those hours stuck in the car. When he finished it, he left the rest on the cupboard next to the books he could tell she hadn't touched. Well, he was glad she didn't. She should just rest anyway. She wouldn't be happy that he put the rest of the apple on the cupboard, not in the basket, especially near the books, but he didn't care too much. It was more important for him now to stay quiet and not wake her up.

After a while, he reached out his hand as lightly as he could to get her hair out of her eyes. If by chance this light movement manages to wake her up, then it would mean that she has already slept enough and that she has had enough rest, so after she comes to her senses and warms up nicely for the outside, they can slowly go.

The golden hair went aside and her eyes showed. Philip hasn't seen anything like this since he knew her. She never slept with her eyes half open. "That's what happens when you sleep uncovered," he thought. "Her body was in shock, so she sleeps with her eyes open."

He slowly tucked his hand under the sheets and reached for her palm to make sure she was warm.

He froze and his eyes opened wide.

Just a moment later, all the birds from the castle took off at the same time, frightened by the animal scream of a male voice coming through the small air vent in the room below the castle.

****

The next day, when Anna heard the door, she quickly lowered Arthur into his crib and ran down the hall. The man's body she met there was Philip's, but her son was no longer in it. He stood with his head down in front of his mother, his tired hands down like wood. Looking at those hands, Ana knelt on the floor and bit her palm to the point that blood started coming out. She was suffocating in her tears, and not even her son knelt beside her and placed her head on his shoulder could stop her. He took her hands in his, and she, heartbroken, kept looking at his hands, dirtier than she had ever seen them in her life.

She managed to look him in the absent eyes and ask a single question:

- Did you already bury her? With your own hands?

Instead of answering, Philip laid and stretched out on the floor and he just wanted to die.

PART TWO

18

Michelle Dvornik

On the round glass table on the balcony of my apartment, my coffee is cooling off as I flip through the newspaper. In our family, reading the newspaper was a daily ritual, so I enjoyed the news, but I also enjoyed the memory of my father, who suddenly left us seven years ago after a heart attack. To this day, I avoid doing it in front of our mother, because although she never said it out loud, but as everyone said about me, I looked exactly like my father and with the same morning ritual like her beloved, late husband, it would be more than a reason for the pain in her chest.

Unfortunately, to my brother, who fortunately did not look so much like our father, I couldn't prove that. I warned him a few times, but the fact that we all spoiled him when he was a child comes back to me and to this day my brother is disobedient. He didn't care that much for the people around him and not just himself, so he read without rejecting the habit we acquired from our father, every day regardless of his obligations or if he was late or if our mother sees him . He did not like to be rushed or told what to do and what not to do.

From my living room, through the open door of the balcony, pretty sounds came to me, a wonderful concert for me personally that I had held two days before, and they had already delivered it to me on videotape yesterday. I played Mozzar's 21 with so much passion that I surprised even myself. For a long time, nothing had filled me as much as the time my fingers flew across the keyboard. My mother, brother and my professor, who was responsible for everything, were my support in the first place, but I think that the main support came from a source visible only to me. I felt my father's presence and the strength he was giving me.

All my life I hid that I thought that I am no better than my brother who excelled in his inexplicable belief in supernatural things. All the time I thought he was right, although I never said it out loud and to cover myself up, I even mocked him in some situations.

The cell phone next to my cup of coffee rang. I put down the newspaper and looked at who it was. It was the professor. I answered immediately.

- Michelle, did you manage to rest?
- Yes, yes, professor, thank you. I feel much better than yesterday. How are you?
- As the years dictate! But I'm not giving up!

I laughed. I knew very well that the professor would never give up and I absolutely supported him in that.

- Did those cameramen bring the materials? he asked me.
- Yes, yes, yesterday, after we spoke. I'm just enjoying the recording!
- Ok, boy, ok, you just be good!
- Of course, I'm learning from the best - I knew how proud he was when he heard it.

The truth is, I learned a lot from him in my life. He motivated me many times, but he often criticized me too. Of course, when everything else was happening, my ears were definitely down, but his criticisms were not of the type - your ears bleeding from constantly hearing the same thing.

His criticisms made me more reasonable. They made me think differently, to give more and be more successful. Of course, I knew that my professor did it out of love for music, but also for me. Instead of making me hate the music, he used criticism to make me like it even more. My professor was a smart man.

Patricia, my unmarried wife with whom I lived together for over five years, did not always think that way, except during the first few concerts that we organized precisely because of his leadership. The professor made hers and my dreams come true, and some time later she began to claim and condemn him that he was doing it for selfish reasons.

- Everyone sees in others what he carries within himself - it would be said. In my life, neither before nor after her, I have dealt with a more selfish person than she was. An only child with rich parents accustomed to being able to do whatever she wanted. She was lucky enough to marry a man who held her like a little water in the palm of his hand, until she rejected him just "because he wasn't educated enough and didn't understand classical music." Those were her words, and that was his only fault.

I don't know how "that" happened between us, but it happened.

My friends, my family, and everyone around me condemned me for interfering in her marriage. God is my witness that I didn't want to, but I fell because I was very attracted to her, and the music connected us. I know I was wrong, but as the professor says, I should have forgiven her and myself.

She had panic attacks whenever I mentioned having a child. I could also understand because it was after the tragedy with her first child. I was ready to wait, but not forever, and I told her that.

Our relationship did not break "just because of that." We just couldn't be together anymore, especially after we became so distant that we didn't even talk to each other around the house. When she moved out while I was in Vienna, I received the news very calmly.

I was alone for a long time and my loved ones thought I was afraid of a new relationship. But no, I was afraid I would make another mistake. That's why I was taking things slowly with Dara and convinced myself that this was the real relationship for me, as much as I can be convinced given that she lives in Paris and I in Zagreb. I am thinking of taking a serious step, because we both want a child, and unfortunately I am not as young as she is. I am almost certain that Dara would be ready to return to Zagreb because of our relationship, but why would she, my mother would ask, as well as my brother, and the professor. I give myself a little more time, and then when I add it all up, I will make the final decision. In the meantime, I want to see how serious Marko would be about taking care of our mom.

What I last heard about Patricia came from a friend of

mine. She works in primary school as a music teacher, and rumors are circulating that it is not easy for her children or colleagues. It is her problem that she still considers herself a Diva, but if she doesn't change quickly in terms of her aggression towards others, she will have problems.

I haven't heard that she is married or has children. I feel sorry for her. I sincerely wish her all the best.

19

Marko Dvornik

Our twins we got, because my wife was also a twin, were hugging my legs. One on the left side, the other one on the right. I taught them that, and then I would walk with them as they laughed like crazy.

This time I struggled to walk with a white sheet over my head, letting out horrible screams, but I noticed that either I was no longer so young and strong, or my three-and-a-half-year-olds were too old to be doing that and it was finally time to stop doing that.

My wife would say:
- Is that the only thing you can play?
For her, the world was full of possibilities.

After several turbulent relationships, I only recognized her as a potential woman for a long-term partnership or, to be even more honest, one who would motivate me in such a way that she would make changes whenever it becomes monotonous and I start to lose interest in us.

Ivana was a person who never stood still. She was constantly changing jobs, the circle of people around her, the genre of books she read, her hair color, but there was something she claimed she would never change because it was sacred to her, and that was her family. So she managed to tame even my restless nature, so all I could do was flirt here and there, but never anything serious since I met Ivana, and especially since we got our twins.

I work as a historian and it fulfills me a lot because I have wanted it since I can remember. I live with my family close to my mother, so we all have lunch with her all the time, because my mother cooks the best, and Ivana doesn't really have a big desire to cook and she doesn't really have the time for that. It is not easy to raise two children at once. Sometimes it is even stressful, especially when the twins are sick at the same time.

I love spending time in the house where I grew up, but I really miss my dad. I guess that's how my brother feels too and especially my mom. Michelle constantly tells me that I don't think about our mom if I keep talking about it so I try to control myself, but he goes to extremes because he is bothered by other things like my reading the newspaper, because it supposedly reminds Mom that Dad is gone. I think that she doesn't need me to spread the newspaper and cross my legs to remember dad, and there are a lot of other things that remind us of him even seven years after his death. Now I am convinced that loved ones never die.

When my dad died, I saw a dead man for the first time because I had no choice. I expected that what people always told me would come true - that when I see that there is nothing left, I will understand that higher powers and life after death are not real. But, to be honest, after seeing my father dead, I am even more afraid and believe in things I have always believed in. And how could I not when I had proof of that. Isn't it strange enough that I never, but never in my life dreamed of my neighbor Mirko again after he gave me that horrible promise?

That's why I can't help it when it comes to these things, my wife would always say that and I agree with her.

We also visit Ivana's parents, honestly she does more than I do, but I will sometimes take the children to them, then pick them up and so on. I avoided being overly close, especially to her mother, because I was never good enough and worthy of her daughter.

Unfortunately, I have it in me, and it is against my will, but I don't get along well with some women, and that relationship usually never improves again. I have such a case with a faculty professor. I sincerely hoped that after I graduated, I would not have her on my way again, but we are still in the same circles in some way, so we suddenly met several times. That things between us could not be corrected was proved by the fact that neither I nor she wished to greet each other along.

Thank God, I don't miss her in my life. And I don't miss the saleswoman in the market who was mad at me years before, and to this day I don't think she was right. I decided, I don't go to that market anymore, so she and I are ok. Ivana even informed me that the saleswoman no longer works there, but I got used to taking risks, so I kept sticking to it.

I avoided another risk without Ivana even knowing about it. I waited for her to untie our twins from my feet, and after they tore up my "ghost" mask, they got a bottle of milk from my mother and took an afternoon nap. Many times I would think about Milena, the girl I met near the Trakoschan castle, especially now that I have remembered my intrusions in discussions with women.

But none of my conflicts with the females couldn't match the one with Elena. I get goosebumps every time I think of it, but I've never told that story to anyone in my life. I think about her from time to time, so when I find such peace and quiet in the house as this one today while the children are sleeping, and apparently their mother has fallen asleep between them, I sit in the chair and let my thoughts fly to the castle that stuck to my heart even before I visited it for the first time, but unfortunately I don't visit it anymore, although my wife insisted on it several times.

I try to get out of her persistence the best I can, and then, like today, I sink into my memories.

I have no adjective for that story to this day. I don't have one, to be exact. Because I have a lot of them. She is both beautiful and creepy to me, then sweet, then morbid, then wonderful, then immediately frightening, then innocent, and then disgusting....

It started quite accidentally, and ended, a little desperately.

Ever since I met an older colleague who studied history in America, Elena, I felt like I was talking to a slightly strange woman. It was not surprising, because she had recently moved here from America, so she had different habits and the way she talked to me was different than all the other girls I knew around me. I had love affairs with a few of these girls for a short time, but never anything serious or long. As they came into my head, they evaporated immediately. I didn't care too much for the women's world.

Then I noticed that something was changing with me as far as Elena was concerned, because I had done something I had never done before - I allowed myself to be taken to the castle again to see her again, although I knew that seeing her again was impossible. I hated having to admit it to myself, but I was even happy to be where everything reminded me of her. I even thought that was enough for me. Until I convinced myself that I can't just meet her there, and that made me feel disappointed, even though I fought well and accepted reality in a rather grown-up way.

Until she appeared in front of me while I was playing the prince in front of little Milena!

It has been even harder for me since then. And this time she was the first to interrupt our socializing under the pretext that she had to rest, although she didn't seem to be feeling well again, as was the case when we met. And why she did that, I realized only when I saw her the third time. That third way, her belly gave me all the answers.

Our second meeting was a gift from heaven, so I could not allow this young woman to disappear from my sight again. I knew she wanted to, but I didn't have the strength to let her. I did a lot of things that would make my dad judge me terribly, and above all I dared to follow her that day.

When she didn't want to talk much about herself, I decided to find out a little more about her. My doubts came true. She was not someone who comes and goes from the castle. She was a little more connected with the castle. I don't know why she hid that she was working there, as I thought then. We were colleagues, I would have understood.

One more thing was confusing me - how is it that Patricia's ex-husband, who also works here, didn't know that? I couldn't really understand that, but after our third meeting, I could believe everything.

The second time I saw her, I followed Elena, hiding in the woods. I discovered that she doesn't enter the castle the way everyone does. Her way of entering and exiting the castle was so strange that the first time she disappeared into the stone wall, I was petrified.

After that, as if I had paid for my sin. I broke my leg and I couldn't travel anywhere for almost half a year. But as soon as I could, I went to Trakoscan again, fearing that I would not find her there this time, but at the same time, hoping that I would.

And I did! Heaven was on my side!

When I saw her walking by the lake, I immediately realized that the woman was pregnant, but she didn't mention that the first two times. I didn't know how I felt about it, but I couldn't even think about it then. I ran towards her full of joy and happiness, and I am not just imagining that, but I'm sure I saw the same in her eyes, only not as overreacted as mine.

We sat on the bench and immersed ourselves in a pleasant conversation and I thought I was melting inside. Then, as when a storm suddenly came, I spoiled the pleasant atmosphere between us when I asked her why she was entering the castle in such an unusual way. At first she tried to convince me that I had misunderstood, but when I proved to her that I had seen everything, that I was right, as well as that I wanted to come after her, but unfortunately I couldn't figure out the way, her face changed.

I don't like when women lie, but I was much milder with her, because…I'm sure to this day, she won me over in a completely different way. I was in love with her. And after all, I admitted to myself that I broke inside because I was jealous when I saw her pregnant, even though I wasn't aware of it at the time.

I'm not a saint, so I just bombarded her with questions. I asked her everything that bothered me, looking her in the eyes, and I spilled all my doubts about her right in her face. She stood out and was different from all the other women I knew, which I honestly think is what won me over, but I wanted to know what all these mysteries around her are about. Why don't people know her, if she's always there, why is she always alone and pregnant? Why was she wearing a wardrobe made of materials that no other woman wears?

I have questioned myself so many times in my life and repeated to myself that I did not attack her. I was just curious, but I didn't point a finger at her or try to blame her. I was just terribly jealous when I saw that she was not a free woman as I had imagined, but I didn't want to hurt her! And she jumped on me like a wounded deer. She raised her voice and threatened me:

- Mr. Dvornik, you have allowed yourself to cross my borders voluntarily and I kindly ask you to withdraw or I will have to take other measures!

When she said that, I had a fit of laughter, and then she became even more upset, to the point that I understood her seriousness and at the same time worried about her child, whom I hadn't really thought about until then.

I asked her to calm down because of her pregnancy, but she refused.

As she stood in front of me, I had the feeling that my neighbor Mirko had come back for me. The words she uttered, I'm afraid to repeat them even in my head, but they explained to me that I should regret coming so close to her. She didn't answer any of my questions specifically, but in just a few words she showed me and proved that she is not an ordinary woman, as I thought. And it may sound strange, I didn't dare to think, but I believed in one thing and I stick to it to this day - if I ever mention her in front of anyone, the curse she put on my life would come true.

To be honest, I am grateful to her because of that, because if I told anyone about her, they would declare me terribly superstitious and a little crazy. I know I'm none of that, but how could I prove that when not all people have the luck to experience supernatural things. Maybe it's their fault and that their disbelief exactly separates them from everything.

I felt a gentle touch on my shoulder and immediately

dismissed the thought of Elena. I always did that when Ivana was close to me, I hid my stories of supernatural experiences like a drunk hiding a bottle when he comes across someone he swore he wouldn't drink again. Because she knew me so well, it seemed to me that sometimes she could read my mind. But I can't let her read my thoughts about Elena. Because that would curse our whole family, and I don't want that.

- Are they asleep? - I asked.

- Yes. I surrendered a little too, but the desire to be alone with you for a while was stronger.

I kissed her forehead.

She is so nice and, although she is constantly restless, she takes care to make me happy. That's why I'm ashamed every time I desire another woman, and it's not that it rarely happens to me. But so far I have never gone beyond "desire". I've never even touched another woman. Except in my mind, so many times... I've touched Elena.

20

Anna

From the first day I gave birth to Philip, he became my heart walking outside my body. I never feared for myself or my life again. He was the only one I cared about. But I also saved my life, precisely because I was afraid to leave him without me in this world. I thought it would be easier for me when he grew up and became his own man, but I was wrong. A child, forever remains a child for his mother.

He grew up and was happy. But my help and love were not unnecessary to him, only the circumstances, in which he needed them, changed. Ever since his dad died, I had even more desire to live longer and take care and sometimes just to watch him and pray for him, for Phillip.

To my satisfaction, I seemed to raise the child I always wanted. I cried a million times because of that. I cried tears of joy. He was so kind, honest, reasonable and compassionate, that I felt I got more than I invested in him. My husband also worked hard, but somehow I was in the lead.

I didn't always approve of all the decisions he made in his life, but I always supported him and fortunately, he knew that if I had to, I was ready to die for him. He was such a grateful child, he loved me and thanked me for everything many, many, many times in my life. He loved me and because of that I was very happy, but I was even more happier because he was convinced how much I love him and that he can trust me to the maximum.

After I achieved that, it was much easier with him. As he grew, he still kept some things to himself, but knowing him better than anyone, I knew I could be calm and even if I wouldn't see him in years, God forbid, I wouldn't hear that my child has ever done harm to someone.

But sometimes things don't go as planned in life as we wanted to. Some things slip through your hand. Sometimes we make big mistakes, but the important thing is that we don't make them intentionally.

It was like that in his life, and I was always there to forgive him and embrace him. I was his first and last stop and he knew he could always come to me, no matter what. I also gave him complete freedom to hide things from me. The only thing I didn't want was him to hide things from me, fearing for me or my health.

Philip has made me the happiest mother in the world twice. Unfortunately, my granddaughter, whose mother was Patricia, died and it all threw us down. It showed us that we don't live many different lives than all other people. Because life consists of ups and downs.

When his marriage with Patricia ended, I felt sorry for her and had a full understanding for her, but I knew who MY child was. Although, even before it was revealed that Patricia was in a relationship with the pianist, I suspected that my Philip was in a relationship with Elena again.

Now I know I was right. He told me everything after he made me the happiest mother for the second time and we got Arthur. But then we hit rock bottom again when we lost Elena. Poor thing, while we were hoping, she knew she was leaving. She knew exactly the day when she would die. If only I knew that that hug was the last.... But that angel of woman knew and kept silent.

Everything was clear to me when my broken son showed up at our door the next day. I would be out of my mind if I didn't have to take care of him and Arthur. If there was someone to take care of them for a while, I would have gone to the mountain and cried out loud for days, until I cried my eyes out.

The pain was even greater, but I needed more strength that only God could give me, while I watched Philip fight for his life. I believe only because he had Arthur and watching Arthur, my sunshine, how he laughs merrily as he seeks our attention, having no idea that I could barely change his clothes and feed him, and his father not that, that the angels were taking care of him those days.

For three days and three nights my son didn't say a word, and then, full of sorrow, he spoke in a hoarse voice:

- She's gone again! And this time forever!

Then I surrendered and cried in front of him and until then I was hiding. I hugged him like a little child on my chest. I have never seen him weaker since he grew up and became his own man. He had never experienced so much pain.

There were still traces of soil under his fingernails. I didn't bother him with questions about why he buried her himself. I didn't bother or question him, but only a few days later, when Arthur fell asleep, I received the whole story as a gift and I only hope that was the whole story. As much as I was in shock, everything became clear to me. I was proud of Philip for loving his wife so much that he accepted her with something that I don't believe anyone would ever accept. I saw his courage when he put his life at great risk, but he buried our beloved Elena where she asked him to, the way she wanted to - in a grave by the lake near the castle, dressed in clothes she had prepared for herself, with her favorite shoes, wrapped in the sheet she had given him for that purpose.

I managed to teach him that love is worth everything and I was proud of him, but my love for him made me fear because it was easy to see and discover the grave. My fear grew because I knew in all that pain he was not able to do it in a way that no one would notice. I was afraid, yes, I was very afraid that he would be caught and we don't need that, not now.

- Mom - he was comforting me - I never believed in her crazy stories, but in one thing I did believe. Elena was the smartest woman I ever met and she knew things very well. She seemed to be writing the script for her death. In that scenario, she tried to protect me as much as possible. I was still throwing the soil in her grave — he was biting his lips in pain — when snow began to fall in large flakes. Mom, I know she wasn't a countess, but I doubt she had the power to see the future. She knew that when she died, snow would cover both her grave and my tracks. As if she could plan everything. After the snow, warm days will come and the grass will hide it. It's not that I'm afraid of the consequences, I'm ready for everything, mom, the only thing I wasn't ready for was for her to leave without telling me that, but still trying so hard to protect me!

It took us a lot, a lot of time to rise again from the ashes, but we had to. We had Arthur. And in him we had Elena too. Our angel was a copy of his mother. And Elena watched us every day from the picture above the fireplace. She watched how happy childhood we were able to give her child. I sincerely hope she was pleased. Because we did our best, not only for her, but for us too. That's why, today we have a wonderful seventeen-year-old who is our pride and joy. His smile is our joy, although it often awakens other types of emotions because the holes in his cheeks remind us constantly of his mother.

He inherited his hair, as well as his body, from his father, so I see my husband young for the third time every day.

A few months after Elena's death, Philip decided to return to work. Not that the reason was of a financial nature. As far as this is concerned, we were still surprised to find out only after her death how much money Elena had left to Philip and Arthur. But the way we raised him never gave Philip to spend the money just like that. He continued to live modestly as before her death. And so he insisted on raising his child, spending as much time as he could with him. And I knew, without him even telling me, that he had returned to work so he could visit her grave every day.

Arthur was raised to keep family secrets, but Philip still hid the greatest secret from him. He waited, as Elena wished, for Arthur to turn eighteenth.

If I could put aside every sadness and tragedy we have experienced, it would leave me with a wonderful life next to the two most important men in my life. And when that day comes, when I close my eyes, although I still don't want to because I still think they need me, I will leave happy and bring a lot of good news to my husband and Elena there.

21

Patricia

I feel like I'm losing the ground under my feet. My mom has always told me that this world is cruel, and now I see that she was right. Unfortunately, she herself started getting into fights with me, so she is not that far from that world either. I used to be a daughter whose decisions were supported by her proud parents. Lately, more and more they are contradicting everything I do.

We have been arguing for ten years about my house in Krapina, which was built for me, and which has been empty for years and does not serve anyone, but they don't agree with me to sell it. That's what I get when I didn't persuade my dad in time to transfer all the documents in my name and so I don't have to beg them now.

I'm doing the best I can. I'm really trying. The fact that fewer and fewer people understand me hurts me, but I don't intend to change myself for anyone. It is not pride, nor spite. I just respect myself. That's exactly what my parents taught me, and I'm very grateful to them for that. I am grateful to them that I know how much I am worth and for not letting anyone humiliate me.

I always had only one dream and with my own strength I managed to make it come true. I became an opera singer, people applauded me, and gave me flowers. Then the professor and the pianist began to use me to their advantage, so I broke off the relationship first with the professor and then with the pianist.

Michelle. I wouldn't say I overestimated him, because I've always been good at estimating people. The man has simply changed. Soon after the professor brought us together, I realized that he liked me very much. I was still grieving my stillborn child, but I liked his attention. It was distracting me from what had happened to me, and it was fun to give him hope that he could get closer to me, and take that hope away from him. My hot-cold play warmed him up even more.

And then followed a period where he did everything he could to impress me. Day by day, I began to feel that I was also attracted to him. It is true that I was married, but my marriage lost its strength when I moved to Zagreb, and it never occurred to my husband to come to live with me. We both saw ourselves moving away. I don't know what my husband thought about it, but I didn't bother too much. Anyway, after the first concert I was ashamed of his education and understanding of music, especially around Michelle's family.

I followed my heart and soon made my life more beautiful, bringing fresh excitement to it. I was surprised when my husband literally caught me in my new relationship with the pianist, but on the other hand he made it easier for me. We had a reasonable and painless divorce. At least as far as I'm concerned. I didn't ask or think about him until I started to miss him.

The longer I was with Michelle, the more I realized that I was not guaranteed that every man would look after me and take care of me the way Phillip did. He had spoiled me so much that not even ten like Michellle would have replaced him. I never confessed to anyone, but I quickly wanted him back. If I hadn't been bothered by his background and level of education, I would have had him back as if I had swung a magic wand. Not even his American girlfriend, with whom my mother told me she was comforting after me, would stop me.

I felt sorry for him when I heard that the American woman had died of lung cancer as their son was only a small baby. I saw him some time after that while I was visiting my parents. I was looking forward to that encounter, but I quickly realized I was wrong. People change. It was no longer the Philip I used to know and he wasn't attractive to me anymore. He was more silent than speaking, and I don't really like that in people. I've seen him two more times since then, but I just pretended I haven't seen him.

Some time after I was in a relationship with Michelle, the professor really started to exaggerate, and I couldn't stand him anymore. I stopped working with him and wanted to make a career for me and Michelle without him. I thought we already knew enough people. Unfortunately, Michelle didn't cooperate. All he wanted was to have a child with me, but it never occurred to me. And even without that, I was already disappointed enough in him, so we just drifted further and further away. Then I felt it was best to move out of his apartment, so I did.

I haven't been in any long relationships since. Nor have I held a job for long. I'm working as a music teacher at a school where everyone thinks they are above me just because I came there last. I will prove them wrong. I will prove to them that they didn't appreciate what they had, and they will brag with me when I return to the opera stronger than ever.

22

Arthur

These were very difficult days for me. I had to go to school, and my blood froze in my veins as I walked through it. I was raised to admit at home whatever I did, and that's how I lived because I didn't know any other way. My family has always been on my side no matter what.

So I explained to them as soon as I entered the house what had happened to me. After all, they raised me that way, I couldn't close my eyes when someone was in trouble and not run to help. That's how I reacted that day, and what did I get in return ?!

I told my father and grandmother the truth:

- Last night I stayed up late. Although I'm not a fan of chemistry, I thought with a little effort I can fix my grade. And there is not much time left, the end of the school year is approaching. It is not impossible, I am aware of that, so I decided to stay up late and study. Even as I got up in the morning, I was aware that I had gone too far, but I hoped that everything would be fine. But I was a little mistaken. In math, I realized I was going to fall asleep. I apologized and the professor allowed me to freshen up a little.

I came to the empty men's restroom, washed my face with cold water, and then wet my hair with my wet hands. I was on the way out with no intention of staying anywhere, when I heard someone snorting from the ladies' room. It was very unusual for me, and although I have never done that before, I looked curiously inside.

Surprised, I said:

- Biba! Wait a minute... Hey! What's going on? Why aren't you in class?

One brief, angry look was all I got from her. I knew I was breaking the rules, but I walked two steps into the women's restroom, asking:

- Biba? Is everything OK?
- Leave me alone and go away - she said over her shoulder.
- Okay...I said cautiously. - Are you coming with me to class?

She tried to laugh, but her voice sounded more painful than cheerful.

- You're crazy - she said shortly.

I knew that Biba smoked, but I thought she would never dare to do it inside the school. But I couldn't ignore the smoke that was spreading, nor the tears she was trying to hide.

I approached her even closer and began a conversation with her, hoping to make it easier for her. She admitted her problems to me, and when I tried to comfort her, she became angry, her hands began to shake, and she began to cry even more.

- You don't understand, you can't understand - she raised her voice at me.

I tried to calm her down. I don't know what I did wrong, but instead of calming down, she felt worse.

- Nobody understands - she cried - Nobody, especially you!

Then she lost control and tried to do a terrible thing with trembling hands. She wanted to put out her cigarette in her flesh. She tried to press it into her hand with her fingers. I jumped without thinking and grabbed her wrists. I separated her hands and she started to fight with me like a wounded animal. I admit, I also raised my voice at her, but I was in a panic...

- Finally - I thought when I saw the pedagogue rush into the bathroom, followed by the art professor.

- What's going on here? - the pedagogue interrupted our struggle.

Biba managed to get out of my grip when I turned in surprise to see who had come and moved aside. It was much easier for me when I saw this wonderful reinforcement. At the same time, I saw that the cigarette had fallen on the tiles, and I naively bent down to lift it carefully so as not to burn my fingers. It was still smoking, so I wanted to put it under the water. Then I heard her awful words:

- He's bothering me - she said crying.

- Draskovich! - the teacher yelled at me. - What's going on here?

I slowly got to my feet, carrying the smoking cigarette butt. I even naively showed it to them in order to say that we have to get rid of it.

- Wow, young man - the art professor called from behind - I thought you don't smoke, especially not in the school!

- It's not.... - I wanted to tell the truth, but I remembered that I would push Biba into even bigger problems, so I stopped.

- It's not like it looks like, yes, I know - the pedagogue said ironically. - All of you are saying the same words. Biba, what's going on here? "

Still fighting for air, she said through her tears:

- Just get him away from me, please!

Get me away? And I just wanted to help her!

She was quickly taken to the pedagogue's office and I to the principal's office. I can't say that the principal wasn't kind to me, but she was a little angry with me when I kept saying:

- Please ask Biba!

They have already asked Biba. The girl I was protecting said that I came to the ladies' room, lit a cigarette and attacked her because she didn't want to share it with me.

- Dad, you have to come to the school tomorrow, please!

- Too bad I can't go today - my wonderful father said

calmly.

He hugged me tightly as he always did, and my grandmother was waiting for her turn behind him.

- Don't worry, honey, Daddy will take care of everything - she told me.

And he did it. My wonderful father, who didn't talk much except with me and my grandmother, came to the principal's office the next day. He insisted on seeing the pedagogue as well. I don't know what he told them, because he modestly repeated that it didn't matter, but they called me an hour later and the principal and the pedagogue apologized to me in front of my father.

The class said that they knew everything, that Biba admitted the truth because she betrayed herself not being in class at all that day, but hiding in the toilet. The school reported her parents for domestic violence. I felt sorry for her, even though she put me in a very awkward situation. The worst thing for me was that she admitted that she deliberately wanted to set me up to be guilty of what I was not because I would never know how it feels when your father is beating you with his belt.

My dad's hair was rising on his head, and my grandmother was crying out the fate of poor Biba.

The rumor in the classroom was that my dad had silenced the principal and the pedagogue with one question. He asked them if they really believed that a child who had never met his mother because she died of lung cancer when he was a baby could afford to light a cigarette at any time in his life. My dad is a very smart man, although he is very silent, as a result of my mother's death. Everyone who knows him better says that.

My wonderful grandmother and father. They have sacrificed so much that I didn't really feel the absence of my mother. They are the source of my energy and my happiness. They deserve their name to be kept clean.

From everything I've heard about my mother, I have no doubt that she would be similar to them.

I never knew what it meant to have a mother, but I always felt like she was there. My father and grandmother fought and fought for it all the time. So far, I have missed nothing in my life, but I know it would have been much better if she had survived.

He would certainly be even happier, and I have no doubt, and so would my father, my grandmother as well, and things in the family would be different.

Grandma says my parents loved each other very much. I believe that. I don't know my dad from when my mom was alive, but all my life I've been watching how sacred to him were the things she left behind. In their bedroom to this day, he still has her dresses, strange in cut and material, I would say, but I suppose she brought them from America. Dad says she was recognizable when she walked by precisely because of her unusual appearance. There were a few woolen scarves that my dad would wrap around his neck and smell when he wanted to be alone. Then there were the two hooded cloaks. They say that she brought me to this house under one of them after she gave birth to me.

Ever since I can remember, I have often stood under the picture above the fireplace and looked at all of us, but I would look at her the most. I remember when I was little, my father would lower the picture to my height, and I admired my beautiful golden-haired mother. Sometimes I wanted to touch her. My father would allow me, but as I touched the glass of the painting he was on guard as if I had his heart in my hands. I had enough reason to be jealous of that picture because they looked after it almost as much as they looked after me, but I didn't, because I had everything I wanted and never lacked anything.

I don't mean material things here, although I had enough of everything. I mean things that are much more important to a child than anything that money can buy - my father and my grandmother were always with me, they played with me whenever I asked one of them, they drew for me, sang to me, they also read bedtime stories to me, talked about things that interested me as long as they interested me, and never showed me that they were bored with me, even though I was quite live and tireless child.

But of course, I always wished my mom would come alive from the picture. To come to us for dinner, especially when we were laughing, to laugh with us because I see that she was a woman who loved to laugh. She smiled so much that it began to leave marks on her cheeks.

- I wished she was still alive and all that smiling made

deep wrinkles on her face - my grandmother would sigh.

I imagined what it would be like if she was able to move instead of standing stiffly with me in her arms. I imagined her in such detail that at times it seemed to me that she managed to touch me, and I know it because I could smell her skin.

- How did her skin smell? -I would ask Dad, just to make sure I wasn't wrong.

He would snatch a sigh from his chest, then say:
- Beautiful!
- But how? - I would be persistent.
- Just like yours, son!

As I grew older, I realized that it wasn't that my father and grandmother were talking to me about everything. I had the feeling that they were avoiding me when I would surprise them with a question such as why I can't visit my mother's grave, because it was normal for people to die and have graves.

In those moments, my grandmother would immediately jump in, because that's when she remembered that she had a very important job to do and that our house would surely burn down if she didn't do it right away.

My father would try to convince me that the cemetery is a sad place and that it is not a smart thing to take small children there.

Then I would remind them that he and my grandmother had once taken me to bring flowers to my grandfather, because it was the anniversary of his death. With that, I just made them not to take me there anymore too. I wondered why we never brought flowers to my mother's grave.

- That's not true - he said. - I brought her flowers from all of us.
- Is that why you're going to America?

He denied with a smile:
- Her grave is not in America, son. It's not that far. You've even been close to her a few times, and I'm sure she was thrilled if she happened to know that you were there or hear you.
- But why don't you show it to me?
- I'll show it to you, just be patient - he would pat me on the head.

From the age of twelve to sixteen, I didn't push too hard. But in the days when I wasn't really in the mood, I argued with them:

- I don't even know where my mother's grave is, so how do the professors expect me to know everything that is written in this book!

And then silence.

After I turned seventeen, I changed my tone and talked respectfully about her grave:

- I just hope that at some point in my life I will be honored to be told where my mother's grave is, so that I can go there, kneel down and thank her.

Not even my grandmother left the room that day, but remained calm in her armchair. My father looked at her, and then with a soft look, as well as a hand, he stroked me, saying:

- She was very smart, just like you! She foresaw a lot in advance, including the fact that, which is not always the rule, you will be mature enough by the age of eighteen to be able to hear everything she wanted to say. She insisted that I tell you everything on her grave.

I was very happy and excited to finally know when I would visit her grave for the first time. I was waiting for that day, not because, like my friends, I thought that who knows what would change when we became 18, but because I would visit my mother's grave. I was happy as I was about to meet her alive that day. I couldn't wait!

And then, one warm day in July, my father literally ran into the house and yelled:

- Arthure!

Grandma looked at him confused, and I was surprised.

- I'm here, Dad - I said.
- Get ready, son, you're coming with me!
- Where, Dad?

He stood between me and my grandmother and with a serious face said:

- We are going to your mom's grave!

When I exclaimed happily, he looked over at grandma who just stood there with a pale face and said:

- Please, Mom, watch your blood pressure!
- What happened? - she asked, almost without a voice.
- They found the grave. I don't know how and I don't know the details, but one thing is for sure - they are waiting for an exhumation permit. Please stay here and take care of yourself. We're going to do something very important, and you know what. Come on, Arthur!
- God please help us - she whispered.

It was then that I realized that my joy was a little bit too soon. Fear overwhelmed me, so I asked my father:
- But it's not my eighteenth birthday, Dad!

As he stepped out the living room door, he turned and glanced at the picture above the fireplace.
- She was wrong for once - he said.

23

Philip

I fulfilled my last promise to Elena on the same day that the bad news came and shook my otherwise truly peaceful life. I arranged everything in the way that would be best for my child and my mother. Watching them being happy, I was happy too. As much as I could, after I barely survived the death of my Elena, only because of our child.

That day, the only thing that made me feel a glimmer of satisfaction was really in what I believed - that she hadn't been able to predict everything. It was the consolation I have been waiting for all these years, and it arrived on the worst day. Her grave has been discovered, I will for sure go to prison, but I will go away convinced that she was a little crazy, although I loved her more than myself. Now all I cared about was our son not falling and believing in her unfounded stories. But I will keep my promise and tell him everything she wanted, and I promised in an effort to make her happy, because I thought that would help her survive.

How was I only deceived and how she slipped out of my hands....

It was still daylight when we arrived by the lake next to the Trakoscan castle, and left in the middle of the night. My mom has called twice on my cell phone to ask if everything is okay.

I can't say that, I don't know. What I can say is that the time we spent there was full of various emotions. The story itself broke my soul, and it turned him from a smart and quiet child into a young man with a lost look. I didn't bother asking him what he thought about it. I emphasized that I can assume how he feels and if he needs to, he should take all the time in the world before he is able to say or comment on anything.

Every now and then he turned what I said into questions:

- She knew I was going to be a boy? Did she know when I would be born? Did she know when her last day was? She came back from the past? The castle used to be her home?

My poor child! Oh my dear Elena, if I hadn't loved you so much, I would have never done this to him! Either way, we're in trouble — if he accepts your crazy stories, he'll be in conflict with me forever. If he does not accept them, the ideal of you will be a shameful story.

If I could choose, I would choose the second variant. Because no one knows our family secret, so if that bothers him, there is no one to mock him. What are you doing to us today when heavy clouds of leaden rains are already over our lives because they discovered you, my Elena? And I just wanted to fulfill your wish and bury you in the woods by the lake, so you can watch the castle, as you insisted. I could never deny you anything. Even today, I am not mad, although I'm trying to convince myself that I'm. I can never be mad at you. Even if Arthur has consequences and even if I have to go to prison, I would do everything for you...

I took Arthur here many times, although he had no idea that his mother was close to him. Several times I drove my mother here too to stroke the grass over the grave of her dear Elena without saying a word.

For me, apart from the place next to my family, this was the second most favorite place in the world. That's why I went back to work. I wanted to visit the grave, which only I could recognize, because I know exactly where I dug it all the time and look at it from the castle. What I didn't want, and that was happening, was me talking to the grave. I hated it, and I repeated it over and over again. I couldn't stop talking to Elena. I wanted to keep her informed about our child. I wanted to repeat to her that she was the only one I could love so deeply ...

I wasn't sure if she would be happy with it or if she would point an angry finger at me. I knew her as I know myself, but I didn't know how she would be now dead.

When she left for the first time, I broke into pieces. Then she came back and put me together. And then she couldn't help me. Not me, not our child, not me. She left, and I'm sure she didn't want to.

Seventeen years without her. Her body is gone. Her smile is gone. Her voice is gone and her deeds resembling the deeds of a good fairy are gone too.

But what is still there, no one has been able to take away from me. I was a regular visitor to our room below the castle. Even the small amount of oxygen there didn't bother me when I would enter our world where nothing visible was there, but I could feel it. Memories of her will remain mine as long as I breathe. They found the grave, but only I still know her secret hiding place, one of the many ways. The other one, I have never dared to use it since I tried and failed to get through it. She didn't manage to explain it to me.

Arthur was barely walking with me when I turned around with a candle in my hand and said:

- Here she gave birth to you. And she left us here before I found her cold.

Our child was silent, and that was to be expected.

It was the same the next day. And then the next, and the next.

After the shock, he started talking, but on the subject of his mother, he would only said:

- Be patient, father! I will tell you my opinion after I have digested all the information!

I was patient. I waited patiently for him to tell me what he thinks and I waited patiently for the police to pick me up, at work or at home, and take me away. I was not afraid of anything. I was only afraid about my mother's health while I was gone. Because Arthur will need her more than ever. I'm scared to think about it, but I think my mom would not survive while I am in prison.

Days passed, and there was no sign or voice from the announced exhumation. I thanked God for every day I spent in freedom. In those days, a new irreconcilable desire moved into my heart - I want to see her when they take her out!

- Don't, my son! - my mother begged me -Don't honey, why would you spoil the picture you have of her in your mind, look how beautiful she is to us! Isn't It enough that you saw her dead? Give yourself peace of mind and don't look at her after more than seventeen years underground. If someone forces me to see your dad like that, I would close my eyes.

Arthur looked at her respectfully, and then, in her presence, said to me:

- I want to come with you! I want to see her too! Take care of it, please, Dad!

I promised I would, but that day never came. And then, quite by accident, it was announced in the castle - "they don't want to do it in the heat. They will do it when the weather is a little bit colder. It's not urgent anyway, the grave is so old that a few days won't change anything."

When they finally decided to do the exhumation at the beginning of the first week of October, I stood in front of the picture above the fireplace, stared into her eyes, and whispered that only she could hear:

- I'm sorry, I didn't know I could still wait for his birthday. Elena, as always, your prediction was right....

That day, looking at her in the picture, she seemed to be smiling at me even more, teasing me triumphantly.

At the beginning of the first week of October, early in the morning, Arthur came with me. I asked for permission and he was allowed to attend the exhumation. We justified it with great desire and interest on the part of my son.

Fortunately, the project was led by Dr. Sinchich, and I was lucky enough to recognize him, which further confirmed that I was ready for anything that day. The doctor who arrived early in the morning did not recognize me, which was not strange, and I remembered him confirming the death of my stillborn daughter a long time ago.

- I'm sorry, sir - he squeezed my hand, then Arthur's.

As they carefully removed the earth and set it aside, I tried to keep track of how Arthur was feeling and whether he could really stand it. He looked braver than I had hoped, but he was very sensitive, just like me.

- Don't forget what we agreed on - I reminded him - just stay without emotions visible to other people.

He nodded.

Shortly afterwards, the clatter of two metals was heard. There was silence, and then someone said louder:

- A hairpin. It seems to be a woman.

Hairpins? That is impossible. She never used them in her hair, much less when she was sick.

I kept quiet and watched, and then I remembered.

The shoes! Her shoes were different from any other type of shoe. Yes, they had little metal pins on the side, I remember very well, how could I forget about it. Elena... They found you, my love! They are coming for you.

I still didn't feel scared, but I was excited to see her. For a second I thought my mom was right and I wanted to take Arthur with me and run away. And then I was excitedly waiting for them to bring my love in front of my eyes. I no longer thought about the time it would take them to find and convict me, or how long I would be in prison. I was interested in nothing but seeing her again.

The endless wait was finally over. Several of them bent down to pull out the body together, and only one of them was downstairs. It's good that I was far enough away and didn't see him if he trampled on my Elena, at least by accident.

Arthur and I twisted our necks as much as we could, and at that moment I stopped thinking about my child because all I cared about was Elena.

To my great disappointment, all I saw was a slightly larger lump of soil. While I was waiting for them to get my love out, they put that lump on the already prepared stretcher, closed it and I just heard:

- Take it away!

Take it where? What? Was that my Elena? Do they really think they found her? The lump was not as big as her hair was! And they still carry it as if they were carrying soil! One of them can't wait to walk away so he can laugh while he throws something at his colleagues. What kind of behavior is it when you have the greater woman of all in your hands?

I wanted to swear! For the first time in my life I wanted to swear! Of course I wouldn't do it, but I sincerely wanted to. I have been standing here for months preparing to meet my beloved again, and they carry it like a stone under my nose with no respect for her! After I finish my prison sentence, I will sue them for this! This is pathetic!

Arthur! How is Arthur?

I turned to him abruptly and saw tears in his eyes that I could not interpret. Fearing that the others would not see them, I pulled him by the arm and we left without saying goodbye. They didn't even deserve a goodbye! They took her away as if they had found an old coat, not a woman who was not a real countess, but she was my queen!

I couldn't get over it for days.

My mom just kept saying:

- I told you! You shouldn't have attended!

Arthur held on bravely, but he was still silent. When asked if he was pleased to see his mother at least in that form, he nodded, seemingly pleased.

It was a whole week before we were told the findings. And then I called Arthur on my cell phone.

- Tell me, Dad - he answered after the first ring.
- My son...
- Yes, Dad. Dad?
- Everything's fine, honey, I just have one request!
- I'm listening, Dad!
- Can you please pick me up from work?

Short silence.

- Dad, just tell me, is everything okay?

- Yes, honey, everything is ok. Trust me. I just don't feel able to drive to Krapina alone.
- Dad, your shift isn't over. Are you sure everything is fine? Dad! Did the autopsy results come in?
- Yes!
- Ok, I get it! I am coming right now!
- Arthure!
- Yes, Dad?
- Drive carefully, please! You are a young driver!
- Don't worry, Dad!

Not that I needed it, but he helped me sit in his car. I stared blankly in front of me. He started driving, and I was neither in heaven nor on earth. Halfway to Krapina, I gave in, I covered my face with my hands and began to cry.

Arthur quickly parked to the side and squeezed me into his arms.

- You said you wouldn't regret anything, Dad! I know it's hard for you, but at least be glad you didn't feel sorry for anything!

I fought back the air, so I yelled at my innocent child:
- You see, that's the thing! I AM SORRY! I'm so sorry I could die!
- Dad - he squeezed me even harder - I'm with you, you know! Mom would be proud of you!
- Mom... - I choked on tears.
- You said she deserved it all, Dad!

I had to calm down. I had to explain it to my child. I had to look him in the eye and admit to him that she deserved it all, but that I did not deserve her love.

I took a deep breath and his grip around me eased. After a while, I was ready to briefly explain my crime.

- Arthur - I said - My dear son! The results!
- Okay Dad, we knew it was going to happen and we know what's next and we're ready, aren't we?
- I wasn't ready, Arthur. I was preparing for what my head had imagined, but I was not ready for what had happened.
- What happened, Dad?
- The results....
- They came, ok! We know that, Dad! And we know what

will happen next. I'm sorry, but we know everything, Dad. You're going to jail...

-Arthur...I'm not going anywhere. They're not taking me anywhere and no one will ask me anything. Because your mother's body... They found out, was there, in that grave... for four hundred years...

24

The fire in the fireplace crackled. Anna was sitting in her armchair drinking tea. Her two men, her two golden boys on the table, were pushing their hands to see who was stronger.

- My God, that is not even fun! Please, don't play like that!

- You are right, grandma, so I won't let him win - Arthur said, grinding his teeth.

At that moment, the table seemed to move as well. Both of them got up from their chairs, with red cheeks, breathing quickly and sweating. Then they began to shout, louder and louder, and then Philip yelled the sound of defeat as Arthur, celebrating his victory, jumped in the living room. He jumped and kissed his grandmother on both cheeks, then returned to Philip, who was still sweaty, and bending over the table, bringing himself into his father's face, he asked in a low and serious voice:

- Who's the Count here, huh?

Raising both hands in the air, Philip surrendered:

- You are, my man, you are!

- Let's stop playing this - Anna repeated her - But, tell me, have you decided when you are going to visit Elena's new grave?

Walking to the family picture, Philip said:

- As soon as the snows fall, Mom. But I know why you are asking and I will repeat one more time - you are not coming with us because you are too weak this time. We want to have you here with us as long as possible. Elena's new grave near the Draskovich family tomb will be visited only by the male part of this family. Dear mom, we will bring you a lot of pictures. Satisfied?

She snorted angrily and continued to drink her tea.

For two months now, Philip had been living differently and couldn't believe it was that simple. Trusting Elena would be so easy. And he refused, until he buried her sad.

That is why Arthur did not follow his example. But he was silent for a short time because he did not want to hurt his father. And when the autopsy results arrived, while his father wept with remorse, he wept with satisfaction that both his father and grandmother would finally trust his mother just as he immediately believed her. It didn't take him much effort to believe her, as Philip called them, crazy stories. They simply coincided so much that, as crazy as they sounded, they justified themselves.

Since then, he kept watching his father come under the family picture, looking into Elena's eyes and whispering:

- Please forgive me, my love!

****

In Zagreb, Marko Dvornik was sitting in the kitchen. He had raised his legs in another chair and was sure he would keep them there until his wife appeared from the room where their twins were still sleeping.

The coffee was steaming in front of him as he was going

through the newspaper as he did every other day.

"NEW, EARLY ELECTIONS IN SPRING" - one title said.

It didn't get his attention. He only lingered on it for a few minutes, because titles of this kind were no longer really interesting to him.

"THE PRESIDENT OF AMERICA, MR. GEORGE BUSH, on an official visit to the White House yesterday, received..."

- Who cares - Marko turned abruptly.

And then he froze. He held the newspaper in front of him, almost out of breath. His hands began to tremble abruptly, and he felt sweat on his back, though he was wearing his pajamas only. His body was paralyzed, and even if Ivana came along, he couldn't move, and he wouldn't even remember to remove his legs from the other kitchen chair.

He felt weak. He felt out of breath and his heart was pounding. In front of his eyes, it began to glow as if someone was turning the light off and on.

"I'm not feeling well"- he thought to himself.

Then he wished Ivana was close because he needed her hand, but the very thought of her closeness made him even worse. He felt like vomiting. Ivana can't see me like this. Even if I pass out, it doesn't matter. It is important that she does not know why.

And then she reminded him that she was, realistically, very close. He heard the creak of the door and her footsteps. He sincerely hoped she had gone to the bathroom, but unfortunately, he saw her red house dress on the kitchen door.

As if struck by lightning, he jumped from his chair, grabbed the newspaper and immediately after Ivana said "good morning", he quickly said:

- I have to go to the toilet!

He flew past her like lightning, and she looked back at him in astonishment.

- And why are you taking the newspaper with you? - she yelled.

There was no answer other than the bang of the bathroom door. So she added louder:

- Don't even think of bringing the newspaper back here later!

He heard her voice, but he didn't care what she said. He put the lid down on the toilet and sat on it. He felt safer, so he could afford to shake his hands again as much as he wanted.

He spread the newspaper in front of him. He could barely breathe, but he saw it very well.

"AT THE TRAKOSCAN CASTLE...."

He was swallowing the letters, then he swallowed the picture, then the letters again, then the picture, and then just the picture.

It was a continuation of a story from two months ago, they explained. How did he miss it then... They publish the details because now they have managed to prove it. They found a grave four hundred years old. A woman was buried in it. Experts tried and succeeded in making a photo-robot. Barely changed, with a serious face and eyes fixed on Marko, Elena was staring at him from the newspaper.

Made in the USA
Middletown, DE
11 July 2022